# Secrets of my Heart's Desire

By

Katrina Chanice

# Stay Connected

Twitter: @katrinachanice
Instagram: @novelist_kc
Facebook: Katrina Chanice

# Dedication

### To My Angel

Forever in my heart will I feel your kicks and while you never got to see the light of day, I know that you are forever in God's arms feeling a love that shines through your family. Thank you for the dreams. Until we finally meet in heaven.

### To My Queen

Forever may you rest in love. I've taken everything you've given me and said to me and I'm sharing it with the world through writing. Thank you for supporting me and encouraging me everything I've ever tried to do. Forever my Queen you'll be.

### To My Prayer Warrior

Thank you for teaching me love. It is because of you and your prayers that I am who I am today. You are and forever will be my rock. Thank you for being an amazing God-fearing woman!

# Table of Contents

# Prologue

Lost in my thoughts, remembering when he said he loved me, knowing I should have never believed him in the first place. I was a fool, tormented with thoughts of losing him every day because of my failure to provide him with everything he wanted and needed. Oh, I just knew that our bond was unbreakable and baby I was sadly mistaken. Eventually, this day was going to come, I just never knew how hard letting go would truly be. Walking away sounds easy when you say it, but I've tried to wean myself away from him. Every chance I got to walk away for good, he lured me right back into his arms. Time never existed but as the years went on, my worries and fears always hovered nearby.

One would think we were perfect for each other. Nothing but happy times and even now it feels real, but all good things must come to an end, so this breakup has to happen. I've had plenty of reasons to walk away, I just always wanted our love to last. Reality slapped me in the face harder than my mama ever could while I was living my best days in sin. Faced with decisions I never wanted to make, I wish he would wrap his arms around me and pretend that I'm his one and only until the morning like he used to do. What's so bad with that? The man will act as though I just hopped into whatever this is by myself. We both know what we have and it's much more than a quick nut or random lay in the hay. I wanted to tell the world but he's too busy convincing me that it's just us and nobody else. Telling him how much I truly loved him would be pointless with no hope for change. So, when in Rome, pretend for just one more night and then let the wife have him until death do them part.

There he was, waiting patiently in the living room by the

fireplace when I walked in and sat down on the couch. The thoughts of how great we could have been flashed through my mind once he sat down beside me. At times I've acted hasty in breaking up and he'll forgive me with compassion saying that he understood me being too young and immature to process what we had sometimes. He reels me in with a kiss on my cheek. His essence is intoxicating, and I need to cherish every ounce of it. Switching from kissing to nibbling on my ear and whispering those words I yearned to hear. Like a fool I believe every single syllable that spills out of his mouth. Still, I allowed him to take control of me by kissing me down into the couch until he had me out of my shirt and jeans. It was years too late to do the right thing and push him off of me. I couldn't wait to feel him inside of me. He's always been a gentle lover, taking the time to show his affection to every part of me. His kisses were driving me into ecstasy while he caressed both breasts, suckling them one at a time like he was a junkie, and they were his addiction.

His excitement bulged out against my legs exercising its desire for this one last high. My mind, body and soul started to enter another realm as he lifted my legs onto my shoulders. He didn't miss a beat as he devoured my juices treating me like I was the object of his obsession. There would never be another man to please me like this. A man who can express his feelings and thoughts with the vibrations of his tongue on my pearl as he slowly fingers me. Only this man could consistently blow my mind like this. I had already started running when he tightly grabbed my hips, pulling me deeper into him. I heard him utter, "Put them legs up. I want to see those pretty toes in the air." My lover's request was granted. Those pretty toes went completely numb at the same time my legs began to tremble as he slurped his last drop. He left my lady throbbing, waiting, and anticipating his next move.

In so many ways he was my own personal chocolate love factory. I could stare at him working out all day and then picture myself just licking the sweat right off of him. He has this sexy smile that makes my lady purr while the waves in his low fade could make a person seasick. Being an older man gives him a huge advantage. I don't have to tell him a thing because he already knows what my body craves for. He glided his member inside of me nice and slow like the beat of the song he was humming. He lifted me up off the couch, still pulsating inside of my walls. He slowly pushed in and out every inch of him and then carried me over to the wall, keeping the same slow pace. I thought my entire body would just melt in his arms, but he held me up with a death grip as my legs wrapped around him. Before I knew it, I was on top of him in the chair next to the radio. I turned it on and *'On Top of Me'* by Tyrese started to ease its way out of the speakers. He needed to know truly the woman I had grown to become. He was going to always remember me and what we had after tonight plus this was my favorite position. I love being in control more than allowing him to be. My body rode him like he was a bull in my rodeo. As the lyrics echoed out instructing me on what to do, I exploded on top of him. His moans were so loud, they gave me chills knowing how good I could make him feel.

Moments later I was going down on my lover. I knew how to please any man thanks to this one man. He loves when I stroke his shaft, while making circles around the tip. According to him, all men loved a warm mouth. Of course, I perfected this for him so that I could hear him moan to me working my gag reflects while catching the rhythm to *'Tell Me'* by Usher. The man was going insane, giving me the ego boost I needed and wanted. His pressure was building up, but he had other plans in mind when he commanded, "Get up." With the biggest smile on my face, these thick caramel thighs stood up. My pudgy stomach didn't stop no show around here. I positioned myself over the armrest of the couch while maintaining the arch of his dreams. He gripped my hips preparing himself for his finishing move. I've never been a fan of doggy style, but he does it so well. With every slow and sinful stroke, my moans became screams of pleasure. As his speed increased, sweat was beginning to trickle down from his forehead and chest onto my back. My moans of pleasure mixed in with the music of my slow tunes as I hit my last climax for the night. Seconds later, he was out of breath slumping on top of me.

There was no time wasted as he quickly gathered his clothes off the floor talking about how much he'd missed me. I watched him get dressed fighting the desire to say I loved him. He made it clear that he didn't want to stop seeing me, but I couldn't force him to stay as I usually do. It was time to move on now. He had a wife to love and cherish which wasn't me.

# Chapter One

It's Mother's Day and I wondered if calling my mother really made me a great daughter. Here I stood in the mirror feeling dead inside as my phone buzzed with a text message of her bragging about James taking her on a cruise. I did not bother to respond, assuming it would be best to just leave her a voicemail seeing as how our conversations constantly take a wrong turn and somebody ends up in their feelings. That somebody is always me. I am already trying to soothe the hurt of my heart and mind in this bathroom mirror depressed listening to all the breakup songs I could find from the 90s. I have felt emptiness before, but nothing could compare to how broken and empty I feel this morning. Granted she is the only mother that I have but listen if I could have picked my parents it would have never been Shirley Ann Ward or that deadbeat Jeffery Adams. This is what loving somebody from a distance looks like. I guess. My mother is one who can notice everything about everybody else's child while neglecting her own. She knew when my best friend started having sex. She knew when some girl down the street got pregnant and was hiding it. She knew who was fighting and cheating and of course selling drugs and going to jail. The neighborhood know it all. The Tea Queen. The very reason all of the neighborhood would hang out with her. They loved her and felt like she really understood them because she did not have to hear a lot or ask much to tell somebody their whole life's story. All she ever told me was she would know when I would start having sex as well because I was going to walk different, smell different, my hips would spread, and all that jazz. When I lost my virginity to Calvin, I tried to pay attention to my walk and wash my body more but after a while, I figured she knew I was no longer a virgin and knew who I was having sex with. As years went on it no longer mattered to me if she knew and that is why I never said anything to her about him. As for as I was concerned, if she did not already know then it clearly was not meant for her to know. Now when I need a mother's love the most, I know I would be a fool to turn to her. Why would I add on to the horrible image she already sees in me? I can be a miserable fat black walrus looking bitch on any given day. I refuse to be that every day just to say I have a relationship with my mother.

All last night I dreamt of the most precious little baby girl that I wish I could meet. I would wake up several times and go back to sleep but still, I dreamt of her. She has the biggest hazel-nut eyes. The type of eyes I could just get lost in. Her skin looked silky smooth with a head full of ginger-colored hair. She is all dressed up from head to toe wearing the prettiest red dress and matching socks with the ruffles on them that I have ever seen. When I look at her, I see myself and the man I loved all wrapped into one with a beautiful red bow like a cherry on top of a sundae. Her smile shines so brightly making it obvious that she is a happy and loved baby. Seems like she was made just for me and yet no matter what or how I did it, I could not hold her. I could not pick her up. Every single time I tried, she started to cry as if I have disturbed her peace. I would give anything to comfort her and calm her, but she rejected every effort I made. This precious baby girl dissolved into a blob of blood in her crib. I was screaming at my loudest, still, no one came to my rescue. I woke up each time with fresh tears rolling down my face. It's been over two months ago that I was at the clinic getting rid of what I thought was the biggest mistake of my life and ever since then I've had these dreams of what could've been with my baby girl. From the moment I saw the two lines on that pregnancy test I never stopped to think, to pray, or even question it. I did not consider any other options because I knew I did not have another choice.

When I decided this pregnancy wasn't for me, I should have pulled my big girl panties up and handled my business alone because when I told Calvin, he cussed me out, broke up with me, and truly broke my heart. I ended up at the clinic by my-self. It felt like my heart was going to burst out of my chest as I waited for my name to be called. They had me go back and forth to different people. A nurse confirmed my pregnancy with an ultrasound while a therapist went over my emotions and reasons for the abortion. For once in my life, I was honest with somebody other than my best friend and I could feel the judgment seeping from her pores. She referred me to Dr. Sim-one Juelz for further counseling if I begin to experience Post-Abortion Syndrome. I tried to be positive while opting for the non-surgical route. The nurse gave me the first pill to stop the growth of the fetus. Somehow a part of me felt like it would be easier. I spent the next thirty-six hours apologizing to this baby until I took the second pill that would force the miscarriage. They gave me a Vicodin prescription for the pain, and I chose not to get it filled. I wanted to suffer for allowing myself to be put in this situation. A decision I later regretted.

Within hours of taking the second pill, I started to feel cramps that got stronger as the days grew longer. It was debili-tating causing me to bury myself under my covers away from the world. I could not walk, talk, or eat. I was losing weight and my grades dropped drastically. It was emotionally and physic-ally draining but seeing my unborn in clumps of blood is what truly broke me down into nothing. I wanted to be a mother. I wanted to love this baby, but I knew this was for the best for both me and baby. The most painful experience of my life. Despite me doing everything I can to forgive myself, it seems pretty much impossible. I almost killed myself from blood loss but apparently this is all normal. I would love to confide in Shir-ley because she is my mother. Just once I wish she could hold me and tell me everything will be okay, but I know that is something she could never do. There was a time when my mother was a mother but that was many moons ago.

Fifth grade is when everything changed. That is when I started developing breasts. It is as if they grew overnight and refused to stop. I went from mosquito bites to a C cup in no time.

My butt was not far behind either. At first, I was feeling myself because the cutest boys were starting to notice me. Of course, I was enjoying the attention but after a while it all turned sour. Older men were noticing me too. Most of them knew how old I was. They just did not care while the rest simply refused to even believe me when I told them I was only eleven years old. They would call me all kinds of liars and bitches as I was walking away. By the time, I started junior high, I was labeled the sixth-grade hoe and had never even been kissed. Everybody just knew I was having sex based on how big my boobs and butt were. Shirley stayed flipping out! She was acting like everybody else. I felt completely isolated and confused all throughout middle school. It was like the entire world was against me because of something I had no control over. It was depressing, and it caused me to cut myself. I would never cut deep enough to end up hospitalized however there were a few times I thought about ending it all. Eventually, I resorted to food and found comfort in eating. Hell, I believed if I was fat, then no man would want me. I would rather deal with fat slurs because I ate too much than to deal with being an unkissed hoe. I knew my mom could not trip about my breasts if I had rolls and a stomach to match. Man, was I ever wrong! Being fat did not stop a damn thing. Older men still wanted me. It was more older men liking me after being fat than it was before. The ones that liked me when I was slim thick, loved me now that I was plump. The guys that did not believe my age, still called me liars and bitches, they just added fat to the lineup of insults. I still got picked on at school and for each pound I gained my mother hated me more and more. There was no escaping the ridicule.

I pushed the pain to the back burner when I heard my phone ringing. Today is supposed to be an exciting day because my bestie boo is coming to stay with me for a week. It has been a couple of years and we have got a ton of catching up to do. Even though I cannot wait to see her, I already cannot wait for her to leave. I did not think any of this would be happening when she planned her visit. Now, I would rather just deal with my demons without having to play hostess to my best friend. I just cannot bring myself to tell her about the abortion or the breakup with Calvin. Aleccia would completely chew me out about even being pregnant. Last time I checked I was grown which means I am free to do whatever I please. Her over-opinionated nature could ruin this ten-year friendship especially with the way I am currently feeling. She knows the last thing I want to hear is anything negative about Calvin, even if we are no longer together. I swear if laying down in bed all day, staring at the ceiling was an option, then I would do it with ease, however life continues no matter what bad choices you have made.

Aleccia should have been here hours ago but hopefully she has stopped by the liquor store to get our favorite Alize. I done cleaned my apartment spotless with her favorite meal waiting on the stove. I answered the phone, "Heffa, where are you?"

"Uh, what?!"

I looked down at the phone and the caller ID read Charms. I laughed and replied, "My bad girl I thought you were Aleccia. What's up though?"

She sighed, "Damn, so you don't know huh?"

Feeling really annoyed, "Know what Charmaine?!"

She sounded kind of out of breath as she said, "Aleccia was just found dead girl!"

"What the fuck are you talking about?!" I was completely confused and pissed. Why on earth would Charmaine play games like that. How could Aleccia be dead when she is on the way here to my apartment?! I hung the phone up and started calling Aleccia. No answer. I called repeatedly and still no answer. I left a voicemail. I sent text messages, Facebook messages, and even Instagram messages. I was all over social media and they all read and said the same thing. My best friend was dead. Aleccia was not dead! She just wasn't! This had to be some kind of sick joke that Aleccia and Charmaine were playing or something. At least that's what I hoped it was. I don't know what is going on, but I know she is not dead. I had no doubt about it. As I paced, I began to tremble, waiting on Aleccia to hit me back up. I tried my best to remember Pierre's number, but it was hopeless. Aleccia did not have much family and the little family she did have, could not stand me. I'm convinced Charmaine is lying. Not everything that comes out of her mouth is trustworthy anyway. The girl is a compulsive liar and if this bitch done worked my nerves up over some bullshit, I'm going to really fuck her up. I wanted to drive six hours to Aleccia's house but what good would that do when she was supposed to have been here at least two hours ago. I felt stuck and helpless. I needed answers and nowhere to truly turn to. I searched WLPA's website hoping there was nothing to see but there it was:

*"Today a deadly wreck has claimed the life of a Jackson native. Our Lindsey Hinton joins us live along I-20 – Lindsey?*

*We are here along I-20 in Vicksburg – Where further up the interstate – A tragic accident has happened earlier this evening – Just past Highway 61. I-20 has been blocked for several hours now. Authorities say the 2014 Mercedes-Benz was headed Eastbound on I-20 when it*

*crossed the median and collided head-on into a 2002 Toyota Avalon – 22-year-old Supermodel and Jackson native, Aleccia Bennet was instantly killed. We'll keep you updated as more information comes in."*

I sat there frozen as my entire world collapsed around me. My best friend. My ride or die.
My homie. My sister. The one person in the world that knew me inside and out was gone.

# Chapter Two

Who knew time could fly by so fast? It's hard trying to be the person I was before walking into that clinic. I know I shouldn't attribute everything to that one moment, but I have so many what ifs. I feel as though it was a chain reaction of horrible events and God is punishing me for killing my baby. First, Calvin breaks up with me and then Aleccia is killed in a horrible car accident. I didn't attend the funeral because I couldn't bear with the last thought and memory of her being dead in a casket. Charmaine wasted no time with sharing the details of the drama that happened with Aleccia's family and Pierre. Of course, they are blaming him for her death since he was the one driving the car and made it out alive. It makes no sense to treat him like that. Shutting him out at the funeral and not even allowing him to attend the repast for his own wife?! It's ridiculous and I'm not mad at him for changing his number and blocking everybody including me. I've known Ms. Lisa for too many years, and I know how she can be, so I paid my respects to the family earlier in the week before the funeral. I told her I didn't think I would be able to go through with the funeral as it was already hard trying to wake up and make it through the day. Surprisingly, she understood but I guess she was more focused on hurting Pierre.

While I was there, I overheard Monica arguing about how her mother shouldn't have to do anything because she just lost her daughter. I had to leave before I said something out of the way. The definition of an unfit mother was Lisa Tate! She shows favoritism to her oldest daughter Monica because she is a pretty high yella light skinned like her father that was killed in Hurricane Katrina. Aleccia on the other hand was a beautiful coffee brown bean. The spitting image of Lisa but for whatever reason

Lisa and Monica hated Aleccia. Now that she's dead, Ms. Lisa has put on the biggest woe is me act. She loves attention and is using Aleccia's death to be the reason she gets it too. Monica put on this huge act as well but according to Charmaine at one moment it seemed like they truly were hurt at her death and why wouldn't they be?! No matter how Aleccia was treated in life, she loved her mother, and she loved her sister. If they needed something, she was just a phone call away and always came through for them. I would tell her all the time she needed to rid herself of them, but she'd always throw in my face how I loved my mother and how I'd do the same. I eventually stopped suggesting it because she was completely right. We had horrible mothers and yet we loved them unconditionally.

I just wish she was here right now. If I could go back to the first day we met, it's so many things I would've changed. School had just started back after the devastation that Hurricane Katrina had left. We all had to adjust to these new students from New Orleans and them adjusting to being displaced from their homes. As an adult it was heartbreaking, as a seventh-grade kid it was straight up bullshit! There were fights every other day between Jackson and New Orleans kids. From the bus stop to the classroom to the park when school let out. Eventually the kids settled down and made friends. The day I met Aleccia, she had found out that our birthdays were less than two weeks apart. Hers had already passed but she gave me a gag gift just because. It was a bunch of journals for me to write about my daily disappointments, rants, and things that annoyed me. I thought it was hilarious and we instantly became friends.

Aleccia was the true example of a best friend and never switched up on me. She made the remainder of middle school bearable. While I had gained all of this weight, Aleccia was a stick. She'd joke about being in the itty-bitty titty committee and twerking her spine because she believed she had a long back and no butt. I used to be dead ass envious of her in eighth grade. There would be days that I would starve trying to lose at least half a pound because my mom constantly compared us to each other. She treated Aleccia as if she was her daughter and I was a stranger, but Aleccia always had my back and by the end of high school I had dropped some of the weight and was embracing my thick thighs. I no longer cared what people thought anymore. Aleccia helped me realize just how beautiful I was, and I took that to heart. You weren't going to see her in the halls without me popping up too. We ran that high school, and nobody could tell us otherwise. Still to this day if somebody sees me in the store, they're asking about my homegirl. It was all good and dandy until she moved to Texas the summer after graduation and started doing modeling.

We had plans to go to Southern Miss, but life had other plans for her. Our school held a fashion show in the eleventh grade, where she modeled for the first time. She received so much praise afterwards that weeks had went by and our classmates as well as teachers were still talking about how well she had done. It made her tap into a talent she didn't know she had. Aleccia finally got the courage up to enter a competition at Northpark Mall and of course she won. We thought we would do at least one year of college together, but the modeling agency wanted her to start immediately after graduation and that's exactly what she did. She packed her bags and didn't look back. Barely three months had went by, before she had her own place and a car. I was surprised when she came and scooped me up and said she was kidnapping me. I certainly didn't argue since I had never been out of the state before and hadn't enrolled at Southern Miss yet, so choosing a nearby community college in Texas wasn't going to be a problem at all. Everybody didn't get options like this, but I wasn't sure what I wanted after that. I was just happy that my friend asked me along for the ride. I was at almost every one of her modeling gigs. If I wasn't there, then I was in class or interning for Robert Micheals advertising agency. Aleccia introduced me to the CEO, Todd Herbert, during an industry party and I didn't know who he was until the day I started interning. Any other time we were at all the parties, clubs, restaurants, and taking road trips just for fun. That first year was truly amazing, then she met Pierre and it all changed.

They met at an afterparty for the NBC draft picks. He was one of the draft picks for OKC. We were there just to party as always. I instantly became invisible. They talked all night and she had already fallen in love. I wasn't mad or even jealous, but I did think she was being stupid. They had just met. Over the next few months, he seemed like a real cool dude. We all got along without a problem. He introduced me to his fine ass teammate Darius so that I wouldn't feel like such a third wheel. I'm fairly certain he was trying to hook us up, but we didn't vibe as a couple. Only because my heart and mind at the time was stuck on stupid for Calvin. I only seen Darius as the big brother I never had. We'd hang out all the time until people were swearing up and down that we were sexing it up and that just wasn't case.

I had my fun while it lasted, but I was ready to go home. I never planned on putting roots down in Texas. Aleccia knew I'd only come back to Texas for her since she was originally scared of this big new life she was living. Of course, I didn't mind helping her adjust to her new amazing life. I'm happy for her and nobody is taking my place. Pierre is just an added bonus and I have no reason to cock block. I could've stayed and gotten my own place but like a fool I was missing Calvin more than anything. Since Aleccia no longer needed me, I moved back to Mississippi. I had saved money up for an apartment that she co-signed with me. She also gave me her 2011 Toyota Camry because Pierre had bought her a new 2012 Range Rover. After I enrolled at JSU, I realized for the first time in my life I was on my own and I loved it! There's no better feeling than having my own apartment. A year went by and Aleccia called me screaming in the phone telling me how they had gotten married, and she was already trying to have a baby. This girl wanted to be a mother so bad! It's the one thing she has always talked about from the day we became friends was how she wanted to have a husband, a baby, and a huge mansion.

She told me she wanted a maid because she wasn't cleaning that mansion either. I always laughed because I am the complete opposite of her. I'm simple. I wanted a family too, but you can keep the big mansion and maids. I'd rather have a lot of land and build on. I give credit where credit is due, Pierre is a wonderful man! He literally caters to her every desire. I bet she got that huge mansion and the maid. They were still working on that baby though. She had a few miscarriages and after so many attempts, she's started to give up on the idea. So, no I would've never told her about the fucked-up shit I had just done. I've regretted from the moment I swallowed the first pill knowing deep down that Aleccia would've probably adopted the baby and raised it as her own. I can't deny that she would've been a better mother than me.

It's been so hard trying to move forward with so much pain and regret pushing me down. I called my classmate up so we could study, because I haven't been studying like I should have, and I don't need a drop in my grades like last semester instead I took this time to smoke my first blunt. How do I cope with all of this? I find myself more depressed than I've ever been before. Omari stays high so I knew he would have a blunt or two on him. I'm tired of pretending as if I'm making it when I'm not. I'm constantly crying and when I finally laugh, I realize I don't deserve happiness not even for a moment. The scent of Mary Jane filled the air as I choked on the first few hits that also produced my first set of tears in front of somebody. I may not always shed tears on the outside, but I haven't stopped crying on the inside for the past four months. I've been trying to focus on finishing this last semester of grad school. I'm so ready to get this degree and move on to the next chapter in my life but that's easier said than done. I needed this distraction and Omari is always down for a free meal, laughs, and good vibes. He's even mentioned being roommates, but I had to decline because I love my little space. Besides, I don't even know what to do after I get this degree. All my hopes and dreams are just floating in the air right now.

Omari has tried to get me to smoke plenty of times since I'm known to stress pretty hard during exams. He says it'll calm my nerves. I've refused each and every time until the point where I almost cussed him out. Before the abortion, I was an emergency room tech, and I couldn't afford to get caught with weed in my system. Now that I gotten fired from missing so many days, I could care less about what drugs were in my system. I hated that job anyway. A bunch of snobby wannabe Instafame models working in a hospital while snorting on the side but thinking they're securing a bag and yet stay in the most drama. Every single day it was something new going on. I was too ready to quit! Now I just need to secure this degree, so I

won't lose this apartment. Omari is the one person I trust to not lace a blunt or spike a drink. In this moment I simply want to stop caring. I want to stop feeling. I want to forget the pain and I'm hoping this blunt will do just that.

Omari broke my train of thought, "So, are we pregnant or what?" I froze and said absolutely nothing.

He waved his hand in front of my face and I finally managed to say, "Dude, what are you talking about?"

He chuckled, "You think I haven't noticed how different you are. You're always in the bathroom and barely eating. You've become very cranky and emotional. You've even lost weight and my sister was the same way when she was pregnant with my nephew so what's up?"

I shook my head and said, "Okay, first of all why are you clocking my moves so hard and second of all who is we?!"

He seemed truly offended saying, "Wow! You don't think this affects me too?"

I replied, "Uh no, I don't. Now stop being silly and pass me this study guide. I'm trying to finish so I can watch Shonda-Land unless you want to be surrounded by study guides, study notes, and formulas all night long. I'm not missing out on Meredith, Olivia, and Annalise for you."

He handed me the study guide while saying, "Harper, not only would I have to deal with the cravings but the mood swings too. You're already crazy without being pregnant. I need to be prepared for this. Shonda and the rest of them won't be the ones

dealing with these hormones.
Do you want me to buy you a test or something because we need to know?"

We both just burst out laughing because we were high and something about the awkwardness of the moment was hilarious to us both. Omari was a complete fool, but he wasn't completely wrong I guess, so I said, "Okay, maybe you're my person and maybe you make a great point, so the answer is no we're not pregnant. Is that better?"

He sighed so hard the papers flew up as he said, "Yes, it is! I don't think we're ready for a baby yet."

I giggled. "You sound more like the father rather than the would-be uncle."

Without hesitation, "Well assuming the biological father is a figment of your imagination, then it's safe to say he'll be a deadbeat. Don't think for one second I wouldn't take care of y'all, Harper."

The thought of Omari taking care of me, and my baby made me cringe. He was too much of a player for me to even picture him in the role of a father, then again, the thought of a man taking care of me, and my little baby made me smile. I'm sure one day he'll make a great father, but it definitely won't be to any kids I have. The very reason Calvin broke up with was because he wanted this baby and thinks I didn't. I wanted him and the baby but sometimes you must realize your wants can be bullshit and it's best to go with your needs. I replied, "Thanks Omari. That's real sweet of you but umm the fuck you mean a figment of my imagination. It's nice to know somebody cares but I don't think Calvin would walk away from his child like that. I'm pretty sure he'd be there."

Omari said in an aggravated tone, "Believe what you want Harper. The man didn't even want a commitment so how is he going to actually want a baby. You need to open your eyes man. He just wanted some pussy and he got that."

I rolled my eyes and sighed. My first high and he was already blowing it with his asshole nature. Calvin may be a cheater but that doesn't mean he wouldn't be a great father. Luckily, neither one of us will have to find out anytime soon. I replied, "You do realize you're a big ass man whore that doesn't want commitment either? What is so different between you and Calvin?"

He didn't have to say the difference. It was obvious. He wasn't married. Omari could be the biggest man whore he wanted to be. Calvin was the one stepping out on vows. I could clearly see that I had offended him. He already knew the difference and I was wrong to box him in with Calvin like that. He gathered his things in silence and when he was done, he said, "You're going to believe what you want regardless. Congratulations I guess." He stormed out the door and I was left feeling angry and ashamed of myself.

I sent Omari a text saying, "Sorry friend. Exams just getting to me."

"You good."

I wasn't but he wouldn't have understood. He's from Madison with a dad that's a pastor and ethics professor at Tougaloo while his mom is the principal at Madison Central. He's the second oldest of five kids and all of them are destined for greatness excelling in any and everything they touch. All of Jackson, Ridgeland, and Madison is his family. He came to J State so that his dad wouldn't be able to clock his moves, and everybody here thinks they know him but only know what he tells them. When he's with me, he's the most laid-back, goofy, pothead that I've ever met. On the outside, he's a standup guy. I mean completely innocent! We have a chill no judgement zone and here I was judging him like I didn't know anything about him. I'm the one that's scared of being judged in ways I'm not ready for if anybody knew the truth about me and Calvin.

# Chapter Three

KNOCK!

KNOCK!

Without even checking the time or asking who it was, I jumped up from the couch and opened the door. Clearly still sleep and dreaming because I thought I was looking at Channing Tatum asking for my signature. I figured if I rubbed my eyes, it would clear my vision however the sun was still blinding. Using my hand as a shield I could easily see this man was more of a Channing Tatum stunt double in a FedEx suit. I signed my name as he handed me this long rectangle box. Instead of closing the door and saving my eyes from the glaring sun, I watched this fine white chocolate walk back to his truck. He was all the proof I needed that those brown shorts do a few men some justice. He gave me the sweetest view as I closed the door.

The first thought I had was to trash it without even opening it. I knew I hadn't ordered anything, but the box sat on my table taunting me! I sat down on the couch after unboxing the package just to be met with a black rectangle box with a card taped to it. It read *'Drop Dead Gorgeous'* which made me smile because it reminded me of Aleccia. We used to say this whenever we felt like we were the baddest and finest things walking the earth. That was our motto and if we seen a chick looking completely stunning, we'd say it to her as well. Calvin was so tired of us saying it, but it wasn't long before he was saying it too. The only thing I could conclude was that Calvin was attempting to apologize for his actions. The man had some nerve to treat me like some random chick he met and knocked up. I got up and took the box to the trash. I stared at the card one last time and threw it away as well. Any other time, I'd forgive and forget but not this time. No, because this time I wanted him to understand he wasn't coming back. He made it very clear that we were over and I for one would love for it to stay that way. He wasn't getting another chance to play with my heart. I wanted it understood that I was moving on. I've been invested in Calvin in ways I shouldn't have been for too long. I'm ready for a relationship where I'm the guy's one and only. I can't help it, if I still love Calvin. I'll never deny my love for him. He will always hold a special place in my heart because he's my first love. I don't understand it myself. I couldn't cloud my mind with these thoughts of him though.

I glanced at my phone, and it was already 3:23pm which meant I needed to get ready for this double date I was having with Omari, Tia and stillarrogant89 from POF. I have never been on a date, and I certainly wasn't about to start with a stranger from the internet. Normally I would've ignored a message from somebody with a username like that, but he sent this long intro and I felt special while reading it. He seemed genuine in his approach, and it was refreshing from the multiple 'Hey sexy' messages that I was getting. Unfortunately, he doesn't know it's a double date, but the most important thing is that neither one of us are getting catfished. I met them at Applebee's on Lakeland because I highly doubt, he'd be stupid enough to cause a scene in Flowood. I should've walked right back out and said fuck it as soon as I seen who Tia really was but nope, I wanted to actually try. Omari truly is my best male friend and I guess I want him happy even if it's with some psychotic hoe such as Hope Natia Magee.

I remember her from high school, but I technically met this simple-minded little girl a couple of years ago at a house party in Virden Addition. It wasn't nothing special. A group of guys in the living room playing spades and spectating while a different group were at the dining room table playing bones. A few guys outside shooting dice and because I showed up with Omari, all of the snobby loose coochie hoes were side eyeing me in the most evil way. Granted Omari was the finest dude there, it was no need for them to turn their noses up at me. I don't even see

Omari like that. Of course, when I first met him, I indeed had a crush on him for the quickest little second. The man is fine as fuck and I ain't blind! Omari's style is always fresh and clean. The boy knows how to dress! He works out like he's done some time in prison making his arms buff with a rock hard 6 pack. He reminds me of a very rough and sexy 50 Cent with the smooth facial looks of Morris Chestnut. I've seen girls literally throw themselves on him. Even the professors done got with him and apparently a few of his old high school teachers done hit him up as well. It's sad because all of them think they're his number one when they aren't even the main one. He's tried running those tired lines and using his piece of game on me and I'm quick to dismiss him. Granted he's got a very good head on his shoulder, works for MDOT, and hella funny. He's a real-life sweetheart and for whatever reason females automatically assume we're together when that's never been the case. We're just good friends. He gives me rides to work, we study together, and hang out. They stay worried about the wrong thing. I don't even let it get to me. It would probably mean something if I was trying to join in his lineup of ball lickers. I'm just happy that I'm not. My plate of personal problems and love interests are enough to last about five lifetimes.

Imagine my surprise when he agrees with this double date saying he can't wait to introduce me to his new girlfriend. I sat down at the table as they sat down directly across from me. Before he started to talk, stillarrogant89 was walking up to the table. He kissed me and sat down beside me. He wasn't a catfish. Bonus points because his profile picture was hella fine and I was ready to get back my apartment for Netflix and Chill. The look on Tia's face was priceless. I'm not sure if it was her makeup making her look so dead and pale or if it was the moment but everything in me screamed it's both! Omari and stillarrogant89 shook hands and Omari began by saying, "Okay y'all this is my girl, Tia."

She interrupted, "Fiancée."

He grimaced, "I'm sorry. Fiancée. Anyway, I wanted you to

meet her because you're like a sister to me. With that being said, I'm very protective of my family especially the black women." His attention directed at my date.

Before I could even reply, Tia had beaten me to the punch, "I don't think she's going to need your protection babe. It's not like she's your blood. Besides buddy over there gone protect her if need be."

I chuckled, and stillarrogant89 cleared his throat. We all knew she was trying me. I looked dead at Omari thinking *Somebody? Anybody?! Please just smack her before I do.* Omari must've known what I was thinking because he looked at Tia and chimed in, "You must be ready to go?"

She was pissed, "Yes! I don't even know why the fuck they're here!"

I truly had to bite my tongue to keep from cussing this girl out. I looked up at the ceiling pondering whether to lie and say to this bitch I'm fucking Omari or to humble myself and let it go. I stood up and replied, "One thing I won't be is a fool. This entire fucking thing is a joke. I'm gone! Omari you know where to find me when you're ready." I got my purse and walked out. Yeah, that friendship is pretty much dead now. I could've savaged it for Omari but for what? I'm too grown for this drama filled childish ass shit. I should've never even entertained it.

Stillarrogant89 was right on my ass though. He caught up with me at my car. "Damn, boo.
I ain't mad at cha though."

I smiled through the anger, "I'm sorry but I can't deal with that shit. That's his problem not mine. He chose her, so he needs to deal with her and all that extra shit she got going on."

He held me and said, "You're right. I'm happy you're better than these other females. All they would've done is get in a fight and end up in jail waiting on me to bail them out."

"I can't afford the jail time. My bills would be like 'Bitch where you at?' and then where would I stay?" We both laughed and agreed to chill at his house while he ordered some pizza. He assured me that all frustrations would be handled.

He certainly didn't disappoint me. Normally I'd take my time getting to know a guy because I always had Calvin to scratch any itch, I had but now that I'm a completely free agent, I no longer cared about getting to really know anybody. I'm just looking to get my back blown out and stillarrogant89 had just the right tools for the job. We'd been sexting for days, and this meetup was bound to happen as long as he was really who he said he was. The sex had potential, but he needed to work on stamina. I didn't think anything of twisting his nipples even though they were extremely sweaty. Maybe for some girls it would've been weird but not for me. It was the roaring like a lion while I twisted them, that turned me off from him. I'm really not into that furry sex shit and him roaring made me feel like I was a step away from wearing a cheetah costume or something.

My walk of shame started at ten that night while he was snoring from the twenty-minute session we had. He couldn't even give me a round two. Lesson learned. It took about 30 minutes to get from McDowell to Ridgewood Rd only because I was enjoying the drive which are the best at night since the roads are so clear. I thought I was tripping when I pulled up to my apartment because Calvin was pulling up beside me. I just threw my hands up. This needed to be his last time popping up at my apartment like this. I don't know if he came bearing gifts or not. He waited by my door as if he knew I was going to let him in. I took my sweet time to get to the door and as soon as I was there, he started lying, "Hey baby. I've been missing you. I got you something special."

I chuckled, "Thanks."

He had this stank look on his face trying to understand why I was being nonchalant with him. The lies continued, "Don't be like that baby. Come on. Let me in and I can make it all up to you."

As tempting as that sounded, it wasn't enough. I'd rather have furry sex than to succumb to Calvin again. I declined his offer, "I'm exhausted, and I do believe you have a wife to get home to."

He walked away saying, "Wow. Okay Harper."

I didn't bother watching him walk away. There was nothing exciting about Calvin to me anymore. He was the oldest old news I had. After entering my apartment, I almost threw away the Victoria Secret's bag he had given me. I looked inside and it was lingerie. Classic Calvin. I wondered about the present from earlier, so I went to the trash to pull the long black rectangle box out and opened it. The contents were shocking and repulsive. I screamed as I dropped the

box on the floor. It was a dead rat laying on top of three dead roses. There was another card on the inside saying....... *'HAPPY 23rd BIRTHDAY'*

# Chapter Four

It's been a week since I attempted to file a police report. It was nothing the police could do. I didn't believe Calvin would send me the black box so ultimately, I had no person of interest, no motive, no nothing. Of course, they kept the box as evidence, so they say. They probably just threw it away. I felt crazy trying to explain that I have no idea why I'd receive something like this. I am completely terrified though. Needless to say, I haven't slept too good but thankfully Charmaine has agreed to stay with me the next few days. She's certainly not the best roommate to have but it's better than being alone. We ended up at the Walmart on 18 feeling more defeated than ever before. I planned on getting groceries but ended up walking out with snacks and wine. I was ready to go home and down an entire bottle of Jose Cuervo and take my ass to sleep. She ran up to the car, hopping in the passenger side with a bottle of Patron in her hand. I already knew what that meant.

I couldn't even get in the car good before seeing my back tire completely flat. What was happening to me? I slammed my car door which startled Charmaine, "Damn girl. What the fuck is wrong with you?"

I pointed to the tire, "Do you see this shit?! I can't catch a fucking break!"

She sighed, "Oh girl that's nothing. At least it ain't ya engine or ya transmission. Hold on let me call my friend. He's a mechanic and he stays right around the corner in those apartments."

Charmaine was right. It was just a tire, but I honestly didn't have the money for a spare tire. I sent Omari a text telling him my problem and where I was. Charmaine suggested we walk to the apartments where the mechanic lived and before we could start walking, I head a guy say, "Hey baby you need some help."

Charmaine was smiling all extra hard which told me whoever he was had to be fine, and I certainly needed help. I turned around and it was Calvin. Instantly, I was pissed and hissed, "What the fuck are you doing here Calvin?!"

He exhaled, "Had to pick up something from Walmart. Why else would I be here? Better yet why are you here? You could've gone to the Walmart in Ridgeland. It's closer to you anyway. If you were hoping to see me then here I am."

I groaned, "You're the last person I want to see."

He smiled, "You're cute when you're angry."

I smiled back, "I'm sure your wife is cuter."

He nodded, "Harper, let me help you. You know damn well you mean more to me than some piece of paper."

I raised an eyebrow with my head titled to the side, "But a divorce is just a piece of paper too. Besides, I have help coming. I don't need nor want anything from you anymore so please go."

He scoffed, "Your ungrateful ass is going to regret that."

I shrugged my shoulders as he turned and walked away in anger. Charmaine and I started walking behind Walmart up the street to these apartments off of Robinson Rd. It didn't take long but it felt like forever with Charmaine asking me a bunch of questions about Calvin. When we made it took the mechanic's apartment, I was completely dry mouth. I was hoping for the coldest glass or bottle of water he had. This man opened the door and somehow my mouth became a watering hole. What mechanic is this damn fine? Looking like a Boris Kodjoe mixed with The Rock. I don't even understand how God could sculpt such a fine specimen. The most important question was why I had never met this man. He lived in Jackson, MS and not once had I even heard his name.

He let us in, and the flirting commenced. I couldn't control the sex demon that lived within. I needed a moment. Just a taste. A tense if you will. He wasn't shy about showing off his skills either. We left Charmaine in the front while we had a meeting in his bedroom and wasn't a thing wrong with his stamina! No weird lion roaring. He was a master in the art of sex. Everything about him was too good to be true. I couldn't let myself get caught up in this guy. He had blown Calvin's sex game completely out of the water. We were interrupted when Omari called saying he was at Walmart waiting on us. He had gotten a spare tire and had already started to change the tire. I needed the distraction because without it, we would've gone all day and all night. He wanted a chance to take me out and really get to know me, but I couldn't risk it. I'm not in the zone for love and commitment. I'm just enjoying life for what it is, and this moment turned my day completely around from shit to shine. The mechanic dropped us off at Walmart and it made me wonder why on Earth would Charmaine have us walk there when he could've picked us up.

It's that kind of stupid mess that I can't get with.

Omari followed us back to my apartment as he was worried considering how the most recent events in my life was going. We all went inside, and I grabbed three glasses from the top shelf and mixed us all some drinks while Omari fired the gas up and went in, "Girl why in the fuck is Rashad back fucking with Javon. His bitch ass think I don't know though. I been knowing since day one. He stay lying and shit talking about she stalking him and won't leave him alone!"

Rotation was on me, and I was tearing up from coughing so hard. I hit the blunt entirely too damn hard. I said, "I don't know. I guess he love her but if she is stalking him why hasn't he called gotten a restraining order or something?"

Man, Charmaine was a pro. Her and Omari could smoke each other under the table. I'm still trying not to die while they're both puffing with ease. She replied, "Girl, he don't love that bitch. He just ain't got nowhere to go since his people done put him out again. He's a fucking freeloader with no job and too many baby mamas. That bitch desperate and so is he!"

"Well why you won't just take the man in and show him the

love he's trying to find in her. I mean how does the saying go? Something about holding him down or something?"

Charmaine just shook her head no. You could tell she was in the zone too. She started to lean back and talk low as she said, "Bitch bye! That nigga can't stay with me. Not now, not ever. I done played the hold a nigga down fool once too many times with his ass. He don't like to keep a job and all he do is fuck off with other bitches. He stays having me in drama so now the only thing he can do for me is eat this sexy plump ass when I call for it."

I just stared in disbelief while feeling the awesome effects of this gas. Omari was in his zone playing games on his phone. It was clear he was only here for the weed at this point. According to him, Charmaine stayed with gas that puts him on his ass. I replied, "Wait, he eats ass?! I can't imagine fucking Rashad. He's just not cute to me and now you tell me he eats ass."

She laughed, "You one of the few because all the bitches trying to get some of him. I taught him everything they love too. I turned that little baby into a grown man."

Charmaine and I continued talking about Rashad, her new boo, our plans for the future, school, and everything else. She lit up 2 more blunts, we had killed the Alize and Patron, and started on the bottle of Nuvo. We were in there! Charmaine turned her playlist on, and we both just started dancing. The drinking and smoking didn't stop. For a moment everything was good. We were all laughing, and I could feel Aleccia there with us. This was something I truly needed. I wish my friend could've died in her sleep at the age of 101 or something, not a car accident. She was too beautiful to die like that. I could easily picture my tatted-up brownie boo with that loud mouth, that everybody who really knew her loved. She had a heart of gold. She was a real sweetheart in every sense of the word. She'd been hurt more times than a few and her heart was wrapped up in barb wire or something. Aleccia hardly ever let anybody in. You couldn't help but fall for her though. The girl could've had any guy she wanted and his woman too. When we met Charmaine is when Aleccia started to show her true colors though. We were on a school field trip our junior year and I met Charmaine first. I wanted all of us to be the best of friends but for the longest Aleccia just couldn't stand Charmaine because she felt like Charmaine was taking her best friend away. This shit went on even after graduation though. It was always tension when we hung out. It got to a point where I couldn't put these two in the same room together without some shit hitting the fan.

Aleccia had just come back from Texas to visit. It was her first visit since taking the modeling deal and I missed her so much even though it had only been about 8 months since I lived there with her. One day we were just chilling at her godmother's house off Terry and McDowell behind McDonald's. We were drinking and talking shit as we always did. It was in that moment that she finally told me why she couldn't stand Charmaine. She took a big ass gulp of vodka, she looked at me and said, "Man Harper, why the fuck do you even hang with that Charms bitch?"

I rolled my eyes because I knew where this was going. I just wanted to get buzzed and chill. I told her, "Don't call her a bitch man. I wouldn't let her call you one and beside she's cool, you just won't give her a chance."

Aleccia slick spazzed out saying, "I don't give her a chance because I know what kind of low-down hoe ass bitch she really is!"

I laid back on the floor. Aleccia was getting ready to go in on this girl and she wasn't even there, but my drunk ass didn't even direct the conversation in another direction. I replied, "What has she done to you for her to be all of that?'

"The girl is a straight up hoe. She fucked all of the football team, sucked up the entire drumline, not to mention she was sucking dick on the spiral staircase and fucking behind the cafeteria. She deserves to be in the Hall of Fame for whoredom at Jim Hill and to top it all off she fucked Elijah and Isaiah."

I bet my overly buzzed ass sat up then. I couldn't believe what she was telling me. Elijah and Isaiah were some fine ass twins that Aleccia and I dated together damn near all of high school. Aleccia and Elijah broke up the day after graduation, but Isaiah and I broke up the night of junior prom. We were both ready to test new waters so to speak. I never knew why Aleccia and Elijah stopped talking. I just assumed it had to do with her modeling career, but I clearly was wrong. I looked at her and said, "When you learn this shit?"

She passed me the little bottle of peach New Amsterdam to me while saying, "Shit, Elijah and I ain't together but we still fuck around and yesterday I went to his house to see him. He came out to the car, and we were talking until Isaiah came out of the house with Charmaine. She didn't know it was me in the car of course. I asked Elijah how they knew each other, and he told me."

That shit pissed me off because Charmaine knew exactly who Isaiah was. I introduced her to him, so I know she knew who he was. That's violation right there. You don't fuck your girl's man. What the fuck man?! I told Aleccia, "Thanks boo. I'll be watching that hoe now. I bet she'll NEVER meet Calvin though."

"Bitch, I wish I never met Calvin! What the fuck?! That nigga is the devil. Straight up pure evil!"

We both just laughed because she stayed hating on the man, but she knew of all the dudes I ever talked to, Calvin wasn't going anywhere no time soon. I was happy to know somebody was looking out for a bitch though. I knew if the tables were turned, I'd definitely let her know what was up too. Friends like that only come along once in a lifetime. Yeah, I dropped Charmaine with the quickness, but some months passed, and we were able to talk it out. I just let bygones be bygones. It was some ole petty ass high school bullshit anyway. Isaiah was a cool dude, but I had been messing with Calvin the entire time anyway. I think I was just drunk and in my feelings at the time I received the information. Aleccia still wasn't feeling her, but she eventually dealt with her for me. Charmaine remained a hoe and I realized over time that if I

was dating a guy then she had to have him too. She swore

SECRETS OF MY HEART'S DESIRE

up and down that I was fucking Omari. We both kept telling her we weren't and just didn't see each other that way. We ended up falling out about him and everything. I didn't give two fucks about it. By that time, I was just so over the friendship. She strongly felt like I was cock blocking because I wouldn't put her on him. Hell, I thought we were all grown. I thought we left our childish insecurities at Jim Hill.

I guess that was only me.

What grown ass woman needs somebody else to put her on some dick? That's the perfect way to lose that dick. He's going to be more interested in the female that approached him and not the one that's standing on the sidelines waiting for the answer. I kept telling her the same thing over and over, if you want him then to go get him. He's a hoe, it's not like he's going to say no. Charmaine is a pretty girl, but she got a few what the fuck face moments in her. It's like certain angles she shouldn't approach because she's becomes Gargamel's little sister but other than that she's cute and from what the grapevine says, she's sucking souls and whatnot. She still refused to approach the man so eventually I told him she was trying to fuck but too scared to say something. He straight up laughed in my face. He was all for it but according to him she wasn't his type. He still got her down and the next thing I know she's acting all uppity after getting the dick. She was walking around here acting like Queen Sheba and shit. Throwing it in my face how big it was and how he made her tap out. She was getting ready to spend her entire little CNA check on the man until game night at my apartment. Charmaine was butt ass hurt when he came over with Domonique. He introduced her as his girlfriend while Queen Sheba was introduced as just Harper's friend. I laughed so hard, the bitch walked out, and we didn't speak for almost 4 months. I couldn't control it. I didn't even feel bad the next day, but I had nothing to apologize for. I warned her. She didn't listen.

I left memory lane where it was and came back to reality. Charmaine was passed out on the couch and that's where she was going to stay. I went to the hall closet and grabbed a blanket and placed over her. I wasn't even going to attempt to wake her snoring ass up, but I like my air blasting and I'm not trying to freeze her. I went to my room where my big king size bed was waiting for me and laid down. Omari had gotten in the bed hours ago and went to sleep. It wasn't a problem. It's a king size bed so it's more than enough room. I just stared at this picture on my nightstand of me and Aleccia on my birthday three years ago. I don't know why it had to be her. I'm still pretending as if I'm okay. I just stared at the picture. We were so happy and so free. I cried myself to sleep going down memory lane. I couldn't let it go. I couldn't let her go.

# Chapter Five

Every woman needs at least one freak'um dress for la-dies' night, but Charmaine's entire closet consisted of freak'um dresses, freak'um shirts, freak'um shorts, and freak'um shoes. I watched her try on a thousand different outfits while she kept repeating the lyrics 'Micros and my stilettos.' It was only half accurate as she didn't have any micros in her head. She was rocking a sleek long black ponytail with a bang swooped to the right side looking like her version of Ariana Grande. Ten outfit changes later and she finally says, "Okay girl we got to hurry up if we still want to get in free."

I tilted my head to the side in disbelief as she tried to make it seem like I was holding her up from getting her butt rubbed on at Freelons. This girl took about five hours to get ready just to wear the first outfit she picked out. I was annoyed but I was more ready to shake and twerk on a cute guy or two. Luckily for her it was free before midnight and she was done by 10:40P. Charmaine lived across from Westland Plaza, so the club was only ten minutes away if that. I stood up with keys in hand and we made our way to the car. The only thing I hated about getting in free was that everybody always showed up after the free period so everybody that shows up before is just standing around with a few people here and there dancing. Charmaine refers to me as a grandma since I'm trying to party and get back home before midnight, but I thought that was the entire point of partying. Staying out too late leads to trouble.

I wasn't surprised to see the line long as hell in the last thirty minutes of being free. Charmaine was the one in dire need of getting in before midnight because she was broke but I had the cover fee for both of us just in case. As soon as we entered, I spotted this sexy hunk of a man talking to some girl in the corner. If I didn't know any better, I'd swear she was Tia. I kept my sight on the guy and wasn't worried about the girl until she turned around and it was confirmed to be Tia. I didn't want her to see me, so I tried my best to steer clear of her while considering sending Omari a text to see if he was coming to Freelons which I knew he wasn't. Omari hated the vibe in Freelons and preferred Mirage with his dance team. All they do is krump and break dance with a few slow grinders. I love the diversity in their group, from the white chocolate to the dark chocolate, they are all fine ass men! They could make the Jackson version of Magic Mike if they really wanted to which is why it's baffling how I see Tia walking around with some coochie cutters and a halter grinding on any dude giving her attention. I would've been at home with my man or at the club with my man but to each is his own.

Charmaine and I started dancing on each other after a while. I placed my hands on her shoulders with hers on my mine and we both started popping and dropping it low. Some dudes walked up behind us as if this was our mating call and I suppose it was because we eventually let each other go and started to just grind and twerk on the guys to the beat. It was nasty hour with all the nastiest songs playing like 'Lick' by Joi. That song is forever stamped in the nasty song hall of fame for any true Jackson native. I turned around to face my dance partner and I was smitten to see the very guy I had my eyes on earlier. He handed me his phone and whispered in my ear, "Can I get your number?" I nodded and saved my number in his phone. I didn't bother calling or texting myself because I was confident that he was going to hit me up later. We continued to party until just before the club closed. We had to fight the parking lot traffic because after partying of hours, nobody is ever ready to go home and go to sleep. The next stop is either IHOP or Waffle House because nothing else is open at two in the morning. I guess I'm a grandma because I took me and Charmaine to my apartment to go to sleep. Drama normally follows after the club, and I wasn't trying to get caught up in anything.

A few hours in bed and there goes my phone ringing. Why was this guy from the club calling me this early in the morning?! Ugh! Not today devil. I was going to ignore it until it stopped and started again. The screen lit up with Omari's name. What was he even doing up this early?! I haven't seen nor heard from him since he helped me with my flat tire. Even graduation as come and gone since then. He's double down on Tia and has completely thrown me away. I almost didn't attend but I worked hard for this Bachelor of Arts degree, and I needed a reason to perk up and smile. I needed a reason to dress up and feel good about myself and that's exactly what I did. Our interaction with each other was like two people forced to meet at a gathering because Tia was there, and nobody needed to catch a case based on stupidity. That awkward and tense feeling of please somebody save me from this conversation stained every word that uttered out of our mouths. So why on earth was he blowing my phone up now? He never stopped calling. I forced myself to answer the phone. Not really trying to be up at seven in the morning unless I'm making money and today was supposed to had been an extremely lazy day. My first off day from my new job and here he was blowing up my phone. As soon as I answered, he said, "Open the door."

Groggy and confused, I replied, "Open what door?"

He sighed, "Your front door."

Was this fool was at my apartment?! I stumbled out of the bed and made my way to the front door. Charmaine was dead to the world on the couch. WWII could be happening around her and she'd sleep peacefully through the gunfire and bombs going off. I wasn't worried about waking her up nor did I bother to put on a robe or house shoes. I had on clothes for the most part but a crop top, boy shorts, and long mix matched Spongebob socks isn't the idea attire to open front doors with. The man laughed as soon as the door swung open. I tried to slam the door closed and he caught it. I wasn't up for the games this early in the morning. I just turned around and headed back to the bed as I said, "I don't have time for you today. I'm tired. I just want to sleep."

He continued to laugh, "You look like you've been thrown away."

"I have by you." I got back in bed and snuggled under the covers. "Where have you been stranger? Thought we weren't friends anymore?"

"I didn't throw you away butt face and if I remember correctly, you stopped answering my calls and text messages but fuck all that. You got some shit going on."

"What do you mean?" He handed me his phone and there I was butt ass naked across the screen. My entire body was frozen stiff. I sat up and said, "What the fuck? Why do you have this on your phone? Where did you get this?!"

"It was sent to me last night on messenger. I knew it wasn't you, so I came over to see what was going on and who I needed to fuck up?"

"If I knew who, you would be bailing me out of jail right now! I can't fucking believe this right now!" I started to freak completely out! I picked up my phone and I had 17 missed calls, 28 text messages, 4 voicemails, and a bunch of other shit. They all read and said the same thing. My Facebook account had been hacked and everybody had all kinds of pictures and messages from me. I didn't answer nor call back anybody. This had to be some kind of perverted joke by some bitch made dude that I don't fuck with or some extra mad bitch but why me? When I finally logged into my page, my heart dropped. The nudes were sent in messenger, but so much more was on my page. Disgusting posts that I would never post and replies to the comments with shit I would never say. I quickly changed my information around and deactivated the page. Fuck social media! If they didn't have my number, then they didn't need to contact me.

"Who did you piss off Harper?"

"Omari, I have not one idea who I could've made this fucking mad. I only sent those pictures to one person, and I don't even know how anybody else could have them right now."

"Who did you send them to?"

"I don't want to say right now but believe me they were some-body I completely trusted."

"Well maybe their phone was stolen or something. Maybe somebody hacked their accounts as well."

"Maybe so. Still, I don't know why this is happening. Just a few weeks ago I received a package with a dead rat and three dead roses. Can you believe that shit?"

"Harper, this has to be somebody you know. Whoever it is they slashed your tire that day I came and changed it."

"I don't know anybody it could be though."

"What about Calvin?"

"What about Calvin? Why would Calvin do this Omari? What does he have to gain from this?"

He raised his hands in defense, "I don't know. It was just a suggestion."

"I'm sorry I'm not trying to lash out at you. I just don't know what to do right now."

"No, it's okay. I'm here for you." Omari held me as I began to cry. I was dumbfounded, hurt, and didn't know what to do be-sides going back to the police to file another report. I knew they wouldn't be able to help me because I had nobody to think of to even suggest but I knew Calvin wasn't the person behind this. It still didn't stop me from calling him. Maybe I did really piss him off but of course he didn't answer. I thought I knew Calvin better than this. I thought he would never do something so foul!

I went ahead and got dressed, Omari went with me to the precinct to file another report. This time I met with Detectives Bibbs, and he told me exactly what I already knew. It was noth-ing they could do for me. There's no surefire way to find out who the hacker is, and the person didn't physically harm me. Once again, I was defeated. This was a wasted trip. They couldn't do anything when I received the rat and roses and now, they can't do nothing while somebody is sending these pictures to every-body from my Facebook page. I feel violated and hands down scared. What if this person is just watching me and waiting to snatch me up? Then again, this is probably just somebody getting off on scaring people and it's nothing I can do about it. Omari took me back home and made sure I was good. Charmaine had been smoking so when we got back, she already had a few rolled up. As soon as I hit it, I was about to cough up both lungs. Omari just laughed and said, "I thought you were a pro by now since you've been smoking with us."

I took a sip of my green tea before I said, "Boy shut up! You know I'm a rookie."

"That you are." He chuckled and then got serious, "I missed your crazy ass. Aside from all of this stalker shit going on, how are you?"

I figured it was best to be honest with him this time. These creep sessions with randoms haven't helped me in accepting the bad along with the good and moving on with my life. I replied, "I've been okay. It's about to be a year now since my life just turned upside down. My best friend was killed in a car accident and at the same time I had just had an abortion. I'm feeling like I barely have a handle on my life now. I feel like I'm just now getting back to me."

Charmaine chimed in with an attitude, "I didn't know none of this."

Omari seemed stunned, "Oh damn. Maybe it'd be good if you found somebody to talk to. You look better than before. You got a whole glow on you. I should've been a better friend though. I didn't know you had so much going on. Charms told me about y'all friend. She was that supermodel, right?"

"Yeah, that was her."

Charmaine continued, "She wasn't really my friend, but she was cool."

"Damn." He chuckled, "Why you never introduced us though?!"

I glared at Charmaine as I slapped Omari's arm and said, "Boy! You know you're a hoe plus she was married!"

He waved his hand in the air and said, "Shid never stopped me before."

I laughed as I got up to cook something to eat.  I replied, "I ain't got time for you Omari.
I'm gone put your ass out!"

He got up and followed me into the kitchen while Charmaine stayed in the living room trying to make my misery about her. Omari replied, "Nah, don't do that.  I gotta keep you safe."

"I'm good.  I'm sure it's just somebody playing pranks and shit."

"You know if I had known about the baby, I would've been here for you.  I'm just a call away."

I lied, "I know Omari.  I didn't want anybody to know.  I thought I could handle it on my own and for the most part I did. I just didn't realize how hard it would be to forgive myself but I'm good now."

The menu consisted of smothered drumsticks, brown rice, and steamed cauliflower.  Omari joked on my healthy eating since I had the smothered drumsticks.  I didn't care.  It was still healthier than what Charmaine wanted which was fried pork chops, rice with sugar, and mac and cheese.  He was lucky to have a friend that could actually cook and loved to feed her friends. We stayed up all night watching scary movies until we passed out.  I was terrified to be alone and no matter how honest I had been with them.  I didn't really want to blurt that out as well.  It was obvious in the same sense though.

It wasn't long before Shirley started to blow my phone up as well.  I walked outside to get away from Omari and Charmaine. Shirley knew about the Facebook hack because she only called me when somebody died or was in jail.  I answered with much hesitation dreading the conversation that was about to take place, "Hey ma."

She screamed, "Have you lost your fucking mind?  You need to take that shit off of Facebook.  I don't need people looking at me crazy because of the dumb shit yo ass is doing?
The fuck is you a prostitute now?!"

I thought about explaining how it wasn't me but what good would it had done?  She was convinced that I was the one behind

the Facebook posts and messages. I attempted to reply,
"Ma, I've already deactivated Facebook. Nothing else to worry about."

She wasn't hearing a word I said, "I don't give a fuck about you deleting Facebook. That shit gone stay on the internet forever. Do you know James received that nasty ass shit? I should come beat your ass since you want to try my fucking husband!"

I shook my head in disbelief at the shit she was saying and hung the phone up without even replying. I wasn't going to deal with this woman today. My phone begins ringing again now that anger had filled inside of me. I quickly answered, "Look, the shit wasn't even me so back the fuck up off of me!"

"Baby, I know you wouldn't do this. Do you need me to come over there?"

I glanced down at the phone in my hand and seen that it was Calvin not Shirley. He couldn't leave well enough alone. He couldn't possibly be in love with me and still married to his wife. Why couldn't he just forget about me like I was trying to do with him. I replied, "No! How many times do I have to point you back in the direction of your fucking wife! Call me again and I will tell her every fucking little tidbit about us."

"Try me bitch! You'll be dead before you can utter a word!"

I laughed, "Do your fucking worse you low life son of a bitch!"

If somebody had told me that I would be in this zone with Calvin, I probably would've fought them for speaking negatively on us. I didn't know I could harbor so much hate for a man I was once so deeply in love with. Maybe I was wrong about Calvin but that's still so hard to believe that he would do all of this when he broke up with me in the first place. Nothing in my life was making sense and it was probably time I started to get some sage or something! Omari stepped outside and hugged me as he whispered, "Everything will be okay." Although my mind was in disarray, I believed him and together we prayed for my strength to endure the turmoil until the culprit is captured. The benefits of being friends with a PK. They're definitely going to pray over you and with you!

# Chapter Six

Another off day just gone thanks to weed, food, and sleep but now that I'm up I needed to get ready for Mike to come over when he got off work. For the past month, everything has been really copasetic. There hasn't been any weird packages in the mail or social media hacking. I guess prayers do work and I have Omari to thank for that. Since this month has been so chill, I'm actually trying to see where things could go with me and Mike from Freelons. I actually want to cook for him and that's a big deal when it comes to me and a man. I cook for friends all of the time, but my man will get a five-course meal if he's really all mines. It's the only thing I was ever able to really do for Calvin and his ass loves to eat.

A couple of days after the Facebook hacking bs happened, Mike hit me up to go to Cracker Barrel one day and we've been hanging out and getting to know each other every day. I love staring into his pretty green eyes. He's light skin with these huge muscles. He gives me Rotimi vibes all day long. He even has the same big juicy lips as Rotimi too. When he left the table and went to the bathroom, an older lady walked by me smiling as she said, "Be careful baby. That's one handsome devil." She wasn't lying. That boy so is too sexy! I got to do this right and make him mine! So, tonight I planned for us to have dinner at my apartment. He has a business meeting about opening a gym in Byram. He said he'd be here a little after seven but for some odd reason somebody was banging on my front door like the police in a drug bust. I just threw my hands up as I went to answer the door. People act like they don't know how to knock or something. I went to look out of the peephole and seen Charmaine popping some gum and screaming at some scrub, about why he can't get

with her. I slung the door open and said,
"Bring your country ass in here. Being all extra loud and shit."

She walked in giggling, "Oh my bad. I forgot you live by the wypipo. I'm surprised you're not at work. I came by the other day, but you weren't here."

I rolled my eyes. It made no sense for her to keep popping up when she knew I had a job now. I just shook my head and said, "If you'd get a job, you wouldn't make wasted pop ups."

She smacked, "Oh it wasn't wasted. My boothang stay out this way but girl what kinda work you do? Do they drug test?"

They didn't but I wasn't telling her that. I chuckled, "Naw na and yes they do." I lied. My job did not drug test, but I wasn't about to help her get a job there. I'm very particular about who I let use my name as a reference when it comes to my coins. I'm an advertising manager at Milron, a real estate investment company. It's not hard getting a job there but since I finally have my BA in Advertising, it was even easier. I've worked my ass off to get that degree and even now I want more. I can't believe I'm in grad school and working towards a Masters. It hasn't been easy getting to this point in life. Charmaine's biggest issue with coming to see me was that she didn't want to get a ticket for not being 10/10 on the road on Ridgewood. It didn't bother me if she came or didn't. Charmaine loved saying I wanted to be white because I moved to what she considers the white area of Jackson. I don't see it that way, I just prefer living as far away from Rebelwood as possible. Granted bullets flew a lot less but overall crime is everywhere, it's just a lot less in this area. The grass is literally greener in certain neighborhoods, then again, some neighborhoods don't have grass at all. I wasn't trying to go for a dip in the water or be a gardener, but I was trying to have something a little better than what I knew growing up in South Jackson.

Charmaine broke my train of thought by saying, "I see you got that glow again!"

I glared at her, "Bitch what glow?"

She started to bounce on the chair singing, "That I just got some dick glow!"

We both laughed. I wasn't the type to tell everybody about my love life, especially not Charmaine. Her track history sucks major ass. The only person I ever really told was Aleccia of course. I forgave Charmaine for messing around with Isaiah because we were young, dumb, and full of cum back then. However, Charmaine has proven that she's a hoe through and through. There's no sugarcoating that. She met Calvin by default. I can get real feisty when it comes to my man. My guard will go up and I'll be ready to smack her because I know the next line out of her mouth would be the reason for it. I wanted her mind off of my love life, "Girl, I'm too busy with work."

She looked content with the answer as she replied, "Oh well bitch it must be that moneymaking glow." I got up and headed towards the kitchen to check on what I was cooking. Charmaine followed saying, "Damn, girl you got it smelling good in here. I hope I can get a plate too!"

I quickly gave her that 'girl stop' look as I said, "You can get a plate tomorrow. This right here is for work."

She started to pout, then quickly realized she was getting nowhere and asked, "Have you heard from Pierre?"

I replied, "No not really. He finally unblocked me before I deactivated Facebook and we exchanged numbers. Sometimes, I'll text him and he'll reply with one or two words. I guess he's just really not feeling anybody that reminds him of Aleccia. I really wanted to help him get through this."

Charmaine said, "Oh, I heard he was coming to visit her gravesite next month."

I said to Charmaine, "Damn, if it was me, I don't know how I'd make the trip. Did you know that the guy in the other car is trying to sue Pierre?"

She shook her head and said, "That's fucked up. That man don't need all of that on him like that. It was an accident. He only doing that because Pierre is in the NBA."

I agreed, "Yeah, you right. All he see is money and we're all hurting too. He should be thankful he was able to walk away from it."

"Girl, who wouldn't though?! We all joke about it. He's just one of the ones that wasn't joking. If I didn't personally know Aleccia, I'd be right there with him telling him to get all that he can. It's just life sometimes babe."

I agreed with Charmaine. She was smart when she wanted to be. I don't understand how she was that smart and such a big hoe at the same time. We continued to talk for about three or four hours, then Mike sent me a text saying he was outside. I told Charmaine it was time for her to go. I wish I had cut this short sooner because now they would be meeting in passing. As she walked out the door, he was walking up. I noticed a weird look he gave her. He probably thought she was staying which was all the more reason I should've cut the visit short well before now. They exchanged a few hellos and she walked on to her car. Mike and I enjoyed our night. We watched Netflix in my bed and that's it. No sex. No fondling. Nothing. It was sweet kisses and laughs all night. I was so comfortable in his arms that I fell asleep for the first time in a man's arms. This was something I longed for, to sleep while being held. So many nights I slept alone. So many times, I wanted to beg Calvin to stay, and I knew he wouldn't. It was nice to have this moment. I felt wanted. I felt loved.

Of course, this didn't last long as we were both startled out of our sleep by a loud bang in the living room. Nobody was supposed to had been here but me and Mike. I started to get up, but Mike placed his hand on my shoulder with a finger to his mouth instructing me to remain silent. He creeped to the door and slowly opened it. I was right on his heels holding his arm, scared to death of what the noise could've been. Immediately, Omari popped out of the kitchen with a sandwich in his hand. I pulled Mike back from swinging on him while Omari said, "Oh damn. My bad. I probably should've called."

Relieved to see it was just him, I replied, "You think?"

Mike was looking like he still wanted to fight because Omari wasn't even acknowledging the man's presence as he continued, "I'll be sure to do that next time."

The vibe was becoming tense from the male egos sparring in the air. I gave a quick introduction, "Well sir, this is Mike. Mike this is my best friend Omari."

Mike extended his hand and Omari started walking to the door saying, "Hey, I need to head on out. I was only here to make this bomb ass sandwich. I'll hit you up later and uh nice meeting you Mark!"

I bit my lip at the utter disrespect he just threw at Mike. I knew Omari could be an asshole, but I didn't think he would've slammed the asshole card down so soon like that. How was I going to explain this erratic behavior to this man who was obviously offended? Mike wasted no time in getting his keys and heading out the door. He told me he needed to get home and get some rest but that he'd hit me up tomorrow. I doubted that he would after what just happened, but I kept a glimmer of hope that he would. I called Omari to tell him about himself. He answers as if he hasn't done a thing wrong, "What's up?"

I was firm, "Did you really have to do Mike like that?"

He pretended not to know who I was talking about as he replied, "Who?"

Annoyingly I said, "Mike! The guy I literally just introduced you to!"

He sounded genuinely confused as he asked, "Oh! What did I do to him?"

I scoffed, "You were rude as fuck to him!"

"How? I don't see anything I did wrong."

"For starters, the man tried to shake your and you not only dismissed him, but you completely jacked up his name and called him Mark."

The audacity of him to burst out laughing on this phone let me know, the asshole in him couldn't be controlled. Omari was so deep in the pool of arrogance that he doesn't even see the error of his ways. He replied, "Ahhh damn my bad. I ain't got no beef with the man. He must be ya new lil fuck buddy."

"No, he's not. We're getting to know each other and no we haven't had sex yet."

"I didn't ask about that."

"Yeah, well I said it! Anywho have you been in my apartment like this before because I'm starting to notice a few things missing."

He chuckled, "Yeah I been stealing ya dirty drawls so I can smell them later."

"What? Boy shut up!"

He laughed harder, "I only ever come by like that when I'm in the area and hungry."

"Oh, but how do you even have a key."

"Damn Harper you late. I been had a key."

Even though he couldn't see it, I was rolling my eyes so hard. I replied, "Whatever. Just call next time. Never know I might actually be having sex and I don't need the awkwardness that I experienced today to ever happened again. Cool?"

"No problem."

After getting off of the phone with Omari, I searched my apartment and couldn't find my MacBook. My hope was that I had left it at the office but deep down I knew I left it on this couch. I should have put it up in my room, but I live alone and wasn't thinking about putting it up. Maybe I never brought it in and just thought that I did. It's clear to me that I've been a little too carefree in my life because I've lost a whole freaking laptop in my one bed apartment. What's really going on?!

# Chapter Seven

A year has passed already and I'm standing over my best friend's grave with flowers and balloons. I've finally accepted that she's no longer here and still I can't help but to cry. So many things I wish I could tell her right now but 'I love you and I miss you' is all I would even say. A year has brought so many changes my way and yet as I look around everything looks the exact same. I sat around and waited awhile. I thought I would've seen Pierre, until he sent me a text and let me know he wouldn't be able to make it today. If there's one person, I wish I could actually sit down and talk to, it's him. The one person that was with her in her final moments but I'm sure reliving that constantly is enough. He didn't need me to help him relive the trauma but since it's Mother's Day I decided to visit her mother. I just wanted to feel close to her in some way and figured why not with spend a little time with Ms. Lisa. They were having a memorial for Aleccia, and it was only right for me to attend. I figured I'd bring Mike, but he was busy with work, so I went alone. I didn't want to take Charmaine since they really weren't all that cool, but she's also become very distance. I haven't seen her since last month when she popped up at my apartment. It certainly didn't stop her from texting me and trying to put all of her issues on me. I wasn't trying to hear none of that. I was good on my end and didn't need the extra drama in my day.

I made it to the memorial just in time. They started sharing her pictures from a child to adulthood. I thought I had seen all the pictures of Aleccia but these cousins of hers had reached way back in the archive and found some I bet she didn't even know she had taken. It was truly amazing. When a few stood up to share stories I was crying laughing. They shared the family fights and neighborhood brawls. They shared her dreams and fears. They made me stand and share a story as well. All I could think of was this one time when we played hooky in middle school. Ms. Lisa looked at me crazy as soon as I started too. I just remember being silly standing at the bus stop. That day we chose not to ride the bus. We wanted to savor the moment and walk to school. We felt like the bus dropped us off entirely too soon and we hated everybody on the bus anyway, so we started walking. Before we even started walking good, we ended up getting chased by dogs. I knew that Aleccia had never been to Africa, but I learned that day that the girl could run! As soon as I said that everybody just burst out laughing and agreeing. She tapped into those African roots and hauled ass from those dogs. Left me straight in the dust crying like a baby. By the time I caught up to her, I didn't even want to go to school anymore but it wasn't no turning around. We had to go to school because we were never supposed to be walking. We walked the entire way and right before we could turn the corner and get on the street that led straight to the school, we started getting picked on by this fat high school boy. We ignored him until he threw his drink at us and somehow, we jumped him and still lost. So, since our pants were wet, we chose to walk all the way back home, just for my mom to curse us out and drive us back to school. Everybody was laughing, even Ms. Lisa. We were some dumb kids but that was my girl!

After the memorial, I called my mother to wish her a Happy Mother's Day. She answered as if she was out of breath, "Hello!"

"Hey ma, Happy Mother's Day!"

She sounded aggravated, "Oh thanks."

"Are you okay?"

"Yeah, just wondering where the fuck James is."

I didn't want to hear anything about the man. My phone started ringing from an unknown number. I ignored it and said, "Do you want me to pick you up and go out for dinner?"

She was definitely annoyed, "Girl, I ain't got my mind on that. Your fat ass is always thinking about food at the wrong damn time. Can't you see I'm worried about my husband."

I replied, "I understand. I'll talk to you another day." I hung up. I wasn't about to deal with the attitude that I didn't place there. My phone started ringing again. At this point I wasn't in the mood to talk to anybody. I just wanted to go home and relax in a hot tub with bubbles listening to my Gerald Levert. I couldn't even make it home without my phone ringing back-to-back. My charger wasn't with me, so my phone eventually died thanks to whoever was constantly calling me.

After getting something to eat, working on last minutes edits, it was midnight and as I soaked in the tub, I heard the front door open and close. Who in the hell was in my apartment?! I jumped up out of the tub and wrapped a towel around me. I came out on the bathroom and eased my way down the hall. I peeked around the corner and there Omari was standing at the kitchen counter fixing a fucking sandwich. I walked in and snapped completely out! "Omari, what the fuck are you doing?"

Calm as day, he replied, "Fixing a sandwich, what does it look like?"

Annoyingly I asked, "Again? You know I only let you keep that spare key for emergencies only!

As he made his way to the refrigerator putting everything up, he replied "And hunger isn't an emergency?"

I rolled my eyes, "Give me my damn key!"

He took his plate and went into the living room and sat down. He had already gotten something to drink and all. He turned the TV on and said, "I've used it plenty of times and it wasn't a big deal then, plus I called before I came, you didn't answer."

So now it all made sense in who was calling me back-to-back from a blocked number. I made my way into the living room, "Why did you call me from an unknown number and seriously give me my damn key back?!"

He didn't budge from the recliner. He just continued to watch TV and eat his sandwich. After he finished the sandwich he replied, "I didn't and it ain't like ya lil bust it baby in the back."

He paused and looked at me, "Oh shit, he is huh?"

I stood there glaring at him, "Give me my fucking key!"

He laid it on the living room table and shrugged, "I made a copy anyway."

"Get the fuck out Omari." I don't even have the words to describe the stalker shit he's pulling right now but buddy wasn't going. He continued to drink his soda just as calm as day. I went to my room to get my phone because he was going to leave either on his own or I was giving his sweet Tia a phone call and messing up his entire relationship. There were at least 10 missed called from this unknown number and before I could make it back to Omari, the unknown number was calling me again, so I answered it. Nobody said anything. There wasn't any background noise and then they just hung up. Everything in me, told me it was Tia making prank calls on my phone. I don't know if she knew or even how she knew he was there, but it was very convenient in how I was receiving these blocked calls and Omari popping up. I stormed back to the front to Omari and asked, "What the fuck is going on?"

"Well Harper, you've been ignoring me. Again, I might add. After everything that's happened, I'm not about to just disappear on you or let you disappear on me. We're best friends so at the very least we should be able to talk to each other even when we don't like the person they're dating."

I folded my arms in defense. He made a good point, but I wasn't the person with the problem. I replied, "So you came over here to talk? About what? Oh, excuse me, about who? That hoe you're trying to marry."

He sighed, "No, I didn't come to talk about her. I came to fix a sandwich honestly but here you are acting all uppity like I can't have a sandwich and shit."

I interrupted him, "I fucking live here! I pay the bills here! This is my shit! I can be here.
You're the one that needs to remember he has his own spot to go to."

"So, what? Any other day you would've caught me eating a

sandwich, you would've laughed it off. Ain't no way this dude you with got you acting like this?! I'm not about to stop being your friend just because you and Tia don't like each other."

And there it was. The truth. I replied, "So this is about who I'm with now?"

He threw his hands up, "No. It's about our friendship. We haven't really chilled since Applebee's. I'm sorry for how Tia acted and believe me I told her about herself and told her that she'd have to get over whatever bullshit she got with you if she wanted to be with me." I rolled my eyes and he continued, "I'm for real Harper. I figured I would just come over and wait until you got home so we could finally talk. I didn't think you were already here."

My phone began to ring again. I pulled it out and placed it on the armrest, "So is she calling me from blocked numbers? This is why I didn't answer the phone. Your girl is fucking crazy and drama filled. I don't have time to play games with her. I can be your friend from a distance but I'm not about to deal with this girl and her games."

He picked the phone up and answered but after a few hellos he put the phone back down.

He replied, "I didn't get a reply. I mean if it's Tia, then I'll talk to her but what if it's not her."

"Who else would it be Omari?"

"The same person that sent the roses and hacked your Facebook. I mean it's not hard now. They got all of your information from Facebook."

I sighed, "Who's to say this person isn't Tia this entire time? She's had a problem with me from the moment I met her if you remember correctly."

"Come on Harper. Yeah, she don't like you but that's her insecurities. The person behind this knows you on a different level. What does she have to gain from doing this? That's certified crazy that I can't even fuck with. Besides why would she send you roses? I might can give her the blocked calls but the roses? And how would she end up with those pictures of you?

Doesn't make sense."

"Whatever, maybe the roses and hacking weren't her but until I have proof that it's not her, you keep her crazy ass away from me. And you need to stop popping up at my apartment like this. It's obvious I'm finally no longer single, and I don't want to run him off because you have no boundaries."

He laughed, "Oh she gets a man and now she got rules and shit! If you had answered the phone maybe I wouldn't have to pop up and dude just gone have to get used to me the same way Tia gots to get used to you."

"Omari, you do realize it's damn near one in the morning and you're at my apartment fixing a sandwich with the spare key I let you have. Best friend or not, this shit ain't cool when your bitch is crazy, and I just got in a new relationship so don't fuck this up for me. I really like this guy."

He shook his head, "I guess Harper. You barely even know this dude."

I shrugged, "I know enough, besides that's the purpose of the relationship."

He looked at me, "I'm telling you, until he knows your deepest and darkest secrets and vice versa, then y'all barely know each other."

He made a good point but even he didn't know my deepest and darkest secrets. I replied, "If that's the case then I barely know you."

Omari agreed, "Exactly. You don't but you'd be surprised at what I knew about you. All I'm saying is be careful but let me get back to my side of town. I got to be at work in a few more hours." He stood up and I escorted his crazy ass to the door. We hugged, and he left. I slick wanted him to spend the night because now he had me thinking about what he knew about me. If it wasn't for both of us having to be at work, then I would've wanted an all-night session of tea spilling. Tell me what you know! Then I realized Omari don't know shit, but he made valid points on this blocked number. What if it wasn't Tia? What if it was the same person and why were they doing this shit? I couldn't afford anymore drama with Tia so Omari spending the night wasn't the answer. I called Mike and got no answer, I figured he was sleep since it was so late. As much as I wanted a hardworking man, I could've settled tonight because I was afraid to be alone. I hit up Charmaine and she didn't answer either. She done probably smoked her day away and now knocked out. I swallowed my fears and took my ass to bed. I got a new account to work on at work and I need to make sure I'm giving it my best.

# Chapter Eight

By the time I made it to Charmaine's apartment, I was pissed. She wasn't even home and was sending my calls to voicemail. I drove from Ridgewood all the way to Clinton, and she wasn't even here but told me the car was messed up. I don't know what was up with Charmaine, but she didn't have to just ignore me like she was doing. I drove around a bit with this manila folder on the passenger seat. I needed somebody to talk to and found myself sitting in the driveway at Omari's house in Byram. I guess if I needed somebody to talk to then he was the perfect person. He seen my car outside and came out and tapped on the window. I rolled it down and with a smile he asked, "What's wrong?"

I grimaced, "But what's with the smile?"

He shrugged, "You don't even like driving to Byram so it's kind of funny seeing you out here."

I nodded, "You right. You got some smoke?"

He leaned back, "You trying to smoke?" He went back in the house for a minute and came back out. He got in the car, fired the gas up. He looked as I pulled and then started laughing, "Wow. You're really out here smoking like it's an everyday thang!"

I started coughing, "Man shut up! I just got a lot on my mind."

"What's up? Ole boy done fucked up already huh?"

I glared, "No! Everything is great with Mike. I got this in the mail today though."

Omari started to cough so bad he started tearing up. I chuckled because I knew what I had said was indeed shocking. He replied, "What the fuck is it?"

I shook my head because I really didn't know and was

terrified to open it. I replied, "I didn't want to open it alone. I know how I can be, and I didn't want to get sucked back into depression."

Omari looked at me and passed the blunt as he said, "Why don't you come in? I cooked some red beans with rice, fried chicken, and cornbread if you want some."

I was truly taken back. The man could cook. I never knew he could even cook. We've been friends for years and I never once seen or heard him even talk about cooking. I got out of the car and went in to eat. I had the munchies anyway. I walked in and his house was smelling so good. I got a plate of food and sat down at the dining room table and started smashing. It was great. Chicken was fried to golden crispy perfection! I told him, "Omari, there's no way you cooked this!"

He laughed so hard, "Why would you say that?"

I washed down a mouthful of food with some red kool-aid and replied, "First of all you can't cook because if you could cook then you owe me a lot of meals from a lot of years where you done ate up all my food and had me cooking all of this time. This is crazy. I refuse to believe you cooked this."

"Well looks like I owe you because I promise I really did cook this."

I'm going to have to watch this man cook because I'm truly shocked right now. Omari has been a freeloader on me all of these years. I thought all he could do was smoke, be a hoe, and pass exams. If I'm learning new shit like this about Omari, I can only imagine what I don't know about Mike. He asked where the package was and went and brought it back to the dining table. I let him open it and he pulled out a thick packet that was filled with letters. He started to read one of the letters aloud,

*To my love,*

> *Every minute that goes by, I miss you more. I search for reasons just to be next to you.*
> *Each thought of you makes me crave you more. You are my fantasy come true. You are my dreams made real. The memory of your*

*sweet soft lips placing kisses in every curve of my body sends chills down my spine. My body heats up and burns with desire with the smallest touch of your hand. as it searches for juices to slip into and explore. I miss the way our bodies glide as*
*the soft sounds of Sade play into the moans created by our love. Only you can take me to a place created with pure ecstasy. I become lost in you as you dig into the deepest parts of my soul. I am yours. Forever yours.*

*I love you,*
*Harper*

Omari just stared at me, clearly lost for words as I sat puzzled remembering the day, I wrote the letter. I broke the silence and said, "I wrote that like 8 years ago. Why is that in the folder?" He didn't say anything as he continued to go through love letters. It would've been a pleasant moment since it was just old love letters, but my biggest issue was who had these letters and why were they sending them back to me. It was the only thing on my mind as I washed the little dishes I had messed up and headed home. On the drive I put my thoughts on Mike and how I wanted to get it in with him. Before I could make it home, he was sending me a text asking if I could come through. I loved how we were always on the same page, and I hoped he would let me spend the night as well. I stopped by my apartment first and took a quick shower because I

wanted to smell sweeter than a flower and taste better than heaven.

When I got to his place in Georgetown, we sat in the room, and I stared at the man that I'd completely fallen for. Amongst the secret dealings I've had with Calvin, I've met a few guys but he's the complete opposite of Calvin. Maybe that's why I fell for him so fast because he's so different. Mike likes to dabble in the finer things in life and he's introduced me to many of those same things. He doesn't entertain childish females and is always dressed to impress. Whatever cologne he wears is amazing and has him smell so lovely. He's a gym rat, so his body is his pride and joy. An educated black man with a love to travel, I was definitely smitten from the jump. Then, I found out he blows just as hard if not harder than Omari. For a moment, I was shocked because I couldn't understand how I keep meeting all of these potheads, but I quickly got over it. The man actually had something going for himself. He was the owner of a gym but a pothead in every sense of the word. We never dated though. We had some really good vibes where we could chill and talk about any and everything. I wanted him, but I've been keeping my feelings to myself.

Here he was talking about his ex who he thought was the love of his life, Morgan, breaking his heart. I laughed to myself because I really cared nothing about it. She done cheated on the man and got him all heartbroken. I think it's safe to say we both need a release. I had issues of my own that I was still dealing with. I know he didn't know about Aleccia, my baby, or this stalker shit and I'm sure he'd be really sad. He'd comfort me and hold me and want to make sure I'm okay, but I wasn't trying to be sad anymore. I just wanted to hang out with a friend and get my mind off of my own harsh realities from dealing with the lemons that life threw my way. I honestly came over for one thing and one thing only. For some odd reason, I didn't know how to approach it, so I just went for it and interrupted him in mid conversation by saying, "So Mike are we fucking or what?"

He was shocked to say the least. His facial expression was priceless indeed. It was like a mixture of a smirk and a raised eyebrow. It made me smile because I knew he was truly confused and in disbelief. You'd think most guys wouldn't need to process what was happening, but Mike was one of the few that had to. It's so amazing how he still gets surprised by the things I do and say. He should know by now that nothing is ever what it seems with me and I'm very bold when I want to be. I guess you could say I was very timid when we first started hanging out because I obviously didn't want him to think I was this big ass hoe that I was being. It was easy to guess that Morgan had done a number on the man because instead of answering the question, he just grabbed his keys and said while shaking his head, "I'm about to grab a bite to eat. Are you hungry?" Highly disappointed in his reply, I just shook my head no and got up to ride with him. I don't understand how he could think I was joking though. Or was he not interested? Is this the reason we never went past the friendzone? Had he friendzoned me and I not know? He's said plenty of times I was attractive but what the fuck? Guys say they want a bold female, an outspoken female, a female that says what's on her mind but when she's bold enough to say she's horny, they just brush it off. I didn't drive over here to hear an hour's worth of bullshit about some stupid little girl. I came for that monster. That beast! Or at least that's what it felt like when we were grinding in the club. I need some act right and at this point in time only he can give it to me. I can't keep fucking around with randoms even if I wanted to. I'm more single than I've ever been! I'm horny as fuck and I don't know if buddy knows this but we're fucking before I leave here tonight. I'm sucking some dick and getting some head and when it's over I don't mind going home to my big ass king size bed and going to sleep.

When we got back to his house from this food run, I looked at him and said, "You playing." You could hear the aggravation in my voice.

He smiled, still looking crazy and confused saying, "What did I do?"

I'm thinking to myself, *How the hell he don't know what he did?* I shook my head and answered, "You still got your clothes on."

What more needed to be said? I bet he started clearing the bed! The man finally realized this was not a game, so I got undressed and he followed suit. Sadly, to say my mind frame had changed just that fast. I didn't think this situation could've gotten any worse. This had now become quite awkward. We're crossing all type of lines. Our friendship isn't going to be the same after this. What am I thinking? My lady not even purring anymore from the thought of crossing lines like this! I stared at the man naked thinking, *When all else fails, suck some dick.* I enjoy pleasing a man. It's a complete turn on to hear him moan but best believe if I'm sucking, then he's eating my lady. There's no way around that. I wanted the full course meal! No teasers and previews over here. By the time we get ready to actually put in work, my lady will be screaming for the dick.

I placed both of my hands on his chest and stepped a few steps forward and pushed him up to the wall. I kissed him as I gently massaged his dick. I wasn't that drunk in the club because he definitely was working with a monster. I planted sweet kisses all over his neck and chest.

Certainly, wasn't hard to do with my short ass. Mike is a 6'2 jolly green giant. I slowly dropped to my knees and began to ease him into my mouth, placing sweet kisses and licks around the tip while stroking his shaft. All he could say was "Oh." I couldn't help but chuckle. I sped my pace up and the only sounds you could hear were moans, oh fucks, shits, and slurping. He grabbed my head and began to thrust himself deeper into my mouth. I loved feeling like a man's dirty porn star. I had a wild side once the door closed and wanted to do all type of wild and crazy shit. The stroking was perfect with my suction. His legs started to buck, signaling to me that he was getting weak. He was getting closer to his moment. Yeah, I was feeling myself. I felt like I had a point to prove to the man. He moaned, "Ooh shit Harper!" and it made me gush. Just like music to my ears. I wanted to leave him with a memory he'd never forget. I went from fast to slow and back to fast again, wasn't trying to make him bust. That's not the goal here. Just giving him a sneak peek on what he's been missing out on, while slick friend zoning me. So, I slowed down to a complete stop and got up. I walked over to the bed and laid back on it.

Grinning from ear to ear he strolls over, gets on top of me and begins kissing me on my neck. He places his hand on my lady and feels his new friend wet and ready. Oh yes! She's purring very loudly now. He grabs his dick thinking he's about to

stick it in, "Oh no sir." I said quickly. I placed my hand on his head and eased him on down to where he was really needed. After the blowjob he just received, He couldn't have thought I would want that last or that he wasn't doing it. No, give me me. He chuckled and smiled, "Yes, ma'am." I think I bit off more than I could chew. Mike had me running all over the bed in pure pleasure. He seemed right at home, and I loved every minute of every drop he savored. He began to caress my body. To feel his hands, rub my thighs and grip my ass was sending multiple surges throughout my body. He was definitely making a name for himself on this day. I was squirming to the point I almost pushed him off of me. The shit was so good, I could barely take it, but I couldn't afford not to get this orgasm. He's holding my hips and pulling me closer as I'm grinding on his face. I'm shuddering as if my body itself were a volcano erupting in blissful orgasmic erosions! He noticed this as well and when I climaxed, he held my hips tighter. He got up smiling with his shiny ass beard. I had no energy or need to push him back down. Job well done friend! He
knew he did the damn thing as he said, "Damn, it's been a while for you huh?"

I rolled my eyes and said, "Shut up and fuck me already!"

Mike pulled me to the edge of the bed and slowly entered me and I couldn't help but grasp. My lady had swollen from his head work, and she was sensitive to the slightest touch now. I bit my lips and scratched his back. Who did he think he was? Giving me the business like this?! He gone fuck around and end up locked in a basement as my sex slave. I pushed him to the side and got on top, then I started rotating my hips in a circular motion and then faster and faster I went. I took him for a ride. I went up and down and back to circular motions and it all drove him insane. By the time I started gripping, he was already moaning and saying my name. That's exactly what I wanted him to do. He uttered, "From the back." Say less! We got up and switched positions again. Why on earth did I agree to this?! I almost cried it was so good. He smacked the shit out of my ass!

"Ooooh shit! Fuck me zaddy!" What was I thinking?! He went harder but I loved it. He squeezed my hips and commenced to beating my lady up! I loved it even more. We were vibing on so many different levels. Our energies had connected, and it seemed like this is where we both needed to be. We kept switching positions and before I knew it, my legs were on his shoulders. This was the position that got him though. For a moment I

thought this fool was never going to nut. I know we started a good two hours ago. I wasn't rushing him to finish. I just wanted a bottle of water or something. As soon as he bust, he rolled over. All I could say was, "Damn."

Completely out of breath, he replied, "Yeah I know."

Well, there was no denying that this was a great decision on my part. We laid in bed together as the TV played the new Captain America: Civil War movie in the background and we both slowly drifted off to sleep in each other's arms.

# Chapter Nine

My office computer screen illuminated a plethora of tabs for cruises to book going to Jamaica. Mike told me to make the Labor Day Weekend plans and that no matter what it was, we'd do it, so I'm going to hold him to that. I've always wanted to go on a cute little trip with my man. From what I remember Aleccia telling me, it's very romantic and they have some of the most amazing activities on and off the ship. What more could a girl ask for? I'm hoping that this trip will open us both up to each other in ways we couldn't have imagined. I have no desire in telling him every single dark secret I have but after three months of hanging out and two months of being in an actual relationship. I think it's safe to say we don't know a damn thing about each other. Not really. He comes over to my place. I go to his. We've been on a few dates here and there but lately work has gotten in the way of everything. Either he's busy or I'm busy but we rarely have time for each other now and it's making me wonder a bunch of things.

I'm hoping that this getaway gives us a much-needed eye opener for each other.

Just as I was about to text Mike, my phone vibrated, and I rolled my eyes at the name that popped up. Charmaine had been ducking and dodging me for the past two months as if I did something to her. I don't know what she's caught up in, but I refuse to play along with the bullshit. I ignored her message just to read *'You dirty nasty bitch'* I just stared at my phone completely confused. What the fuck was going on now?! This was getting out of hand. I ignored the message until another came in saying, *'Bald-headed hoe ass dick breath bitch'* Clearly somebody was playing on my phone and who would want to do that? I wanted to reply so bad only because I still felt like this was Tia. Somehow, she done found out I was at Omari house and now she done got her panties in a bunch. This girl know she knew how to ruin a wet dream. The same way she had been tripping about him being around me, here she was again tripping over nothing. He needs to let her go. It makes me sick how stupid he is just by being with her. She acts like a baby instead of a grown woman. I'm sure she can't even wipe her own ass without needing Omari to hold the cheeks. I'm not sure what she got on him, but I truly miss the manwhore my best friend once was versus the extra gullible dumbass he's turned into.

I gathered my things and headed out for the day. My mind was only on one thing and that was some good ass E&L BBQ. I had already ordered a rib plate over the phone, just had to go pick it up. By the time I pulled up, I seen Tia and some extra buff dude walk in. I walked in and stood in line behind them. He did a doubletake when he noticed me and smiled. I smirked back. I assumed the guy was her brother until he smacked her ass and she giggled like an innocent little school girl. I said nothing. I didn't even chuckle. I had no intentions of bringing attention to myself. After they placed their order, they turned around to head to a table and have a seat. Tia looked me dead in my eyes while I smiled at her. She looked at me as if she'd seen a ghost. Her facial expression was priceless. I laughed to myself as I picked up my order. I wasn't going to report back to Omari either. He knew she was a hoe when he started fucking with her, no need for me to remind him.

The plate didn't even make it out of the parking when I had started to taste just a piece of utter delight before heading home. I could have eaten the entire plate right then and there but I'm going to try my best to make it home first. I probably should've ordered two, so I'd have one for later. The fat girl inside of me never rested. She stayed hungry, but I wasn't getting out to get another plate, so I took my fat ass on to the house. My phone vibrated over and over again during the entire drive home. When I made it in the house, I still didn't check the phone. I ate my rib plate until I heard knocking at my front door. At this point it could only be Mike or Omari since Charmaine wasn't even answering my calls or text messages. I guess I done pissed her off since I somewhat dropped her thanks to this relationship but I'm not apologizing for finally being happy. If she was a true friend, she'd be happy for me too but not Charmaine. She'd only be happy if she was able to say she fucked him first. I really got to get some new friends in my life. My thoughts were interrupted as I seen Omari walking into the kitchen. I was stunned, "I thought I asked for my key back?"

He smiled, "You did, and I told you I had a spare."

I sighed, "So why are you here this time?"

He ignored my question saying, "Oh you got some E&L and didn't get me none."

"Dude, I didn't even know you were coming over, but I would've if you had called." I stared at him as he made circles on my countertop. It was obvious that he wanted something that I wasn't really trying to give. I asked, "What do you want?"

He quickly replied, "Nothing. Not really. Well maybe a little something."

He continued stammering as I said, "Spit it out man.'

"Okay. I got Tia in the car, and I was hoping she could come in."

I squinted my eyes and just looked at him. I'm sure he thought I just hated the idea of the girl even stepping into my apartment, but I was really trying to figure out how did Tia end up in the car with Omari so damn fast. I know I just seen her with some other dude like an hour ago, if that, so I replied, "Sure she can come in."

He went back to the car to get her, and she walked in with the humblest look on her face. I

guess she thinks I'm about to spill the beans. I'd rather watch her sweat. Spilling the beans is only going to cause a bunch of bickering and they can do that on their own time instead of mine. Tia came in and sat down in the living room as I made my way to the couch. Surprisingly, she spoke, "Hey. I like how you got this set up. It's real cute."

I thought to myself girl bye! Don't try that friendship bullshit now! I replied, "Thanks. You're looking better than you did earlier."

Omari looked weird and said, "What you mean earlier?"

Before I could reply, Tia said, "I seen Harper at E&L earlier."

Omari joked, "Damn so everybody got some E&L today but me?"

I laughed, and Tia replied, "Aww baby if I had some money, I would've gotten you a plate, but Travis had gotten us a plate."

I chimed in, "Oh his name was Travis? He was real cute and buff looking."

Tia had this pained looked on her face as Omari said, "Harper, you actually trying to get hooked up? I thought you were taken?"

I smiled, "Hoes are having more fun nowadays." I walked back to the kitchen to get my peach soda and turned around in Tia's face. I asked, "Thirsty as always huh?"

She chuckled, "I see what you're doing."

I tilted my head and smirked, "Oh do you?"

She shook her head, "You need to chill out. First of all, Travis is just a friend. The same way Omari is just your friend."

I nodded, "I didn't ask for an explanation; however, Omari as never smacked my ass the way Travis smacked yours."

Tia jumped as Omari came into the kitchen saying, "Oh wow."

Tia smiled, "Baby you can't be scaring us girls like that."

He had a blank look on his face as he said, "I'll see you later Harper."

Omari was already headed out of the door without even telling Tia that he was leaving. Tia looked at me and said, "You a ole miserable ass bitch."

I laughed, "But I'm not the one getting caught up so take ya hoe ass on before he drives off."

She walked her simple-minded ass out the door and slammed it behind herself. I should've drugged her ass, but I think Omari heard us talking anyway so she's already in the doghouse. Hopefully, they'll break up after this or he can stay a fool listening to her lies the choice is his. This just needs to be his first and last time bringing her to my apartment. I only wanted to get under her skin this time but next time we might have to fight it out. I doubt she'll be convinced to come back though. Omari will probably be distant now as well, but it is what it is really. I decided to forget about them both and hop in the shower. It was much needed. Words cannot describe the hatred I have for sweating. I hate to sweat, and August in Mississippi is still a hot ass month with mosquitoes that'll suck you dry through your clothes. If I walk outside for three seconds, then I start to sweat while getting ate up. Just a drive to the store makes me angry because of the heat and sweat. I stepped into the tub and turned the showerhead to pulsate. I let the water beat on my back, neck, and shoulders. It's the next best thing to a massage at a spa somewhere.

I heard my phone vibrate until it fell off of the bathroom sink. It really needs to be Mike confirming this cruise to Jamaica. Hearing from him right now would really make my day. I finished my shower, dried off and checked my phone. I had five new messages and not one from Mike. The messages were from the same number that texted me earlier. They all had the same tone.

'Bitch you a slut!'

'Get your own fucking man'

'Loose pussy ass bitch'

'Probably got gonorrhea in the back of ya throat. Nasty hoe!'

'You a nothing ass bitch'

Who else would be telling me I need to get my own man? Who else would be this mad? I

mean they are going off on me but hiding behind some textapp number. It was obvious to me that it was Tia, simple and scary. Tragic. I finally replied. Had to let her know that she can hang the drama up. Nobody cares about her insecurities. When I called the number, she refused to answer so I went an extra step further. I put on my sweats and running shoes, threw my hair into a ponytail, rubbed Vaseline on my face, grabbed my keys, and made my way to Omari's. I wasn't trying to fight anybody, but I was ready for anything.

Within about 30 minutes, I was knocking on Omari's door. It was more like banging but I wasn't trying to lose my cool just yet. He answered looking completely stoned but I just stormed right past him. I was on a mission. I searched all over the house but didn't see the bitch at all. By the time I made it back to the front, Omari was just standing beside the couch with his arms folded across his chest. I could tell he was a little gotten off with. I tried to explain, "I'm sorry Omari but I'm so tired of this bitch playing with me!" He just stared at me. He didn't say a word. I pulled out my phone and begin to show him the messages, "Do you see this?! What is her fucking problem?"

As calm as day he replied, "Oh this again. You think Tia is doing something to you? I thought we went over this already Harper. Come on now. You're better than this. Why are you so caught up on her like this?"

I was appalled, "Caught up on her? She's harassing me! Who else would be telling me to get my own man and just snapping out like this? Who?"

He shrugged, "I don't know Harper. I just know it's not Tia though. You never know who you done pissed off now that you're dating that gym dude."

"Wow! So, you're just dismissing the thought of it being Tia? Are you that in love that you can't see the person she really is?"

Omari shook his head, "All I see is you being crazy. You just bombarded your way into my house looking for my girl as if I was cheating on you. If you didn't want her at your apartment, she didn't have to come in and honestly, how do I know you didn't text this shit to yourself. Be for real with yourself Harper. You are losing it and I just can't keep up."

Hurt by the accusations he threw at me, I nodded my head and walked out of the door. Yes, I was convinced it was Tia, but he should be able to see it's her also. I drove through the city on the way back home. I just wanted to drive and clear my head. My music kept interrupting thanks to Mike finally calling me, but I ignored each and every call. He can kiss that cruise goodbye! I had no desire to talk to him. I just wanted to drive. I've pretty much lost my best friend to a crazy tramp and my other best friend has been ignoring me for whatever reason. All I needed was to drive and clear my head, so that's what I did.

# Chapter Ten

After not hearing from Omari for a good six weeks, my phone chimes with a message from him saying, *'Happy Birthday Chump.'* I had no reason to reply until hours later he showed up to my job with flowers and a gift basket filled with all my favorites and dressed to impress. He had on a crème-colored turtleneck with a brown vest and the slacks to match. He was looking like a dark-skinned Jidenna fresh out of an Atlanta photoshoot. He made every last one of my female co-workers go googly eyed as he walked past them to my office. It was like watching a cartoon as they all turned following his scent. I just laughed. They started whispering and I knew they were thinking he was my man. I would have to shut those rumors down quick. His first words to me after entering my office were, "Take the rest of the day off, so I can treat you to a long lunch."

Still filled with resentment, I asked, "And why would I do that? Because you came up here with a basket full of goodies?"

He smiled, "Yes, that's exactly why. Now get your stuff and come on."

I gathered my jacket and purse while rolling my eyes. It's my birthday and I'm certainly not turning down gifts and free food, even if Tia is there, I'll make the most of it because it's my birthday! We walked outside and he was much more of a gentleman than he's ever been. He opened doors for me and just treated me like a queen. Omari was really an amazing friend to do all of this, and we hadn't spoken in weeks. Whether it was my birthday or not, he didn't have to go all out like this. I was actually surprised when we pulled up at Olive Garden. It's my favorite restaurant. I mean I know all of his favorites as well; I just didn't realize he knew all of mine as well. I was on the lookout for Tia and yet she wasn't already in the car or at the restaurant when we made it there. That was a shocker truly.

We sat down and I was silent. It wasn't awkward but I didn't want to be petty before the food arrived, so I let him control the next few minutes. He chuckled, "I guess you're still mad at me."

I shook my head no as I buttered my roll.

He sighed, "Well that's good to know. I have some pretty good news to share with you and I wouldn't want anger to get in the way of that." While munching on my roll, I nodded in agreement.

He continued, "I proposed to Tia for real this time and we're getting married next month!"

I spit my roll out and choked on the rest. The man straight up started laughing in my face as I said, "Are you serious?"

He could barely speak amongst the laughter, "Hell nah!"

I threw my napkin at him as I finally caught myself, "Why must you play so much, Omari." I gulped down the water I had and asked the server for a refill.

Omari had laughed so hard, he had tears rolling down his face. He replied, "I knew no other way to get you to speak but nah I ain't proposed to nobody. There isn't a woman I've dated that could ever truly make me want to marry them. You know that."

I sighed, "Are you telling me my man-whore of a best friend is back out to play?"

"No, he's very much still in a committed relationship. I just don't see myself settling down any time soon."

"Why are you in a relationship and don't see marriage in the future?"

"I prefer to see a person in all of the seasons. A lot of people like to compare relationships to test driving a car, but I could settle down with a car faster than I could a woman. I like to see how she is in the summer and the winter. She's probably evil in the spring and sweet as pie in the fall. I can't see my wife in her during one only season but kudos to those that can, just saying it's not for me."

"That's very profound."

"Well, I'm a very profound guy but for real, I do have some good news to tell. You're the first person or rather the only person I really wanted to tell, and I know it's your birthday, so I wanted to really do something special for you first." He took a deep breath and said, "You're looking at the new cloud data architect of JDL!"

"Congratulations! I have no idea what that means but you seem really excited about it so in return we must drink!"

He laughed, "It's like literally my dream job and I'm barely qualified for it as for as education goes but my experience makes up for what I'm missing and it's always good to know a few people in high places."

"Yesssss best friend!!! I'm so proud of you and what do you mean you're not qualified?! You have a bachelor's in computer science, wouldn't that make you over-qualified? Okay, not that it's needed but what's the starting salary? Benefits?"

"You would think that however we just graduated, so if it wasn't for the experience I've put in as an intern, then I'd just be another dude with a bunch of student loans. They're starting me at 150K a year with all of the benefits. I mean medical, dental, health, vision, 401K, and a bunch other stuff."

"Damn! I should've been a computer science major if they're giving money away like that."

"Harper, you're great in advertising. I'm going to need those skills one day and instead of trying to learn them, I'll just hire you to do the job for me."

I nodded, "Say less."

We continued to talk and eat and when it was over, he wanted to drive to Vicksburg so we could test our luck at the boat. As tempting as that was, I needed to get home. Mike was going to come over tonight. I didn't know what he had planned but I knew it was going to be great and I was more than happy that Omari and I were back in each other's good graces. As we pulled up to my apartment, I spotted Charmaine's car first. I see this birthday is going to be one to remember. Both of my friends done came through for me! I'm in a wonderful relationship. I got a good job and for once everything is going pretty dang good. I hopped out the car waved bye to Omari and beat Charmaine to the door. I waved for her to come on in as I went and got the Alize ready. I haven't spoken to this girl since April and here it was October, so I know the tea is about to be all of that and more.

She came in and sat down at the table and said, "Well, bitch I'm pregnant."

Stunned still holding the Alize bottle in my hands I exclaimed, "Oh wow! I can't believe you're pregnant!"

She explained how sick she had been and just wasn't feeling up to hanging out with anybody. I felt horrible to know how sick she had been and here I thought she was avoiding me because I had a man. I couldn't have been more self-centered but I'm so happy she's not angry with me and that she has finally come over so that we could catch up. She started with, "Girl, I didn't know what was going on. I thought it was the stomach flu at first. I was throwing up everything and wasn't realizing that Aunt Flo hadn't come yet. I went to the ER thinking nothing of it and here they come back talking about I'm pregnant. I said, 'Who pregnant?!' Girl I was floored you hear me!"

I couldn't help but laugh. Picturing Charmaine in the ER for what she thinks is the stomach flu isn't hard to do at all. I replied, "You didn't curse the nurse or doctor out?"

"Of course, I did! I told them they needed to check again because these got to be somebody else's results. Girl I was all kinds of uncontrollable. I mean crying and cursing, cursing, and crying. I got home and still took tests. I could not believe this shit!"

"Looks like you've finally accepted it for what it is though. Are you happy now?"

"Yeah, I guess so. No other choice really. I just didn't think it would happen so soon. I don't think I'm really ready for it but it's kind of exciting as well", she sighed as she rubbed her growing belly.

I nodded, "I understand. It's scary but I think you'll be a great mom Charms. Have you told Rashad and is he excited?"

She rolled her eyes and replied, "Girl, fuck him. He ain't the daddy no way. I told the nigga though. I don't know how he feels but he claims he wants to be in the kid's life. He just ain't trying to be with me. Had the nerve to say, 'We're just two friends that got caught up' what the fuck does that mean?!"

I shook my head in disgust. I hated this for my friend, but Charmaine was a well-known hoe and how many times must I warn her about the consequences of her own actions. I dipped out into the hoe world for a hot minute, but Charmaine was the queen of the hoe world. Honestly, this was bound to happen but regardless I wish it could be different. I hope she sees the error of her ways and changes for the better. I won't even put all of that onto this little baby that's growing inside of her. Why do people do that? Hope that a baby, an itty-bitty baby will change somebody for the better. Most of the time it makes them worse. They become carefree in their actions and now they're hurting them and the baby. In the end it's another adult with daddy issues or mommy issues blaming their bad decisions on everybody around them. If people sought-after therapy the way they do a crack pipe, blunt or bottle, then maybe just maybe there would be less depressed people. Maybe not. It certainly wasn't something I had been doing. My therapy was being in the hoe world and smoking blunts like everybody else.

The decision to get an abortion was the simplest yet hardest decision I have ever made. The thought of my baby being penalized for my actions is unbearable. I remember this girl I met a few days before Aleccia died. I was at her house getting my hair done and she was more of a hair therapist than a hairstylist. I felt comfortable enough to tell her about my abortion. I instantly thought I had offended her as she said, "God, still loves you and you're still a mother." She broke my heart with those words. Me? Still a mother? Her words helped me to feel sad that I didn't have my baby. At first, it seemed so wrong of me to feel sadness with basically committing murder. I didn't know how or what to feel and I felt more alone each day, but her words were like daggers in my heart. How could anybody still love me let alone God. I quickly dismissed those words, but she said, "You did what you thought was best for your child." I was surprised to hear her say those words. She was clearly a woman that loved God and yet she wasn't chewing me out about getting an abortion. I had to hug her when it was all over with. She really turned me around and helped me accept all of my emotions. It was after Aleccia died that I

shut down and didn't care anymore. I had more issues than just getting through an abortion I decided to have.

"Harper!" Charmaine broke the trance I was in. She was looking highly aggravated as she said, "You haven't heard a word I said!"

I shook my head and sipped my tea, "My bad girl. I'm listening! Just speechless for the most part."

She rolled her eyes and tilted her head back, "Girl, I fucked up. What am I about to do with a baby?!"

"You're going to take care of this baby. You're here now and it's no turning back. How far along are you though?" I replied as I leaned in and rubbed her back to ease her of the many emotions that she was feeling.

She stood up and gathered her stuff. I knew I had upset her somehow, "See, I knew you weren't listening. I literally just told you that I'm four months pregnant and here you go asking again. I'll see you when I see you." She stormed out of the door but left her sonogram sitting on the table. I picked it up and seen the words 'IT'S A BOY' with an arrow pointing between the legs. Tears rolled down my eyes as I realized I never made it to this point and frankly I doubt that I ever will considering my track record on love. Granted Mike and I have something nice going on but who's to say it will last. As much as I hate to admit it, my heart still desires Calvin. The one person I should've never been with in the first place. Amazing how people tell you to be true to your heart and yet your heart deceives you the most. It confuses the brain into believing that what you're feeling is right and even when you know it's wrong, who cares because you're being true to your heart. You're being a fool and blinded by lust. Your heart will love who you tell it to love. Hell, it'll love who you tell it not to love. With no guidance you'll end up married to a tree and that's not a metaphor!

I looked at the time and it was seven o'clock and knew I needed to be ready for Mike. It was still my birthday and yet he hadn't called or texted yet. I poured me a glass of Alize and mixed it with a few other liquors. I sat there reminiscing on the past year and time flew right past me. Within minutes it was already 11:34 PM so I called him. I prayed he answered and then again, I prayed he didn't. What was his reason for not calling or texting or anything on my birthday? We've been talking about me turning twenty-four since October rolled in so how could he forget something like my birthday?

I had to call three times before he finally answered in a whisper, "Hello."

"Were you sleep?"

Still in a whisper, "No."

Annoyed, I asked, "Okay, why are you whispering?"

He sighed and there was a pause. In that moment, my heart sank as he spoke, "I'm sorry Harper but this isn't going to work out." As soon as the last word left his lips, he hung up the phone. As if that wasn't enough to break my mental state, I received more messages from this textapp number. It was a picture of a Backpage post that was supposedly me offering all kinds of nasty shit. It even had pictures of me completely naked. The pictures were at least two years old. How did these pictures get on the fucking internet?! Who was doing this to me and why?! I had no answers. My birthday officially ruined in seconds. All I could think was damn, I should've gone to Vicksburg.

# Chapter Eleven

Another night, another dollar as I've grown accustomed to say. In the past month, I've buried myself more into my work. I've made it my mission to be the first one walking through the door and the last one out. My boss has applauded me every chance she gets. I've literally dominated each and every assignment I've been on. I couldn't be more of a boss ass chick if I tried! As I finished the last bullet on my to-do list and as always being the last to leave the building, I headed to M-Bar to have a few drinks with myself. Everything that happened a month ago is hitting me like a ton of bricks. I truly didn't know Mike at all all. Yes, he's successful and fine as hell. He knows how to please a woman. He can cook and he's attentive. We've talked about the future only a couple of times. Apparently, he does want to get married and have kids but only two. The man was doing and saying all the right things, but it was just a façade and once again I was in too deep, the other shoe dropped, and my entire world was once again turned upside down. At first, I thought the break was so sudden and completely out of the blue until I realized Mike was just a fun time. He was something to occupy the hole in my heart and in all honesty, he was never needed. I just needed time to look in the mirror and see the beautiful girl that had blossomed into a woman. Surprisingly, I haven't even given any other guy a second thought. At this point in my life, they're all distractions. I'm at the point where I wish I never met him. Since meeting him, my life has been hell. I was just blinded by his devilish looks and wearing rose colored glasses to really see him for the snake that he is. It's amazing the things you do and call love when you've never been loved before. I've learned to start loving myself and out of nowhere came this amazing strength.

I'm happier with myself than I've been for a long time.

While I waited on my server with my order, I pulled out my iPad. After getting everybody in my office on the same page with this big account, I had a few last-minute finalizations I needed to go over. Gwen Stubbs already loved the concept and couldn't wait to see the finished project. As I worked on my iPad, I heard a familiar voice say, "Hey Harper." I looked up and there stood Calvin. I looked around for his wife and he let me know he was alone. He asked if he could sit down, and I let him. I'm not the type of person that likes to cause a scene in public. He sat down smiling as if everything was all good. I don't know what made him think that. I just stared at him waiting on him to speak. I hadn't seen or talked to him in over a year. So why even approach me? I would've gone the other way and prayed I wasn't seen but not Calvin. No, he must make his presence known. He asked, "How have you been?"

"I've been great. What about you?"

He nodded, "I've been missing you."

I wasn't surprised, "You've been missing me? Why? It's been over a year now."

He replied, "I know. I was hurt at first about the abortion. You know that was my first kid and probably my only kid."

I shrugged, "I understand. It was my first child also but now it's been over a year. It took a whole twelve months for you to acknowledge this and even now this is just a random moment in time."

He agreed, "You're right. I should've been there for you better. I just didn't think we could continue. I wanted to give you so much more and I couldn't. I wish there was a way for you to forgive me."

I sighed, "I forgave you a long time ago but that doesn't change anything. You're still married, and I no longer want to be your secret fuck buddy."

He looked so sad, but he knew I was telling the truth. He just stared at me but before he could reply, my phone lit up and started to vibrate on the table. Across the screen read Omari.

Calvin was quick to say, "Who is Omari?"

I was surprised he even had the nerve to ask but I could tell he was in his feelings to even see his name on my phone. I replied, "My business and not yours. Allow me to direct you to your business." I pointed to the ring sitting on his wedding finger and he just stared at me. Those sexy brown eyes were burning a hole in my soul as they slowly drew me back in. All of the feelings I had buried and locked away was slowly creeping back up.

He said, "Whatever, Harper. I hope he's making you happy."

He couldn't really say much. The man acts like he done forgot his wifey was somewhere waiting on him. I replied, "Bye Calvin." I thought to myself, Man fuck Calvin! He can hang that shit up. I guarantee he'll never even sniff this cooch again. I can't believe I even agreed to let him sit down. I hate that I still loved him though. I wish dudes could see how much a woman loved them before they broke their hearts and lost them. When she's down for them no matter what but they still choose to fuck over them. I still have dreams of the day where he's all mine and we're raising our family together but I'm not stupid anymore. I can clearly see that those dreams were shot dead the day he got married. I've been lost in love with the man since the day he made me a woman. He's my first love and I wanted him to be my only love. This jumping in and out of bed with Calvin, I could no longer do. I finally grew up and let it go because the man I loved was somebody else's husband. The shit hurts but what else can I do? I thought about fighting for his love and telling her the truth but nothing good would come from that. I truly did not want the baby daddy/baby mama drama with a married man. So really it wasn't shit left for me to do but walk away and that's what I did. I gathered my stuff and walked away. I couldn't stay in this place not a second more.

Nothing really compared to a night drive, while listening to Secret Garden as I think about how nice this bubble bath is about to feel. The weekend is upon me, and I've said forget Alize and started drinking wine more. It was going to be perfect until I walked up to my door and there sat a box from UPS. It was small and considering the last package I received. I didn't even want to open this one, so I picked it up and took it inside. I went ahead with my plans of an amazing bubble bath with a glass of wine. I wasn't about to allow this amazing month I've been having just go up in flames like that. First thing on Monday, I'm scheduling a therapy session with Dr. Simone Juelz, even if it's nothing but a regular package, I just refuse to be triggered by something as simple as a package.

In the middle, of reading a book and drinking my Moscato, I randomly started to smell food cooking. I must be tripping so I quickly hop out of the tub, throw a robe on, go into the kitchen and there Omari was cooking, while Charmaine sat on the side munching on chips. All I could say was, "Uh, what the hell?!"

He sighs, "Just sit down. It's almost done."

I couldn't deny, it was smelling good, so I went and got my Moscato and came back into the kitchen. I looked at Charmaine and said, "So y'all doing break ins together now?"

"It ain't a break in if he got the key boo. Besides, he was here first."

Omari chuckled, "Okay, listen, I'm trying to cook for y'all and y'all ain't appreciating it."

"Okay, but did you have to break in to cook? It's literally 1 in the morning and you're cooking. Are you high?"

They both laughed and said, "Hell yeah."

All I could do was put my head down and say, "First of all, Charms you're freaking pregnant and Omari how are you going to smoke when you just got that good ass job a month ago?"

Charmaine replied, "Well bitch maybe because I'm grown and this weed ain't hurting my baby in the least bit."

Omari shrugged, "My job ain't checking for weed." And went right back cooking. It didn't take long for him to finish cooking. He made beef tips over noodles with asparagus.

Charmaine had to ask, "And you learned to cook like this where? You know what don't even answer that. I tell you what, if you're cooking like this, I'll make you a copy of my key. Me and baby boy need to eat good like this all of the time."

I mumbled, "It's good but I'm changing my locks after this."

With a mouthful of food, Charmaine says, "Damn, you're drinking wine and changing locks? I thought he was your best friend?!"

I glared at her as Omari said, "She in a relationship so now she acting uppity. Wouldn't even go to the boat with me last month."

He poured me another glass of wine while I sighed, "I'm actually no longer with Mike."

They both stared at me in shock as if we had been dating for years. Charmaine interrupts the randomly awkward silence with, "Damn sis."

I shrugged, "That's just how the cookie crumbles. So why the hell are y'all over here again
I ask?"

Omari dropped his head and said, "Just needed to clear my head and maybe needed to talk to a friend."

Charmaine looked at him and said, "Damn, you okay? What's wrong?" "Relationships are stressful." He replied.

Charmaine got her big belly up to fix a second plate while saying, "Damn, son you single too?"

He shook his head, "No, but it doesn't change the fact that they're stressful."

I just stared at Charmaine and replied, "Okay buddy needed a friend, what do you need?"

It was obvious that she was appalled when she replied, "I just wanted to see you damn bitch but it's cool. I see you've become salty now that you're single. I won't pop up no more." Once again, she stormed out. At this point I was used to it. She needed to figure her and little baby out instead of popping up at my house eating up all of my food. Her dramatic exit gave plenty of room for Omari to explain himself. I stared him down until he finally said, "If you want me to leave, then just say it. I'm not trying to disrespect you. I really didn't think you cared."

I took a deep breath and replied, "It's not a problem Omari, I'm just in a mood. I seen
Calvin earlier today and I also received this package and it's got me a little out of sorts."

He asked with concern, "So how did that go?"

I shook my head because I really didn't know and replied, "I guess he just wanted to say he missed me, but I didn't sit around to hear too much more. I know how I can be, and I didn't want to get sucked back into the bullshit."

"Yeah, especially with him being married."

"How did you know he was married?"

Omari looked at me and passed the blunt as he said, "I told you before I know more than you think I do besides Jackson is small. Everybody knows everybody and staying in Byram doesn't stop a person from knowing you or somebody you fuck with. If you went to a Jackson public school, then you know somebody that know somebody that know somebody. It's no way around that."

He was telling the truth. Jackson was small. I've had so many people come up to me talking to me as if they truly knew me and I had never seen them before. I'll ask them how do they know me and every single time it was 'I met you through Aleccia or I met you through Charmaine' but you don't truly know me. You've only heard of me. I wondered if Omari knew who Calvin was married to. It wasn't his marriage that stopped me from being with him. It was who he was married to. I didn't want to continue disrespecting her and I didn't want it to all come out and hurt her. I looked up at him and replied, "So what all do you know since you know so much?"

He smiled, "I'm not at liberty to discuss."

"The fuck you supposed to be now? The police?"

He shrugged, "Call it what you want but I ain't telling nothing else."

"Man whatever. You'll slip up again."

He noticed the package beside the trashcan and motioned towards it. I shrugged and he picked it up to open it. Inside of a shoebox was just a bunch of pictures. Welp here we go again. His reaction to the first picture was, "Damn, this mother-fucker watching your every move!" I snatched the picture from his hand there I was once again but instead of being completely naked, I was fully clothed. The pictures were from the last few months. These were pictures that I hadn't taken but somebody was clearly watching me and taking pictures of me at work, in the tub, and even sleeping. There were pictures from when I went out with Mike and even pictures from the birthday dinner with Omari. This was real life stalking, and I was no longer in the positive head space I was earlier.

How did these pictures get in this box? Where did this box come from? There were what seemed like millions of pictures, new and old. It felt like it was never ending and what made me cringe the most is that I remembered each and every moment in the picture. Yes, I sent some these but why were they being sent back and by who? Then that moment came. The moment when life becomes so surreal that you become so speechless as if silence would erase what's actually happening. The moment where whispered words are too loud, and it feels like the entire world can hear when in reality it's just you freaking completely out. Why did I let him open the box? Why didn't I just throw it away? What the fuck is even happening right now?

Omari was still looking at the pictures as he asked, "Isn't this your supermodel friend that died?" He handed me the picture and sure enough it was Aleccia in her bed wearing a black baby-doll with heels. She was on her knees smiling while being kissed on the neck by another female. Seconds had barely passed when Omari said, "Damn, I think I've seen too much." I was silent. I couldn't speak. My mouth was completely dry. I couldn't move. I knew what this moment was, and I was frozen. He stood be-side me and showed me the picture as he pointed saying, "Is this real?" I looked at the picture and there Aleccia was licking my stomach as I smiled into the camera. What was I supposed to say? Did he really want clarification? What exactly would that sound like? Do I kick him out and deal with this on my own or do I confide in my friend and try to seek his help? How would he even help me when I don't even know why this is happening? I was afraid to even look at him no less answer him. I was afraid of what he was thinking. Omari is truly my best friend and now he knows one secret I thought would never see the light of day. I don't know how to face him.

My mind is racing a million miles per minute, and I can't form the answers he needs. He took everything out of my hands and placed it in the box. I watched him place the lid back on and he took the box to the living room. He started the fireplace and placed the box inside the fire. I never moved. I simply heard and understood his actions. It was the smell of my past burning that I realized just how good of a friend I had. Omari came back and walked me to the couch. We sat down together, and he just held me as I cried into his arms. I don't know how he knew what to do. I don't know how he understood what I was feeling or maybe he didn't know.

Maybe, he didn't understand.

We sat in front of the fire in silence until the box was completely gone and I found the words to say, "Thank you. I don't know what's happening or why but thank you for that."

He wrapped his arms around me, "I got you, Harper." I wanted to explain but that's a closet full of skeletons I don't think he's equipped to handle. I knew opening that damn package was going to be bad. Omari went on to say, "I know you're not ready to talk about this now. I get it. I understand how private you are, but you have to understand, somebody else knows about y'all and they're torturing you because of it." He looked me in my eyes, "Harper, I don't think you're safe. This person is watching your every move. You've been hacked on Facebook, receiving blocked calls and horrible text messages, and didn't you say you got some dead rats in the mail? Let's not forget your tire being slashed. Somebody is out to get you and I'm guessing it's because of you and her but I got you, okay. I got you!" I began crying again and he held me tighter. I understood everything he said. He was right, somebody knew, and they were angry with me. What am I going to do? Omari spent the night and decided to stay the next few nights. He catered to me and never left my side but come Monday we both had a job to be at and there's no telling what could happen next.

# Chapter Twelve

My first session with Dr. Simone Juelz had me more than ready to sing like a canary because I needed to get some help in facing some of these demons. Just the other night I was sloppy drunk after downing a few bottles of Takka. I don't know if I simply wanted to sleep without dreaming or to not wake up but either one would've been just fine. I knew immediately that this therapist was some siditty white woman looking to commit me to Whitfield because her office is deep in Flowood. I walked in and sat down just as nervously as I did at the clinic on the verge of having an anxiety attack. I mean just the thought of airing my dirty laundry out to a complete stranger has me wanting to run for the hills but I'm sitting here 24 years old in need of a miracle. I need to do this. If not for me then at least for the baby that haunts me every night in my dreams.

I entered Dr. Juelz's office and did not in the least bit feel any comfort as I examined the room. Her office looked better than my living room. She was so well educated with all of her degrees and different awards plastered over the walls. My initial thoughts of her were wrong, instead she was some siditty black woman all extra proud of her African heritage. She had a couple of Mother-in-Law Tongues in the corners, abstract paintings filling the walls, fertility statues beside the door, and this beautiful water fountain next to the bookcase. She was even dressed like one of those women from my mother's church that think they're from Wakanda or somewhere, so the first thought that ran thorough my head was that she's probably going to tell me to pray about it! It's just one session though. I done filled all these insurance papers out and done gave her my little coins to hear my problems, so I might as well get my money's worth. I politely smiled, "Good evening, Doctor. It's nice to meet you. I'm Harper Ward."

She didn't skip a beat, "Hello, Miss Ward. I'm Dr. Juelz."

"Please call me Harper."

"No problem, Harper. Please sit anywhere you like. Or don't sit. Whatever you prefer."

I sat down on the couch and said, "Should I lie down on the couch and make this official?"

She smiled, "If that makes you more comfortable."

I was nervous and really didn't know what to do or what to say. I mean do I tell her about the bottles I downed last night, or do I tell her about the many new men in my life? She'd probably be more interested in how I've started smoking weed every day now. So many avenues here, it's hard to decide. I sighed, "I'm sorry, I hope I didn't offend you. I don't know. I guess I'm just a little weirded out by being here."

She nodded, "I understand. I know it must be difficult, but I'm glad you are expressing your feelings. That's a good start, Harper. Why don't you tell me what brought you here?"

I fumbled with my fingers as I replied, "It's kind of hard to explain really. I was given your number by another therapist who suggested I come see you if I felt I needed to"

"Have you been in therapy before?"

"No, this is my first time. I got an abortion almost two years ago and the counselor at the clinic referred me to you."

"Well, I'm happy you came in. What made you get the abortion?"

I replied, "I didn't feel I was ready for a baby. The father is married, and pregnancy should've never happened. I didn't think I would regret it so much at the time. I really didn't think about anything but getting the abortion. I just thought that over time I would be okay and for a while, I was doing okay or at least I thought I was. I started having these very vivid dreams of the baby and that really started messing with me. I've been constantly crying, and I've become angrier. It's starting to affect my relationships with friends. I've cut everybody off, but a lot has happened since the abortion and I'm just trying get through everything. I don't feel like anybody really understands how hard this has been."

"Did the father ask you to get an abortion?"

"No. The crazy thing is he wanted me to keep the baby. He broke up with me when I told him I was getting the abortion. I'm not sure how he'd raise a child with me when he wasn't going to leave his wife. I didn't want to bring a child into that kind of environment. If I would've kept the baby and tried adoption, he wouldn't have signed over his rights. I'm sure his wife would've been hesitant to accept his outside child, so it felt like a lose/lose situation. I did what I thought was best."

"I see. Harper, experiencing a host of different emotions from depression to guilt and even suicidal thoughts following a traumatic experience such as an abortion is actually very common. Post Abortion Syndrome is not listed as an actual term by mental health and disorders, but it is very real and happens to a lot of women. I take it very seriously because it's so taboo. The first step in the healing process is forgiving yourself."

I put my head down and started to fumble with my fingers again, "That's easier said than done. Doctor, I've had a really bad couple of years so far and I am just trying to move past it all."

"What are some things you're trying to get past?"

I chuckled, "The answers to that are honestly endless but the main thing would be the fact that I lost my best friend in a car accident. She was the one person I would've confided in. It's crazy because she was on her way to stay with me for a week. I didn't want to tell her about the abortion and now she's gone too."

"I'm so sorry for your lost. I know how hard that can be to try and cope with one thing as so many other things are happening. I believe it's very understandable to feel as if your emotions are all over the place. You mentioned that this was affecting your relationship with friends, do you have any family here?"

"Yeah, I'm from here. I just don't fool with my family. My dad walked out of my life when I was three and I'm not really close with my mom even though I try to be, but it only got worse after she was married."

"What do you believe caused the distance between you and your mother?"

I shrugged, "My birth."

"You feel as though your mother did not want you."

"She hardly ever acted like she was happy to have me. I always was a burden on her. She constantly put me off on other family members even when she knew I didn't want to be there."

"Were you having issues with other family members?"

"Aside from her brother molesting me and her mother abusing me, no."

"I see. Did you ever tell your mother what was happening?"

"I did when I was 7. She didn't believe me. I found out from my cousin when I was older that it was more about protecting her brother rather than not believing me."

"What about the abuse from her mother? Your grandmother?"

"She made excuses and told me to stay out of her way. I don't know how I'd do that when she was constantly dropping me off at her house."

"Did she continue to take you around your uncle?"

"No, not to stay like before but he was still around. I just secluded myself from the family and when I got older, I refused to associate myself with them. I still try to talk with my mom but as I said we've never been close."

"Why do you still try to talk to her?"

"I don't know. She loved her mother so much, but her mother seemed to hate her too. It's just what I'm used to I guess."

"A cycle of abuse where the daughter loves her mother, and the mother hates her in return?" "Sounds about right."

"How did the relationship change after she was married?"

I chuckled, "Everything I wanted to do had to be pre-approved by him. She wanted me to call him Dad, and I hated that. She wanted to be picture perfect, but I was too fat to fit into the picture she created. According to her I was a fat lazy nasty bitch."

"That's horrible."

"I mean, I didn't think it was abuse then though. I just wanted to be a good daughter. I just wanted her to love me the way my aunts loved their daughters. Man, they could go and kill the president, and nobody would know but no matter what I did I was talked about and to like a dog. My cousins snickered and talked about me behind my back all because of stories she had told her family about me. I was considered the worse child, and nobody cared for me. I had nowhere to go. I was happy to have a friend like Aleccia, even when she tried to run her off. Aleccia didn't let her get under her skin. She was my friend through it all."

"Why do you think your mother told stories about you?"

"I'm honestly not sure. Up until I was in middle school, she adored me. I was the ideal child. I obeyed. I catered to her. I just wanted her approval. It was after I turned 13 that I just started living my own life and no longer caring about her approval."

"Why 13?"

Dr. Juelz sat silently as I started to pace back and forth in her office while attempting to change the subject by spilling my guts out, "Okay, I think I'm being stalked or something. I've received dead flowers with dead rats in them. My Facebook account was hacked. They shared all of these nude pictures of me to my friends. Then somebody started just cussing me completely out in text messages and before that I was receiving blocked calls, but I never answered. Not to mention somebody has slashed my tire and I think they've been in my apartment stealing stuff and watching me." I took a deep breath and continued, "Just recently I received recent pictures of me along with some old ones of me and my best friend that was never supposed to had been seen by anybody. There was even a Backpage post of me soliciting sex for money. Dr. Juelz this has me completely freaked out. I tried going to the police and they couldn't help me. What am I supposed to do?"

She calmly replied, "I'm sorry that this is happening to you

Harper but there's nothing you can do without knowing who this could possibly be. It does sound like you have a stalker; however, you don't have anybody for the police to look into. How about we dig into what's happened. What stood out the most in the first incident? What was it?"

I sat down and replied, "It was some dead flowers and a dead rat with a note saying, 'Drop Dead Gorgeous' I thought it was from Calvin at first. The father of the baby." "What about that made you think of Calvin?"

"The note. It was a joke between me and my friend Aleccia. I just assumed he was apologizing about the breakup and that wasn't the case."

"Who else knows about the joke?"

"Our friend Charmaine and I guess my friend Omari. Sometimes me and Charmaine would use jokes with it, but it was mainly a thing between me and Aleccia."

"Have you associated the dead flowers and the note with one familiar with the saying such as Charmaine or Omari?"

"No, it's not them. They were both just as shocked as me and has been there for me through all of this."

"I see. What was the next incident?"

"My Facebook account was hacked. They sent nude pictures of me to people on my friends list."

"Who was with you when your account was hacked?"

"Technically, nobody. Omari came over and showed me what was sent, and I had missed calls and messages in my phone after that."

"And the next incident was text messages?"

"No, it was blocked calls, old letters and pictures, a Backpage post, and then text messages which I accused Omari's girlfriend, Tia of doing it but that had us not speaking for a while."

"Harper, what made you dismiss Omari, Charmaine, and Calvin?"

I shrugged, "I mean what would they gain from this?"

"A resentful stalker gains pleasure from frightening you or distressing you. Who would be resentful of you?"

"Between Omari, Charmaine, and Calvin. At this point, all of them would have a reason but it's not them."

"You seem pretty convinced it's not. Please tell me why."

I didn't think I was ready for this moment but at some point, what's done in the dark must come to light. I sighed, "Okay." I started to rock my foot as my nerves started to take control, but I continued, "Aleccia hated Calvin but that's only after we all used to have threesomes together.
It started when Aleccia kept questioning me about sex. I had already started having sex with Calvin and she was asking every question in the book. I ended up telling Calvin and he suggested that he be her first because he'd be gentle with her and ease her into it. I trusted him and so did Aleccia. He rented a room and I sat in a chair as Aleccia had her first time with Calvin. Afterwards we also had our first threesome. It was the first of many, but something happened during high school and Aleccia just started hating him. I don't know what happened. They never told me what happened. He even acted like he couldn't stand her. I just never questioned it. I loved him and I loved her."

"He sounds validated to host some resentment. What about Omari?"

I chuckled, "He didn't even know about Aleccia until she had died. What resentment would he hold?"

"I see and Charmaine?"

I cringed, "Yeah, Aleccia couldn't stand her either. She actually hated her, but she was cordial because I considered her a friend."

"You know Harper, these two people may very well hold resentment towards Aleccia and because of the bond you two shared, you are their target."

"Okay, I hear you loud and clear, but I have no proof of it being either one of them."

"I understand and until this person makes a mistake or causes physical harm to you it's honestly nothing you can do, however, be careful of your surroundings and trusting every-body isn't something you can afford to do. At this moment, everybody is a suspect."

"Dr. Juelz, what's the worst-case scenario in situations like this?"

"The worst-case scenario is the stalker becomes physical and harms you. If the suspect was one of these people, do you think it would become violent?"

"I don't know. I didn't think I'd ever have a stalker either." I put my head down and there I was fumbling with my fingers again. I looked up at the clock and it was 4:17PM, "Am I going to get charged extra for going over the hour?"

Dr. Juelz looked at the time and said, "No, there's no extra charge. Will you be returning next week for another hour?"

I sighed, "I might. It felt good to just talk so yeah I guess I will."

She smiled, "Well, I will see you next time. It was good talk-ing to you Harper."

Leaving Dr. Juelz's office and I felt worse than when I walked in. I'm sure that's not the point of therapy. I kept thinking of how nervous I was to talk about Calvin and Aleccia. These are se-crets that should've died with her and here they are resurfacing again. The last thing I needed is for this man's wife to find out about any of this. What would she say aside from I

seduced her husband? Maybe I did! I've convinced myself for years that it was love and that maybe he'd one day leave her for me, but I was fooling myself to think that. What he look like leaving his wife for a child? I grew up. I realized our relationship was based on lies and that he took advantage of a child and called it love. Realizing that didn't change how I felt about him. It didn't stop my heart from skipping a beat when I was near him. It didn't stop the memories from flooding in when I thought about him. Somehow, he was still my knight in shining amour no matter his age. His marital status was more his concern than it was mine at that time but since the abortion, I've started to see a lot of things differently. It's more than wrong of me to parade around town with a married man. Especially a town as small as Jackson. It's crazy to think that we thought we had this thing hidden so well. It's very obvious that one other person knows everything and there's no telling who else.

What if this entire time his wife knew everything? I suppose her question would be why or even what was I thinking. I've asked myself this multiple times within this last year. What the hell was I thinking? When I met Calvin before he was married, he was one of the many guys that tried talking to me when I was in the fifth grade. At first, he didn't believe I was eleven and in the fifth grade, but he wasn't a jerk about it either. He still took the time out to get to know me. He'd always sit at his cousin house which was just a couple houses down from the bus stop and wait on me to get off of the bus. As I walked past the house going home, he'd try his best to talk to me. I ignored him as much as I could, but it didn't stop him from trying to spit his game. He was very respectful and even corny at times and yet in the midst of me ignoring him, he never once called me out of my name. I eventually warmed up to him and we started talking nonstop. At the time, I didn't know his age. He looked like he was in eighth or ninth grade, which was still too old for my eleven-year-old self to talk to, but he was cute so why not? I felt like a big boss having a boyfriend in middle school or high school even.

After my fifth-grade class day, he realized I really was eleven. He tried to stop talking to me and man did that crush my little heart. He was my first real boyfriend. My first real crush. He was the first guy I actually tried to like and just as random as Mike, he broke up with me. He said we were too different, and he didn't want to get in trouble. I didn't understand what he was saying then and by the time the school started back, he had disappeared on me completely. I later found out he was twenty-three with a baby face. I was shocked to say the least. Here I was barely even in middle school and completely in love with a grown ass man. I understood completely what he had said and accepted it for what it was. It's strange how small Jackson can be. I had gone on living my best middle school days with Aleccia. Granted I was picked on left and right because of my body, I still had book sense. I still had common sense. I never once allowed a guy to use me or control me. It was easy to get caught up in our neighborhood and luckily, I had steered clear of that until I seen Calvin at his cousin house.

My heart skipped a million beats, and the biggest smile flew across my face. It had been two years and I was in the middle of my eighth-grade year. I had my eyes glued on him and of course, he locked eyes with me in mere seconds. I didn't know if I wanted to run into his arms or sashay right past him. I should've walked past him and in all honesty I did try. He ran up behind me and asked if we could walk and talk alone. I missed him. I missed his charm and the respect he gave me. I missed being seen for more than my big breasts and fat butt. So yeah, I took him up on his offer. We walked Aleccia home and then we walked to the park and just chilled. He explained to me he had been seeing this woman and that things were getting serious. He didn't want to hurt her especially when the one person he really wanted to be with wasn't even the legal age. It made me feel guilty for missing him. I respected everything he said but I

cannot explain why I still kissed him.

I could lie and say he kissed me but that was all me! I wanted that man. I craved that man. That one kiss led us down a path I truly regret. We tried to be friends, but the attraction and the chemistry controlled us. Before I knew it, I had given him my virginity and was planning our future together. I couldn't have imagined a more terrifying moment as the day when, I seen him walk out the house with his wife. My world crashed around me. I was done. I replayed every moment of every conversation in my head for days and still I couldn't put two and two together as to why I still had these feelings for him. There was a small, very small moment when we tried to respect his vows. We were civil. We attempted not to be in close quarters with each other. The attempts were futile. They lasted maybe six months at the most. Once we stopped trying to avoid each other and just gave in to our desires, we couldn't be away from each other.

Eventually Aleccia joined in for the fun, but I guess once she got her fill, she was done with him. She wasn't done with me, and our fun continued until her death. I missed the threesomes we had. I had the best of both worlds. It was the most carefree moments of my life but when that damn stick became positive is when a ton of bricks came crashing down on my head. What the hell would we do with a baby? There's absolutely no reason why after I turned eighteen, he couldn't divorce his wife and marry me. I had no right to continue believing his lies. It took an abortion and Aleccia's death for me to see Calvin for who he really was. A piece of shit. My heart may desire Calvin but continuing to love him after all of this would be a slap in the face of our child. I chose abortion for a reason, and it wasn't to continue carelessly loving a man that clearly did not love me.

# Chapter Thirteen

The holidays are upon us and thanks to the last month's package, Thanksgiving sucked. I was filled with nothing but fear and regret. I mourned for the days when I at least thought I had it all together and now I feel as though I've completely lost control of everything around me. The only positive I can find in all of this is how great of a friend Omari has been to me and how thankful I am for him. I needed space though. Surprisingly, he hasn't asked me a thing. He's just been very considerate and when I told him I wanted a little space, he eased off. My mother has been blowing my phone up. I've declined all of her calls because of the fact we barely have a relationship. In fact, some refer to it as highly toxic, but her antics is not why she's getting rejected. I just don't have the energy to argue with her as well as keep my sanity while waiting on the next package from this crazed stalker of mine. It's a lot to deal with and talking to my mother would only make it worse. Not to mention I haven't spoken with Charmaine since the night she popped up and I hurt her hormones, but I have no need in chasing behind this girl like I was the one that got her pregnant and now I'm just trying to see my son. I'll leave that for the fool that thought sleeping with her was one of his better ideas. I didn't even trip when she popped up totally forgetting my birthday as if it's not the same day every year, but I let her hormonal issues slide and ignored her, just to get dumped on my birthday. I didn't dump all of my emotions on her and frankly I don't need her dumping hers on me. She needs to realize the world does not revolve around her just because she's pregnant. I think I'm better without her or Mike at this point.

Research says that exercise helps relieve stress but the first day at the gym had me in pure hell. I had no idea where to start or even how to use the machines so I started with something I thought would be easy and even that was a challenge. Technology and treadmills don't really need to go together like that. I mean press start and walk or run. The extras had me going up mountains and it was touch screen for what reason I don't know. It was pretty obvious how lost I was because I didn't have cute workout clothes, nor did I have headphones. By the time I did 7

sit ups, I wanted the biggest juiciest greasiest Stamps or Beatty St Burger they had. I contemplated just learning to love my big, beautiful frame for what it was and not ever do another freaking lunge in my life. The end of my session didn't come fast enough. I was beyond sore and could barely walk up the three steps leading to my apartment from the parking lot. I think I cried a little as I tried to ease myself into the tub. Each day was a little better than the last and eventually I started to see the small rewards like more energy and feeling better. I didn't think I'd ever actually like working out, but the research didn't lie, it really is an amazing stress reliever. It's made me truly put this stalker stuff out of my mind as much as possible. Just being focused on the workout itself really helps me get over the anxiety I feel of being stalked. I've bought a taser and I've signed up for self-defense classes as well. I really heard Dr. Juelz when she said trust no one. It's crazy and scary to know that whoever this person is, is somebody I know. Somebody I've met. Somebody I've invited into my home. That's not many people but of the ones I've invited I couldn't possibly place them on a suspect list of people that could be stalking me. I just want to be prepared for anything and anybody, but I still wasn't prepared to see Omari in this gym. He walked up to me smiling, "How was the workout?"

"Uh, it was cool, but I thought you went to Planet Fitness. When did you start coming here?"

He hesitated, "I'm here sometimes. You heading back home?"

That was the plan, but I didn't want him to know that. When I said I wanted space, I thought he respected that, and I could easily say sure come on over, but this entire moment right here is kind of weird. It made no sense for him to be here. He literally lives at Planet Fitness when he's not eating me out of house and home. I wanted to ask more but paranoia started to get the best of me, and I see no reason why I shouldn't let it. I replied, "Nah, I got to go check on my mom. She's been feeling ill, and I've been a little distant lately with everything going on, but I'll catch up with you later."

As he said, "Okay cool. Be careful Harper." I was already halfway out the door. I went straight to my mom's house to check on her. She had been blowing my phone up and, in the end, she didn't want nothing of course. I didn't tell her the ins and outs of what was going on in my life nor did I stay longer than needed. I just wanted to make sure that this stalker hadn't started messing with her as well. As I headed home, I started to resent myself. I'm acting completely crazy. Omari is not the stalker and for me to act that way around him is absurd! I hope he didn't notice how funny acting I was. This shit has me all dis-combobulated. When I'm working out, I get a temporary release from my troubles but seeing Omari at the gym messed me up. I shouldn't have treated him that way, however, I really can't trust anybody at this point. I don't know if I'm going or coming.

When I made it home, I lit some candles instead of turning the lights on. I sat on the floor and attempted to meditate. At this point I'm trying any and everything to keep my sanity in check and after 30 mins I was having a nice glass of wine in-stead. I've noticed my phone will ring during the very second where all of my charkas are in balance and that phone call will have the most drama filled individual on the other end. I fig-ured it was my mother. I just left her place, but she could still find reasons to blow my phone up regardless of the time frame in which she had just seen me. I should've placed it on 'Do Not Disturb' or 'Airplane Mode' but silly me thought vibrate would suffice. She called over and over and over again until my phone vibrated off of the table. I was just about to move when it stopped. 'Cool,' I thought, 'It can stay there.' I thought that lit-tle meet up with Omari in the gym earlier was weird but when my phone chimed while somebody knocked on my door, I knew then maybe drinking wine wasn't the smartest idea. Should I ignore my phone and answer the door, or should I answer my phone and ignore the door? They knocked again and then I heard the keys enter the lock. I stared at the door. I didn't move, I just stared at the door. Omari entered and said, "Oh shit."

I jumped up, "No, not oh shit. What the fuck?"

He quickly came in and closed the door while saying, "Listen, you said you weren't going to be here. I was just checking the place out for you."

I glared, "The fuck you mean checking my place out?"

He was taken aback by my anger as he raised his hands in defense, "Yo, Harper, I didn't mean to scare you for real. I know what you're going through, and I was just checking for packages and making sure whoever this stalker is hadn't broken in or something."

"Omari, you need to leave, and you can absolutely expect my locks to be changed."

His expression quickly changed to a frown, "Wow really! I'm just trying to look out for you! It ain't like the police gone do anything."

"Dude, I asked for space. Does this look like you giving me space? Popping up at the gym that you don't go to and now at my home. Who's to say you're not the stalker?!"

Anger had surfaced, "That's what you believe." He begins walking toward me, "Me? Stalk you?" As he came closer, I started to back away, "This shit got you fucked up in the head and burning sage ain't gone solve shit. Since I'm stalking you, buy a gun and shoot the motherfucker. You better hope I'm the one you shot because you just lost the one nigga that actually fucking cared about you." He threw my key on the table and stormed out of the door. I had no idea what to think. My phone started to chime again but I felt it was best to run behind Omari. I couldn't lose the one friend I had left in this world over my nerves being shot! I made it to his car and wedged my hips between the door to prevent him from closing it and driving off.

His voice was firm and still filled with anger, "Move Harper."

"Omari, please. I. I. I am so sorry. Truly I am. I'm not trying to lose you over this. I'm just scared, and I don't know what to do. I don't know who to trust. I just don't know what's going on. I don't know what's going to happen next and no matter how much I try to stay calm; shit gets worse. Please don't leave like this."

He sighed, "You could've trusted me. You chose not to. Now please move!"

With a broken heart of my own doing, I stepped aside. He quickly slammed the car door and sped off. How do I fix this? Better yet how do you lose every single person in your inner circle and a piece of yourself as well. I stepped back into my apartment and laid down on my couch. The only good thing I have going for me is my job and I'm scared to even leave my apartment. Hell, I'm scared to leave my job or even the gym. I'm scared to just be me. I have no idea where this person is or who the person may be. I'm a sitting duck everywhere I go, and nobody cares. The one person that did care just sped the hell off from me. I'll let him cool off before popping up at his place. I've known him seems like forever at this point and I've never seen him mad. Lately, his little girlfriend will be in her feelings and having us not talk. I back off because I respect him even if I don't agree with his relationship choice, but nothing has ever gotten under his skin enough to really have him bothered no less mad, so I know I messed up big time. I'd be surprised if he ever talked to me again, but I wouldn't be me if I didn't at least try to reconcile with him. I just hope he can understand where I'm at. I hope that he can put himself in my shoes and see that it's more than being scared. It's more than anxiety. It's more than a bad break up. I've found rock bottom and my breaking point isn't far behind.

I cried myself to sleep realizing how messed up my life has gotten and before I knew it, I was dreaming of a toddler saying, 'Help me mommy!' She was being taken away and I tried to save her, but I couldn't get to her. She was crying and her words just echoed. I jumped out of my sleep and hours had passed. The things I'd give for any kind of escape from my reality and dreams. If I'm awake, I'm stuck with the constant fear of this stalker and if I'm sleep, I'm haunted with the consequences of my actions. At this point just throw me in Freddy vs Jason. I may have better luck fighting them. There was a time when I wasn't allowing the dreams to affect me as much but everything these days has me rattled. I scrambled to my phone to call Omari. I just wanted to apologize and try to explain where my head is, but he didn't answer. I checked my missed calls in an attempt to call my mom back, but it wasn't her number that had called me earlier. I recognized the number just fine. I'm not understanding why this number would be calling me. Do I call it back? At this point in my life, what the hell else could happen? It's probably the wrong number and still I called the number back. It went straight to voicemail. I hung up the phone before I realized the voicemail was still the same, so I called again. It went straight to voicemail but this time I listened as it said, "Hi, you have reached the voicemail of Aleccia Tate Bennet. Please leave your name, number, and a brief message and I'll be back in touch with you shortly. Thank you." Was I high? I called Omari again. He still didn't answer. Maybe it was Pierre using Aleccia's phone to contact me. I called again and to voicemail it went. I started to send a text until I seen I had a message that read, 'Help me Harper' Help who?

Pierre? Why would Pierre need my help though?

I pulled out my laptop and searched for Pierre Bennett. His entire life was on the internet, but I guess that's what happens when you're an NBA player. It's honestly too easy to get information on famous individuals. None of this man's life was private. The best thing I could do was try to meet up with him in January for his charity event. He would be in Memphis and at least then I could see what he needed my help for or show him that somebody is playing on Aleccia's phone. The charity event is next month which gives me plenty of time to take off work, book my room, and prepare my speech so that I'm not sounding crazy. I really don't know what I expect to do for Pierre, but he loved that girl more than I did and if there's anything I can help him with then I'm all for it. It'll be a nice escape from my current messed up reality. Fear arose as I wondered if he was the stalker. I quickly dismissed the thought as I know Pierre doesn't even have the time to stalk anybody with basketball season in full effect.

# Chapter Fourteen

"Baby, I want you to come over for my Christmas dinner party. It's going to be a bunch of my co-workers and a few friends from church, so I need you not to look like you've been thrown away!" My mom exclaimed over the phone.

"I just seen you like two weeks ago and mom I've just been really busy with work is all."

"I made your favorite." She said in a sing-song way. Cheesecake was not my favorite. I grew tired of that as a child but for some reason she thought I really just loved it. She makes two and expects me to eat them both just to fuss at me all of next year for being fat. The irony. She continued, "I made an extra cheesecake so you could take home too."

"I have to see if my car will make it. It's been acting funny lately." I hated to lie on my baby like that. This lie would be the very reason it starts to act up on me and I really didn't need those added on troubles."

"Oh, baby I wasn't expecting you to drive. James is already on the way to pick you up so be ready. Now listen I got to go and check on my greens."

She hung up the phone and all I could do was sigh. I went and showered to prepare for this Huxtable style Christmas dinner. All I wanted for Christmas was to be home sipping on some mixed drinks as I sorted through the wreckage that I call my life. I think the best decision I will ever make tonight is to eat my special brownie before this man picks me up. It didn't take long for me to reach the skies between my brownie and perfectly mixed 'Fuck Me Up' I was more than ready for these holiday shenanigans. I seen him pull in and I didn't let him make it out of the car good before I was locking my door and making my way to him.

He had this ugly ass grin on his face. I just wanted to punch him in it.

My first mind was to sit in the back seat but when the hell did, they get a two-seater?! I got in and felt cramped all the way up. I've never been claustrophobic before but there's a first time for everything. The drive was awkward as the radio played all of the wrong songs. We didn't talk and luckily, had made it to their new house in Terry in no time. It was a beautiful house. My mom was happy and for once I was actually happy for her. She had decorated the inside to look like every single hallmark Christmas movie invented. Boys II Men's Silent Night played in the background as a bunch of people I never knew existed tried to remind me who they were and how we met. My mom had been working at the chicken plant since I was born but I couldn't remember a face to save my life. I stayed civil and played the role assigned. Some would say fake it til you make it, I'm doing anything to not face my own reality so why not share some laughs and sip some eggnog. It's better than being alone on Christmas.

The night was a beautiful distraction, and nobody was arguing. It's what you'd want family and friends to do during the holidays. If only it wasn't just a holiday moment but an everyday thing. I couldn't end the night without another attempt at talking to Omari. I fumbled with my phone all night after sending Omari a long apologetic 'Merry Christmas' text. He was still not talking to me, and it hurt more than anything. I no longer have the energy to hate Tia. I just want my friend to answer the phone. I know I messed up, but can you really blame me. It's a lot and I've really been trying not to go crazy.

Three hours later and my mom was kicking everybody out. Classic Shirley indeed. I had my cheesecake, and I was ready to go. I tried to bum a ride so that I wouldn't be cramped in this car again, but just my luck nobody was heading my way. Everybody had other places to go make plates at so back in the two-seater I went. The drive was even more awkward than cramped as we headed back to my apartment but that's probably because I was no longer floating off of that brownie. I should've had one in my purse for the drive home. I stared out of the window and was more than thankful as we pulled into my complex. Easy-peasy. Nope. Always a negative with this guy. He was out of the car by the time I closed the car door and followed me into my apartment saying, "Hey, can I use your bathroom."

I sighed, "Sure."

As I poured myself a glass of Rosé, he walked into the living room and said, "Harper, can we talk?"

"About what?"

He stared at me for a bit and went on to say, "I know that no matter what I say, you won't believe me but Harper you know I would never hurt you. I tried to give you space and I'm sorry if that offended you but baby, I want to show you just how sorry I am."

I chuckled and shook my head, "By fucking your wife's daughter on Christmas night?"

He rolled his eyes, "Harper what the fuck is the problem? We've been fucking for years, and you never cared before so why are you caring now?!"

"Calvin when did I not care? I've asked you to divorce her several times and what was your reply? Huh?!"

"Here, we go with this shit again!"

"Yeah, here we go again! Answer me this though, if I had kept the baby, then what? Would our baby had been enough to make you divorce her or would I have to send my child to its granny's house so she could play stepmom? I mean really how would that had worked?!"

His words were calculated and cold, "You killed our chance of being together when you killed our baby. Now you throw it in my face because I didn't leave my wife." He scoffed, "Trifling."

"Oh, wow I'm trifling now?! Exactly what are you, Calvin?"

He chuckled, "I'm the only man that was willing to love you. I wasn't perfect and you knew that, but I gave you all of my heart. You played me."

I chuckled, "Calvin, I'm twenty-four years old. I'm not

that eleven-year-old little girl you met thirteen years ago. You couldn't possibly think I would still be as naïve as I was back then."

He smirked as he looked at me with lust in his eyes, "Baby, I know! I see the woman you've grown into. Hell, I helped you grow into her. I'm just trying to say I'm sorry for any hurt I caused you."

"What are you sorry for?"

He was on his hands and knees begging, "Baby everything. I'm sorry for everything."

I knew every word was a lie. I knew everything about him was a lie. I didn't want to get reeled into his lies or wrapped into his charm. So why did it feel like my heart and mind wasn't on the same page? Why is it so hard to walk away from the very thing you know is wrong? He crawled closer until he was centered at my feet. He began to ease his hands up my legs as I said, "Please Calvin just go home." He began to kiss my outer thighs. A desperate plea for sex is all it was. I pushed him off, got up and walked over to my mantle and said, "Why did you marry my mom?"

He groaned, "I told you why already. I've apologized a million times for that. I didn't know she was your mom, Harper. I really didn't."

"Dude, you don't see anything wrong in what we've been doing? I mean most of, if not everything has been in the same house. How are you okay with that?"

"Harper, do you hear yourself?! Do you really think I enjoyed doing things this way? I'm not trying to hurt you or your mother. I didn't plan any of this."

I looked away, disgusted with his arrogance, "I didn't really see you saying no either."

He got up and walked over to me. He placed his arms around me and spoke softly in my ear, "I couldn't say no to you because I loved you." His breath on the back of my neck brought back every single memory I worked hard to rid myself of. He started to plant kisses of seduction along my shoulders as he whispered,

"I still love you, Harper."

I broke free from his grasp and walked to the other side of the room. I should've known this night would've ended like this, with him trying all of his slickest moves to snuggle back inside my crevices. What the hell is wrong with me? I should've never allowed him in my apartment. I took a deep breath as I walked away saying, "Just go home Calvin."

I made it to my bedroom and hoped he would leave. I wasn't up for the complex love he had to offer and yet in this very moment I craved every inch of him. I've been a fool for so long with this man and it wasn't until I got pregnant that I realized just how much of a fool I've been. Calvin could've left me where he found me and instead, he married my mom. How could I tell my mom that her new husband is also my boyfriend? As wrong as it was to continue, it was harder to stop. I tried staying away from home but that only made things worse with my mom. Regardless, I never tried to tell her the truth. I knew she'd feel like I seduced him and took him from her, and I can't face the fact that she's not lying. For years, I felt like he was mine! I felt like she took him from me and now he's caught up in a situation with her. I thought that as soon as I turned 18, he'd divorce her, and we'd elope. He told me he couldn't do that to her. I didn't understand why. I believed him when he said he loved me and that he needed time to come up with a plan. I guess he's still trying to figure the plan out, but he has a new car and a new house, and my mother is still his wife. It's not hard to figure out that he's exactly where he wants to be. I've learned to let go but I didn't calculate close encounters with the one man I've loved for thirteen years. Maybe it would be easier if he was beating my ass or even if I hadn't met him first. Regardless of the reason, he still holds a place in my heart, and I hate it.

I made my way back to the living room and there he was waiting on me. I hoped he'd caught the hint and just left but I knew him better than that. I played right into his hand and allowed every slick move to work. It ended the same way it always did, with him leaving to be with his wife. I wasn't going to force him to stay. This night is the last of many nights. I've finally closed a chapter in my life that was long overdue. It was time. I don't know if I'll ever be able to tell my mom the truth and frankly, I doubt Calvin would even own up to his wrong in any of this. He doesn't see anything wrong with it. That means it all falls on me but I'm sure this would be embarrassing for her as well as hurtful and I honestly don't want to be the one to hurt her with the truth. How would I explain any this? She might be understanding to the teen years but the adult years I don't see her understanding. If she could sympathize my adult years, then how would she take in tonight's actions? Telling her it's the last time isn't going to make her feel any better. Telling her I tried to say no but eventually gave in isn't going to just roll over nicely with her. She's going to be pissed and I for one don't want to deal with the anger that Shirley can throw out. Regardless of what she believes, tonight was absolutely the last time. I'm ready to love a man that's man enough to love me back the right way. I can't do that if I'm still sleeping with my mom's husband.

# Chapter Fifteen

The last thing I wanted was to travel by myself, but I boarded a Greyhound bus and made it to Memphis within six hours. I would've love to drive here and saved some time, but I'd prefer to sit back and ride when it comes to trips instead of driving. I love to take in the scenery. Nature is one of the most beautiful scenes that is often duplicated but nothing can be as beautiful as the real thing. I would've also loved to make amends with Omari on this trip. He talks about road trips a lot, and this would've been all on my dime, but he was still declining my calls. He'd sent a text here and there but as far as talking on the phone or coming over, that was null and void. I wonder what Dr. Juelz would say I do to make amends with him. She's part of the reason I have anxiety now. The stalker being the main reason but her words 'Trust nobody' just echoes over and over in my head. That alone is making me crazy. It's probably best I just keep trying the way I know he would if it was me and him which is why I left him a voicemail telling him I would be out of town and that I'd probably be back next week sometime. I have an appointment scheduled with Dr. Juelz next week and I'm going to have to tell her that her suggestions and my anxiety doesn't mix well.

Regardless of how this little meet up with Pierre goes, I have a lot to share with Dr. Juelz, so I hope she's ready to hear about who Calvin really is. Besides, it's not much I can do for Pierre except be there for him but that's the least I can do for him. I've been calling Aleccia's phone and it's still going straight to voicemail. It seems foolish to show up to a place and nobody knows I'm here, not even the person I'm coming to see. I'm adamant about calling or texting before popping up at my house and yet here I am in my hotel room getting ready to head out to a charity event I wasn't invited to. I've heard nothing about Memphis except that it has great food and swap meets. I'm staying at a hotel near Beale Street just so I can experience Memphis and all it has to offer. I would've called an Uber but chose against it. I just wanted to see the city for a while. There's still a little time before the event starts so I went sightseeing and came across some pretty good places that I can't wait to really check out when I go shopping tomorrow after I've seen Pierre. I might not get to see him but being away from my own drama is beauty within itself. This trip was well needed. I just wish I had a friend to share it with.

Imagine my surprise to see Darius walking out of the Beale Sweets Sugar Shack. It took a lot to maneuver my way to him. There were a bunch of people trying to get his autograph, a picture or chat it up with him. By the time I made it to the front of what seemed to be a line for his attention, his bodyguard says, "Sorry, Mr. Flemmings isn't seeing anybody else."

I rolled my eyes and attempted to be nice, "I have some personal business with Darius."

The bodyguard wasn't going for it. I wonder how many people had used that line with a celebrity before. As this Rock wannabe tried to turn me around, Darius noticed me and placed his hand on his bodyguard saying, "Yo, chill. I know her. What's up Harper? What are you doing here?"

I straighten my denim jacket and went on to say, "Came to see Pierre and I guess I found you."

He looked startled as he hugged me, "Listen, I'm heading to get a bite to eat in a minute. Why not catch up over dinner if you want."

I replied, "No problem." As I waited, I realized his definition and mine of the term 'in a minute' is quite different. I figured he'd leave in about twenty more minutes; dude was there for another hour and a half. I waited, nonetheless. How would I get in contact with Pierre if I walked away? We left and made our way to Wet Willie's. I done traveled over two hundred miles to eat at a place called Wet Willie's but I ain't complaining. His bodyguard stayed close but not too close, he gave us space to talk freely. It was a must that we caught up with each other first. It's been almost two years since Aleccia's death and about four years since we've seen each other because anytime Aleccia came to visit, she always came by herself or with Pierre. Thinking about this charity event that's tomorrow had me reminiscing about the first time I ever met Pierre.

I noticed him before he ever met Aleccia. Light skin brothers have never been my cup of tea, but I couldn't deny that he was a very good-looking man. His muscles made him look more like a WWE wrestler rather than an OKC draft pick. He had a low fro with hazel eyes. There were many groupies swarming over him at the industry party. At the time I thought it was so crazy to see models acting like that, but everybody was trying to get an NBA draft baby by somebody. I just let them have that. I was in love, and I just knew I was going to be Mrs. James Calvin Kersh one day soon. Aleccia was the only model at the party that wasn't trying to bag her a baller. She was just being her and men just gravitated towards her. She was very picky on who she slept with and when Pierre came up to her, she quickly dismissed him. It was like watching Lucy Lu in Charlie's Angels.

Hilarious is what it was. He was shocked as he walked away but, in her defense, he was like the twelfth guy that had walked up to her. It wasn't until we were ready to leave that Pierre tried his hand again. It was clear that he'd asked around about her. He already knew her name and mine and he didn't come on strong. He just wanted to be her friend. It was pleasantly different. We left the party and went to play pool as if we had all been friends for years. Everything after that just flowed and when Darius entered the picture, I no longer felt like the third wheel even though it was never anything they did to make me feel that way. I wasn't surprised when Aleccia called me the next year saying they had eloped. I was happy for her. Pierre seemed like the man of her dreams, and I couldn't have picked a better guy for her. He catered to her every want and need. Aleccia was just that fairy tale come true. I looked at her life hoping that one day my fairy tale would come true too.

Darius was never that guy before but in this
moment, he reminded me so much of Omari.
Just being able to chill with a friend was refreshing and what
made it better was that he wasn't Omari. Sure, we never seen
each other in that way before but in this moment his smile was
enough to get the ball rolling in the right direction until he mentioned he had a new lady on his arm, but he wasn't sure how
serious it was. It was still pretty new. I was sadden at first until
I realized he was talking about Pierre and not himself. It's great
that Pierre is moving on with his life. I wouldn't expect him to
be single forever, however, he should probably move out of that
mansion he shared with Aleccia. If I was the new lady on his
arm, I'm not trying to share the same bed that your dead wife
used to share with you. It's common courtesy I suppose. Pierre's
newfound relationship was the very thing that made me ask,
"Darius, what new lady is on your arm?"

"I'm taking it a day at a time. Still single and
not rushing it. It's good to see you again."
I nodded, "I'm here because I received some interesting
phone calls from Aleccia's phone. I thought it was from Pierre
but when I tried calling back, I only got the voicemail."

He shook his head in disbelief. He seemed completely rattled by what I was saying as he replied, "No, Harper it wasn't
Pierre. He thinks you hate him the way Aleccia's family hates
him."

My heart dropped. I've come this way only to cause drama
and turmoil. I could've stayed home and done that. I mumbled,
"Wow. I definitely don't hate him, and I feel so bad that he thinks
that I do."

He placed his hand on mine and replied, "Don't be. It's good
to see you again and honestly, he wanted to reach out to you, and
I told him not to. We all should've been sat down like this. It's
something she would've wanted us to do."

He was right. This is something Aleccia would've wanted
and here it has been almost two years but better late than never I

guess you could say. Since I had the chance, I asked, "I know this is a lot to ask, but do you know what happened? I know about as much as the rest of the world and it's still seems so surreal."

He sighed, "I just know they were arguing. It wasn't nothing major. They'd been dealing with trying to have a baby and at the time had just experienced another miscarriage. It was the second one and she just wanted to be around you. He wanted her to stay home and rest, but she wasn't having it, so I offered to drive her. She didn't want me to drive, and Pierre didn't want her to make that drive by herself, so he let her drive with their friend Victoria. I didn't understand at the time that it was grief, and she didn't want to be around Pierre or me. In her eyes, he was the cause of her pain and she wanted to be as far away from him as possible. They argued over the phone during the drive, and she ended up blacking out when the car swerved." His eyes started to water and together we fought through the tears.

I hated myself for asking. I could've lived with a simple car accident but to know all of that broke my heart. I replied, "I shouldn't have asked. I'm sorry."

He sniffed, "It's okay. You deserved to know. She was like a sister to both of us."

I got up and hugged him as I said, "Thank you for telling me."

We shared a few tears and sniffles, but we pulled ourselves together and the rest of the night we shared laughs and memories of Aleccia. It was a great turn around and at least in those moments I no longer felt like my trip was wasted. We exchanged numbers so the next time we were in a city together, I wouldn't get detained by his bodyguard. Luckily, Wet Willie's was just down the street from my hotel, so I decided to walk back. It was only about a 20-minute walk and that's including the multiple stops, I needed to make as I took in the beauty of the city. I feel free here in Memphis. There's no stalker here. There are no packages waiting for me at my room. There's no baby daddy drama here. I can be me here or at least discover who I truly am without the chains of my past hindering me from achieving my goals. Nobody knows me here which means starting over would be a breeze. I'm considering the move heavily because I've always wanted more, and this is a beautiful city besides at the end of the day it's not Jackson.

I was almost at my hotel when I felt a spell of dizziness come upon me. I had a few drinks, but I didn't think I'd feel the effects so soon. Everything around me started to spin and sitting down felt like the best idea, before I could decide on what to do, someone had grabbed me from behind. I struggled for a moment as I tried to get away, but my attempts got me nowhere. They tightened their grip while placing me in the backseat of a black car. I knew exactly what was happening, but I never thought this would be happening to me. Time moved so quickly, after minutes had passed, I finally blacked out.

# Chapter Sixteen

Here we are face to face not making a move. He's standing there with some trashy slut dangling from his arm. She looks like a one-night stand gone wrong. You can clearly tell this chick means him no good and yet he parades her around as though she's God's gift to the world.

I can hardly stand here faking this smile, while he introduces her, as if I really care who she is. Sweetly, I reply and introduce myself. Now she's thinking we're friends, because she's hammering on and on about anything and everything. I'm more concerned with how he's burning a hole into me. I wore this sexy purple, strapless, hugging all the right curves, can't help but notice me dress. You could say I wore it just for him. Everything is sitting just right as it shows off my smooth legs, and hugs my thick thighs, giving reason to look at this ample ass even more. I didn't think this purple color would be so enticing but I couldn't find a bomb red dress for this moment.

The man had it going on with his tux. Nothing was better than a man that could do both. I could melt in his arms. He's looking like a chiseled god and it's getting me hot and bothered without even knowing it. I had to cut his little girlfriend off, "I'm sorry boo but I'm needed elsewhere." I made my way to the guest bedroom in the back of the house. Looking at his fine ass got me flowing and I need relief! I knew I wouldn't make it through the night without bringing my bullet. I locked the door and got good and comfortable on the chaise by the window. I slid my black lace thongs to the side and started making circles with my bullet on my pearl. All I could think of was Omari's hands all over me.

I heard light tapping at the door. Who in the hell could that be?! I didn't want to stop because I had just started but I didn't want to cause a scene, so I rushed and put my bullet up, fixed my hair and opened the door. Of course, it was Aleccia. She asked, "Are you okay? Why are you hiding in here?" She walked right in and closed the door. We've known each other for too long and I get that she's concerned because of how I just ran off from Omari and his girlfriend but I'm on a different mission right now. It's just kind of the wrong time to care! All I want to do is jump some bones and rock somebody's world. I'm trying to be good though. She looked at me weird and said, "Were you leaving?"

I forced a smile and said, "No, that's not my plan. I was just trying to go to the bathroom dang Aleccia."

She had this funny smirk on her face, while locking the door. Somehow, I instantly knew all of the impure thoughts racing through her head. She walked up to me smiling, saying, "You are looking mighty fine in this dress young lady." She started softly running her fingers up my arms and around my neck! As if I wasn't horny enough?! I do want to respect her marriage but too much of me just don't care right now. While my heart and mind figured out the best way to say no, my body had taken control causing me to grab the back of her head, bringing her to me. I

wanted her right then and there and I wanted her to know it. She grabbed my ass as we kissed, squeezing it like she missed me. It had been so long since we'd been in each other's arms, we were already sharing moans.

She pushed me on the bed and with ease slid this skintight dress up and ripped my thongs off. I just laid back and prepared myself. I felt her lower down to her knees. I knew what she wanted, so I placed my legs on her shoulders. A trail of her kisses started at my thighs and ended at my lips. She pressed my thighs open and went to suckling on my clit. It seemed as though instead of running like I normally do, I slid deeper into her mouth, like I wanted her to suck my soul out. My head went back, and man was this way better than my bullet! I could barely control myself when she slid her finger inside. It never takes long for me to reach my moment when I'm with her. I started to shiver and in went another finger; my hands pushed her right on in. I could barely breathe but that didn't stop my hips from swaying on her face. I wanted to scream! That hallelujah moment! She sent my body to another world. She didn't stop and that's when I began to run. I couldn't take it!

She got up, smiling and shit. I felt the need to show her up because she was feeling a little too sure of herself. I pulled her to me, kissing her and rolling onto her, still weak in the legs but a heart full of confidence. I unbuckled her sexy white shorts and pulled them off with boy shorts intact. My old friend was already dripping wet. I licked and stroked her with only my tongue. I took all the time in the world, slowly sucking and stroking her pearl. She was squirming and moaning which turned me on even more. I pulled out my bullet and gently rubbed it against her clit while fingering her. My mission was to make her remember me when she fucked her husband. This girl was going to be mine when it was all said and done, even if only for one night.

She tried to hold in her screams as much as she could. I never stopped licking and fingering her. I had to be the pro that I am. She was losing control. My ego grew because I knew I had her. I sped up the motions, both hands now gripping that fat ass. She was trying to run. I gripped tighter and pulled her closer. This mouth service was on point! Her legs were shaking, and my old friend was oozing all over my face. Just like clockwork, her moment was vastly approaching. She squirmed and moaned. I loved to hear her moans. She squirted a load out of this world but no need in stopping. I knew she was sensitive, but I didn't care. This is what she asked for.

Another damn knock came on the door. I completely forgot about the fact we're at our friend's party. It felt like it was just me and her this entire time. I didn't stop though. They could wait. This man got 3 other bathrooms. We both didn't want this freak show to stop but the knocking continued. Aleccia looked at me and before she could say something, I opened my eyes to realize it was all a dream.

Pierre knocked on the wall behind me as he said, "Wake up

sleepy head! We've been waiting for you to join us." I could barely make out where I was and maybe I was still dreaming. I felt fuzzy and a tingling sensation over my entire body. I tried to rub my eyes because what I was seeing, and feeling wasn't real, however my hands and feet were tied to the bed posts. Recalling the night before was a total bust. I could remember being at Wet Willie's but nothing after that. When did I leave? How did I get here? What the hell is going on right now? My eyes got more focused, and Pierre was sitting in a chair in the middle of the room between my bed and another. He continued, "I didn't think I would have you here so soon." He chuckled, "I've wasted a year trying to intimidate you when I could've just called and cried to get you here." He looked at me with a devilish smirk, "I have so many wonderful things planned for you." His phone started to buzz, "Oh, look at the time. I have to be at practice but don't worry ladies I'll be back."

After he left out of the door, I turned my head to the bed on the other side of the room and there laid Aleccia, staring back at me. I tried to break free until Aleccia spoke, "It's no use, Harper. He does this shit for sport."

"Am I really seeing you right now?"

"Seeing me is the least of your problems." She scoffed.

"Oh, seeing a dead bitch is the least of my problems? What the fuck is going on with Pierre and nigga did you fake your death?"

She sighed, "I didn't fake anything. Pierre is a fucking sociopath! I don't know how he faked my death; I just know he came back happy that the shit worked out."

"Okay, so he's crazy. Why are we tied up like this though?"

She turned her head at me and replied, "Because he knows everything about us and the shit we used to do with Calvin and he's not happy."

I sighed, "You told him?"

"He's my husband Harper! I confided in him about Calvin because he took advantage of us. Of our age. He was a grown ass man, and we were barely teenagers and then he goes and marries your mom and thinks he can have his cake and eat it too. I wanted to be honest with him. I didn't want secrets in my marriage. You know how my family is. I tried to do this marriage shit right. Did I know I would enrage a fucking sociopath with a God like complex? Hell, no but that's exactly what the fuck I did! Now, I'm tied to a bed with no clue as to what's going to happen next. How did he even get to you?"

"I thought he needed help. I got a text from your phone and assumed it was him. I came here to Memphis to see him and talk. I ended up seeing Darius and we went to Wet Willie's and now I'm here. Where are we?"

"We're in Newton. It's where we'd come to get away when things were good. Now, it's my prison that I'm so lucky to share with you."

"Sounds like it's all my fault Aleccia?"

"Well, I wouldn't know Calvin, if it wasn't for you."

"Wow. Okay." I wasn't angry with her for speaking her truth, but I was hurt. She was completely right about Calvin and if I knew then what I know now, I would've never continued any kind of conversation with Calvin, let alone an actual sexual relationship with him. I was completely at fault for her first time with Calvin and all the multiple sessions thereafter. I already felt terrible for how my mom would feel if she ever knew the truth. I didn't know Aleccia was hurting the way she was, and yet it makes sense as to why she started to hate him so much after a while. I always wondered but never asked. I was too self-absorbed in being able to sleep with my friend and basically my stepfather to really care how this was affecting either one of them. I didn't see how damaging this was to her, nor did I see how he was a real-life pedophile. Everything we did, we did by choice. There were no threats from him to kill our family or to keep our secret. We didn't think things through. Calvin was sweet and careful in his gestures. For the most part I sought him out and he went along with everything. He didn't deny me anything. He gave me everything I wanted and more. It was the thought of having his baby that I couldn't accept. That's when I started to really see how wrong everything that we'd been doing was. I wish I could've seen it sooner then maybe Aleccia and I wouldn't be in this predicament. I glanced at my friend, "Aleccia, I'm sorry. You're right about Calvin and I should've realized it a long time ago. I'm just happy that you're alive. We can find a way out of this; we just have to work together."

Without hesitation she replied, "There's no way out of this Harper. Whatever Pierre is going to do next, he's going to do it, whether we want him to or not."

"We can't just give up."

She yelled, "We're tied to a bed in the basement in the fucking middle of nowhere. What about that don't you understand?!"

"I understand it just fine Aleccia! How about you answer me this though, if he's so angry about Calvin, then why are we the ones tied up to the beds? Why not just go after Calvin?!"

She laughed, "There his bitch ass is tied up!"

I frantically searched around the room. My position and being tied down, hindered my sight in more than a few places, but I was able to see Calvin pretty much hanging in the closet bound by his hands from the corner of my eyes. I could only assume he was unconscious since he hadn't moved or made a sound since I woke up. Or maybe he was dead. I wanted to ask Aleccia more questions, as I had about a million things to ask, instead I choose to be silent. I waited for the next moment whatever it may be.

# Chapter Seventeen

The way this day ended was no surprise. I could feel the vibe change as soon as Pierre entered the room this morning. He was unusually frustrated as he spoke, "You know James, I have been wanting to meet you for some time now. Do you remember your ex, Kimberly Moore?" Pierre had replaced our constraints with shock collars and dared us to escape. We stayed put like trained dogs and every time he came back; he would sit in the center of the room and stroke his Glock as if he was jacking off while directing the scene to his liking. Aleccia had already shared all the horror stories she had about him while he was away at his games. The abuse ranged from being beat to being raped and so much more. She told us it was not long after she had confided in him that his entire demeanor changed. He was no longer the sweet and charming guy he was when they had met. Everything that went wrong was somehow her fault. She tried to find different ways to please him and win his affections back, but it only made him angrier. He started to openly see other women and of course she allowed him to, thinking this would bring back the once caring guy she had married. It did not. She had placed herself in a polyamorous relationship with a sociopath. They all played house for a while until he grew tired of it and apparently killed the girl and used Aleccia's identity to cover up the fact, he had just murdered their girlfriend.

With the NBA season happening, I didn't think we'd see him so much, but I also didn't think he would have time to be the stalker either. When you have your own private helicopter, it makes it easier to travel to your remote cabin in the mosquito filled woods of Newton where you have three people held hostage or secretly deliver packages in North Jackson. He is very thoughtful and well calculated in every action he performs. He does not like to make a lot of mistakes and when he does, his wrath rains down on us. I am not sure how long I have been here. A couple of weeks. Maybe three. He keeps Calvin tied to a chair naked with a gag in his mouth and forces him to watch me and Aleccia having sex. If at any point in time, Calvin is aroused, he uses a taser gun to inflict pain and control over what Calvin is allowed to enjoy and what he isn't. The same is said for me and Aleccia, if we refuse, complain, or act as though we aren't enjoying ourselves, he presses a button on a remote causing the collars around our necks to shocks us. I used to adore Aleccia and every moment I ever had with her I craved more. The days when we would all enjoy each other were the happiest days of my life and I could not wait to one day experience that again. I never imagined it would have been like this. How can I enjoy being forced into this with her? Nothing about this was pleasurable or desirable, however, you would not have known by how we both faked it each time.

Calvin was in a daze and could comprehend the events surrounding him. I had hoped he would eventually master how to control his erections but that certainly was not the case. In mere seconds of us kissing, he would get aroused. Before we finished, he would have passed out from being tased so many times. Aleccia mentioned days before that she could see him growing tired of us all and today was the day, he made it very well known. While Aleccia and I just sat in our beds waiting for directions, Pierre continued, "Come on James! I know you remember." Calvin mumbled, "Yeah, I remember."

"I knew you did. I bet you remember her daughter too. What was her name?"

Calvin looked confused as he replied, "What?"

Pierre punched him in the face like the man owed him money and said, "Don't play coy with me James. What was the daughter's name? It's a simple question."

He groaned, "I don't remember."

Pierre smirked, "You don't remember huh?" He pulled out his

Glock along with a picture out of his back pocket and held both up to Calvin and yelled, "What's the little girl's name?"

Without hesitation, Calvin replied, "It's Trinity. I remember now. Her name is Trinity."

Pierre chuckled, "I bet you do remember." Calvin did not say anything. He just sat there trembling and watching Pierre as he took out another picture and said, "This is Trinity too." Pierre seemed normal for just a moment as he looked over the picture with sadness in his voice he continued, "This was the last picture I took of her. It was her 18th birthday, and she was excited about being legal. She finally felt free from Kimberly. This was the happiest day of her life until it was the last day. I threw her this huge party. I invited family, friends, and all. My biggest mistake was inviting Kimberly's sisters. Kimberly and her sisters hadn't talked since Kimberly left you. That didn't stop them from being family though so of course they showed up and showed out. It didn't take long for them to start arguing. I tried to diffuse the situation, but they just kept going on and on. Messed up a perfectly good party with some old ass drama. When Trinity started going off on Kimberly, that is when I learned some wild shit. That simpleminded bitch said that Trinity was the reason she had to leave you. She said if Trinity had kept her big ass mouth shut that y'all would still be together now. Trinity started crying and ran away. I tried everything I could to find her and eventually I did. She had overdosed and was laying dead in a ditch on Hooker St. I guess being the reason for her mother's misery was too much for her to bear. Do you know how Trinity could be the reason that you and Kimberly had to break up? What you didn't want kids or something?"

Calvin stuttered, "I I I I have no idea what that's all about."

Pierre asked, "Didn't she leave you?"

Calvin replied, "Yeah man she did but I never knew the reason why?"

Pierre chuckled, "Oh cause fucking a 5-year-old ain't a reason?"

Calvin shook his head, "Nah, man that wasn't me."

Pierre stood up as he replied, "It wasn't you?! James Calvin Kersh?! Do you know how messy it was to learn about you? I remember begging my mother to tell me who you were. She deflected. She gave me a bunch of sad mumbo jumbo about how she would've never imagined the son she raised would treat her like this. All the extra drama and misery behind a dude I didn't even know existed. It wasn't until I tied her ass to a bed and doused her with gasoline that she finally told the truth. It was a secret she'd take to her grave, so I had to put her ass in the grave to get it. My mother was sick and should've been locked away in prison for allowing the shit to happen to my sister. I didn't fault Trinity or my aunts. She was nothing but a child but to know you took advantage of my sweet sister. It really did something to me." We were all shocked to say the least, but nobody said a word. We just let Pierre keep talking, "I mean dude, seriously, my mother created you. When she realized how close she was to meeting her maker, she started spilling all of her secrets, thinking it would save her. I could barely stand to hear it as the truth rolled out of her mouth. It was never a secret to her. She knew the entire time. What's worse than knowing? Setting it up. Her disgusting ass gave my sister to you. She did and said stuff to make it damn near impossible for you to say no because what happens in her house, should have stayed in her house. Did you know she hated her own daughter because she thought she was more beautiful than her? She said she had to beat Trinity whenever she tried to talk about the shit you were doing. Kimberly thought that would shut her up, but it didn't. That's why Trinity went to my aunts and told them. My mother created this bullshit cycle but what the fuck is wrong with you? To go along with some shit like that?! You even took my wife's innocence!" He looked at Aleccia and continued, "He made you his fucking whore to share with his slut daughter!"

Calvin tried to explain while Pierre pointed his gun in his direction, "What you want me to say man?! I don't know why I like little girls. I don't know why I did it! If I could take it back, I would. I really would. I'd never touch her or another little girl. I won't even look their way. I'm sorry man. Please man!"

Aleccia chimed in, "Baby it wasn't all him, I didn't do anything I didn't want to do. We could just leave. Just me and you. I'm sorry about all of this. We could go anywhere! Baby please put your gun down. We don't need any more blood on our hands."

POW!

Within seconds Pierre shot Calvin in the head as he said, "He's a grown ass man. He knew what the fuck he was doing. Why do you think he kept getting hard when y'all fucked? He still like that shit and if he could, he would've fucked you right now. He's not remorseful. He wanted me to spare his life and for what? He was only going to fuck up another kid's life. You were a child Aleccia. What's his excuse?!"

Calvin sat there lifeless with a bullet hole in his head. The blood splattered on the wall behind him while some oozed from the hole and down his face. I was staring at him, and his glassed eyes stared right back. Aleccia was already sobbing as Pierre started to untie Calvin and haul his body away. I couldn't speak. I couldn't move. I wasn't sure what to do really. I couldn't seem to form the tears that I thought I would've had. I sat there emotionless as the one man I'd loved for thirteen years was put down worse than a dirty dog. Those last few moments played over and over again in my head in slow motion. His voice I couldn't erase. Just like that it was over. What would Pierre do next? When would he grow tired of me? Soon, I'll have to answer for my sins as well. I'll have to look this crazed man in the face and beg for my life as he's the judge, jury, and executioner. I can count the days down until I'm no longer any use to him.

The next few days quickly turned into a complete whorehouse, and I was at the center of it all. Pierre started bringing in all kinds of men from pretty much everywhere. They did whatever they wanted to me and forced me into things I thought I would never do. The collar only enticed the men more. At one point there was a homeless guy that Pierre had met as he was leaving the grocery store. He invited him back and I could hear him being the perfect host, offering him drinks and food and eventually me. It's sad to say but I considered Aleccia lucky. She only had to endure Pierre while I endured the million-man march. Between the thousands of men, there were thousands of women as well. I wasn't allowed to wear clothes since they were a nuisance for what Pierre wanted to happen. He controlled every second of every day and the collars never left our necks. When he couldn't find other mates to join in, he'd simply have his way with us both. Is it crazy that I missed Calvin? I didn't know about Aleccia, but I hated Calvin for molesting a 5-year-old and yet at least with Calvin, it was all by choice.

Pierre started drugging us at night to make us sleep so he wouldn't have to worry about us trying to escape. These were not the days we'd hoped for. No, these days were complete nightmares that we couldn't wake up from. Aleccia had been pretty standoffish to me from the moment I arrived as if I wanted to share this torture chamber with her. She made it quite clear that introducing her to Calvin was the reason and frankly how could I blame her? Pierre was a loose cannon waiting to attack anybody that defied him. I see that all she could do was obey and stay on his good side. I've certainly done the same. She finally opened up and broke the silence between us, "Harper, I'm sorry for the way I've treated you. I never should've blamed you like I did."

"It's okay Aleccia."

"No, it's not Harper. You're my best friend. We're like sisters and I should've treated you like that. I don't know what Pierre is going to do next and I don't want to see you in the same position as Calvin. I just want you to know I'm sorry. I am. I never meant for any of this to happen."

I turned over to face her, "How could you have known this would happen? You can't predict shit like this so why beat yourself up about it?"

She sighed, "I knew things would get worse. I tried to leave him, and it set him off in ways I've never seen. The moment when I actually tried to walk away and get to the girl I used to be, is when he thwarted every effort I made. Now I'm stuck and I was fine being stuck. It's better than being dead but seeing you and seeing Calvin pissed me off. I felt like everything would've been better if I'd never met him. I regretted meeting you too. I regretted every decision I made in life that led me here but I'm sorry for that. Regardless, nobody made me choose Pierre. Ultimately that was my decision and my decision alone."

"Aleccia, you cannot blame yourself for any of this. I don't know why this is happening, but we'll get through this."

She whispered, "We need to plan our escape."

I shook my head, "We have shock collars on to prevent that and he drugs us every night until we're too sleepy to even try to escape. It's not possible."

"Harper, all we have are shock collars. We're no longer tied to the beds. All we have to do is take the collars off and make a run for it. We'll eventually get to a gas station or a store or something."

"I don't know. If we get caught, it's going to anger him so bad and he's not going to up and kill you next. That's going to be me and I'd rather we not do that."

"If he's going to kill you, it's going to happen whether we try to escape or not. Calvin was killed and was still tied up. He's going to get tired of us soon Harper. We need to make a run for it while we can."

I sighed as I rolled my eyes, "Do you even know the code to the alarm?"

She smiled, "Of course, I do. I told you this was our little get away spot."

"You don't know his schedule though. You don't know when he'll be back."

"I know enough, besides it's still the middle of basketball season, which means we have plenty of time to leave after he leaves for his next game."

I nodded as I started to doze off. The drugs were taking effect. We used the next few days to plan our escape. We scoped the house out every time we were allowed to leave the basement. The front and back doors had deadbolt locks on them. We needed a key to get in and out, but he was the only one with the key. There was an alarm system on top of two big ass red nose pitbulls guarding the house. Aleccia had lost her ever loving mind thinking we were about to escape this house, but she was confident that we would be able to escape through the garage door, so we carefully planned to make a break for it as soon as he left for his next game.

# Chapter Eighteen

We watched in horror as WLPA reported that a body had been found in the Mississippi River near Biloxi. I guess it had been about a month when everybody had finally learned of Calvin's death. I watched my mom on the news crying and asking if anybody with any information to step forward. She wanted justice and understanding but if she knew the true reason behind his death, would she even be able to live with herself. Pierre sat between Aleccia and I as if we were watching an action movie. He just laughed the entire time while eating popcorn. I stayed silent because I didn't know what would tick him off and it was clear as day that he still had a few things in store for me. I realized nobody was looking for me or even cared that I had been here all of this time. He began to rub my head as he read aloud the letter, he was had started writing:

*Dear Shirley,*

*You don't know me, but I thought it was best you knew the truth about your husband. The man you adored and spent your hard-earned dimes on has been secretly having an affair with your daughter in your house. Right under your nose. I'm sure you won't believe a word I say which is why I've included a bunch of pictures and letters between the two of them as supporting evidence. My favorite picture is the one with your husband bending your daughter over in the bathroom. It looked like the master bathroom too. It wasn't just your daughter in there either. It was her best friend Aleccia as well. Did you know he was fucking your daughter and her best friend? Be sure to look at the picture of them all together enjoying each other as if you don't even exist. Your husband was a filthy disgusting pedophile and he deserved to die. This was nothing new for him. He's*

135

*been fucking little girls and teens since well before he met you. I hope you're not like some women that knew and didn't care because that makes you a trifling low life bitch like your husband. Anyway, I hate to dump all of this on you now as I know you're grieving for this scum bucket but there's no need to mourn a bum ass nigga like James. He didn't deserve to live, and jail would've been too good for him. Don't be mad at me as I'm just the messenger but you have a good day.*

*Regards,*
*The Messenger*

The letter brought tears to my eyes. It's not the way I wanted my mom to find out. I should've told her when I had the chance. When I could've explained myself better but really what could I say? I hated my mom when she married him and still managed to love Calvin. Even to the bitter end, I still had place in my heart for him. Do I regret everything about him? Absolutely and that still changes nothing. Now I'm pretty sure she'll never want to see me or talk to me again. That is if I ever get out of here. Pierre noticed my tears and began to mock me, "Aww is the slut daughter sad? What's wrong you didn't want mommy to know you were sucking your dad's dick?"

Aleccia tried to defend me, "Pierre that wasn't her real dad though."

Pierre quickly turned his sour words towards Aleccia, "Aleccia, my sweet, does it really matter if he was her real dad or not?" He turned back to me and asked, "Did you ever once call him dad, daddy, or pops in front of people as if to say he was your real dad? I know you call him daddy in bed, but we all know that's different."

I didn't want to answer but I didn't want to get shocked either. I replied, "Yeah, I called him dad in public as if he was my real dad." It wasn't something I wanted to do. My mom would bitch so much about me not calling him dad, so Calvin told me to just do it anyway. He said it wouldn't be any harm done if I called him dad. As soon as I had said the word yeah, Pierre was laughing as loud as he could.

He went on to say, "So what exactly is the difference Aleccia?"

It was obvious she wanted to say a mouthful but instead she spoke softly, "There's no difference Pierre."

He scoffed, "My point! Nobody fucking cares about the technicalities. She fucked her dad. She's daddy's little whore. Don't argue with me about this shit." We both knew to stay silent as he went on ranting about me being a whore. The topic had hit a nerve with him as he started to express his feelings about his own mother, "I hate my mother for giving my sister away to a grown ass man. She should've aborted us both as soon as she found out but instead, she let her fucked up life ruin mine ours. What kind of woman wants to see her man fucking her daughter? She thought this shit would never come. My dad died thinking he married an angel. If he was alive, I bet he'd wanted nothing to do with her or us. You already know she hated me because I looked like him. Oh yeah, I was another reason she couldn't keep a man. Trinity is the reason she couldn't be with James. It was nothing we did but we were the reasons behind her failed relationships. She treated us like shit until she had another dick to lay beside. None of those niggas stayed though. Every last one of them dipped and every time we were the reasons why. I remember the night I finally killed her so clearly. She was laid up in the bed fussing about the dishes being dirty. Dishes she had fucked up. She just wanted a servant, and I was the only person around. I wasn't angry at her. I was curious. I asked her calmly to tell me why Trinity ran away. I wanted to hear her side and find out who this James nigga was. She cursed me completely out like I was somebody she didn't even know. So, I waited until she was sleep, grabbed the gasoline can, and her keys and went to the gas station. When I came back, I went straight to her room, and started to pour it all over her and the bed. She woke up cussing and shit while I was laughing holding a torch lighter."

He chuckled at the memory, "I held the lighter up and asked her again about Trinity and she spilled her guts. She thought pleading and begging would've stopped me from lighting her ass up, but it didn't. I felt pure delight and freedom when I heard her stop screaming."

Pierre stood up and started pacing, "I couldn't wait to one day meet James, but I couldn't meet him empty handed. I needed to meet him with a truck full of my favorite weapons. I was sixteen when I killed her, so they placed me in an orphanage. Came across some decent people but I stayed to myself. I knew for the most part they were only in it for the check. I let them have that shit. All I wanted was to beast in basketball and that's exactly what the fuck I did. One of the youngest NBA drafts straight from high school. Everybody wanted me. Everybody loved me. I just wanted to meet James though."

He stopped and looked at Aleccia, "But I met you first. For a moment I gave up looking for James. What did I need him for when I had somebody as unbelievable and amazing as you?" He turned away and started back pacing, "Then you ruined it. I bet you haven't even told your whore ass friend a fraction of the truth. A lying bitch like my mother. You had the nerve to bring another nigga in my house. You'll never understand how fucked up I was to see James fucking you. To hear you moaning in pleasure to a bitch made fuck boy like him was more than disgusting to say the least. But then I was like wait a minute is this the nigga I've been searching for? The nigga that molested my sister? This nigga is fucking my wife?!"

I sat there speechless and shocked, hoping I had heard him wrong, but he yelled, "How could you fuck that dude in my house? How could you Aleccia?" When I turned to look at Aleccia, she was once again sobbing. I wanted to ram her head into the window behind her. She straight played me and so did he. This entire time they had their own thing going on and I never even knew. I refuse to believe this was some random moment and lust just took over. They pretended to hate each other for years so how could he end up fucking her in the house she shares with Pierre in Texas? I was so angry tears started to roll down my face. Pierre noticed immediately, "Yeah I figured her lying ass hadn't told you the truth. Look at what you have done Aleccia! You've gone and upset daddy's little whore. I guess my work here is done." He walked out of the door laughing while Aleccia pleaded, "Harper, I'm so sorry."

I shook my head, "Sorry for what? Lying? Sleeping with Calvin behind my back? You being the real reason we're knee deep in bullshit? What are you sorry for exactly?"

She sniffled, "Please forgive me."

I scoffed, "Were you ever going to tell me the truth?"

"Yes! I swear! Listen, I wasn't lying when I said I was trying to leave Pierre. Yes, he caught me and Calvin and that's what made me tell him everything about us. He changed and everything I told you happened afterwards really did happen. When I tried to leave, he faked my death. I don't know why he didn't just kill me instead."

All I just heard was a bunch of bullshit. I used to confide in her about all of our problems. I told her all of my secrets. She was the person I ran to for everything and yet here she is with this sad ass look on her face. They went out of their way to hate each other and there was never any hate. The lengths they went to just to have this little affair is what is amazing to me. I relived every conversation Aleccia, and I ever had, and I glared at her, "Did Calvin get you pregnant?"

She hesitated, "Harper."

"Just answer the question." I replied sternly.

"Yes, but I lost the baby every time."

I choked on the words as they fell from my lips, "Every…. time? How many fucking times?"

"Three. The first one was in high school. Pierre doesn't know about that one."

I shook my head, "Wow. Did Calvin know? Did you try to pass these babies off as
Pierre's?!"

She dropped her head in shame, "Harper, of course he knew. He wanted the babies. They weren't accidents but I was stupid. I didn't know the damage I could cause from thinking I was in love with Calvin."

I shook my head in disbelief, of course his bitch ass wanted the babies. Sarcastically I replied, "In love?! Wow!"

"Okay, don't believe me. It's fine but it's the truth. He was my first too Harper. He would cater to me as if I was the only one. I wanted to tell you. I really did but he said he could never be with you because of your mom and that you wouldn't understood that. He said you were crazy and wouldn't take it well. Was I wrong for not telling you? Yes! You're my best friend. I should've said something but what can I do now? Calvin is dead and as you can see for yourself, Pierre has completely lost it. All we have is each other." She leaned in and whispered, "We have to stick to our plan before he kills both of us next."

Before I could say anything, Pierre had barged back in the room saying, "What plan Aleccia?" She couldn't speak. She was frozen. She looked at me. I looked back at her. Pierre turned his focus to me, "What fucking plan huh?" I didn't say a word. I didn't know how to reply. What was I supposed to say? It was obvious that anger had consumed him. I prepared myself for what was to come next. He came closer to me and began to snatch off my collar. A million thoughts were racing through my mind. Was there a line up at the door waiting to sodomize me or maybe he's about to take his anger out on me because I didn't answer him. That's exactly what he did. He began to choke me as I felt him force himself inside of me. This was something new. Was he into necrophilia too? His violence wasn't as intimate as it was in this moment. He's been very particular in feeding me with a long handle spoon while allowing others to abuse me, so why am I being choked and raped. In front of Aleccia no less. His love for her denied him of being with me unless it was with her as well. I'd prefer he just kill me already. I still tried to fight him off of me. A reflex I suppose. I couldn't do anything but cry and gasp for air in the end. Eventually, I gave up, closed my eyes, and accepted my fate.

# Chapter Nineteen

SPLASH!

"Wake yo ass up!" As I jerked from the freezing cold-water Pierre had just doused on my face, he began his rant, "I can never be nice to you. You always fucking it up somehow. Don't you know that all I want to do is be nice to you? You know I'm not a bad guy. Yeah, maybe some anger issues but I'm only angry when you go and fuck up." I have no idea what he is talking about! What could I have done last night to make him this angry today?! I cleaned the kitchen and the living room. I didn't go into any other room and even though Aleccia was finally ready to escape, I wouldn't join her. I've been doing everything right and I thought things were getting better, but every new day brings with it another surprise from Pierre. It's starting to look like I'm the unicorn, I never wanted to be in. Now it's just me and Aleccia while Pierre is gone away for a game. No more random strays waiting by the door. No more neck collars. I mean the last week has been some pretty easy days compared to when I first got here. My first little ray of sunshine in all of this! We can walk around for a bit. There is a little more freedom now. I still want to leave. I just don't know how to get away and at this point I'm just going with the flow which is why I didn't understand half of what Pierre said until I heard, "So you fucking this Omari nigga?"

Completely dumbfounded by the accusation, the only words that came out of my mouth were, "Am I fucking Omari?

He was already pissed walking through the door. Why on earth would I repeat the question? I've lost the battle before it even began. He drew his hand and slapped me. It felt like I had gotten hit with a hot cast iron skillet. Immediately, tears started to fall but breaking down I refused to ever do. He's tried countless times to make me beg and sob and I refuse. Since the day I learned the real reason behind all of this, I've shut down. Unless I do something now, then no amount of physical pain will make me break down and I can cruise through the days as if they don't even exist. Today, I fucked up. I've been doing everything right but here he is inches from my face yelling about Omari. I sat there with my eyes closed as he continued screaming. Feeling his hot breath in a mist of sour cheap vodka, I've learned not to move a muscle on my face. I didn't mean to repeat the question. I wasn't sure I'd even heard him correctly. Why is he even mentioning Omari right now? And sex? He stepped back glaring at me in silence awaiting my reply to the original question, "No, I'm not fucking Omari. We've never had sex."

He scoffed in disbelief, "Let's see here, from what I know about you and correct me if I'm wrong, but your mother has been horrible to you, no daddy around, sleeping with your step daddy, and eats your best friend's pussy on the side. What did I miss?" "Nothing." I spoke softly.

His hostility grew, "Oh yeah I missed something. Who the fuck is Omari?!"

"He's a friend from college. That's it."

Pierre mocked me and started to pace the room, "He'S a FrIeNd FrOm CoLlEgE. tHaT's It. Bitch lie again! Ain't nobody else in this fucked up world worried about you but this pussy ass nigga." He stopped pacing and leaned into me, "He's the only person making this big fuss about you. Going out of his way to file a missing person's report on you. Not ya mama. Not ya job. Not any other so-called friend. So, I'm going to ask again, who the fuck is Omari?"

"Nobody."

His foul chuckle aimed at Aleccia, "Do you know who Omari is? Have you heard anything about him?"

Aleccia's teary eyed focused on me and then at Pierre and back at me, she mouths to me,

'I'm sorry' and quickly answers, "No, this is my first-time hearing anything about him."

Pierre sighed and began to rub his forehead until seconds later when his entire mood changed. He started to smile and laugh completely out of nowhere. He walked out and told us he would be back soon. Aleccia came over to me and helped me off the water-soaked bed. She did not waste any time with her questions as she whispered, "So who is Omari for real?"

I could barely contain the hostility I felt when talking to Aleccia now. I have accepted my part in what got me here long before I got here. Since our newfound freedom, she has become so clingy to me. My resentment does not last long and eventually turns into sadness for her. Regardless of how long I've been here, she's had to endure his wrath even longer, so I allow her to be clingy sometimes. I replied, "He really is just a friend. That's why you don't know anything about him. If he was somebody important, you would've been the first person I told." The words could not leave my tongue fast enough before I realized one very important moment, I hadn't told her about. The abortion. I looked at her and smiled and continued to put new sheets on the bed. I wasn't about to tell her today either. This shit wasn't a competition of who gets pregnant by the pedophile and that's all it would've turned into had I disclosed that piece of information. I knew getting the abortion was the right thing to do. I don't even want to think about how this would've went had I told her right after the test turned positive or even if I'd kept the baby. And to think I thought she would've made a better mother. What a foolish little girl I was! If I could just get out of this hellhole, I would do so many things differently.

Her questions didn't stop, she went on to ask, "How long have you known him?"

I shook my head, "I don't know. Like I said, he's a friend from school. No more than a couple of years."

"Does he know about me?" She asked in a flirty kind of way.

I faked a laugh not understanding how she could be in a flirty mood when a serial killer walked the halls, "He knows you're dead plus you were married, and I was trying to respect your marriage."

Her response wasn't suited in a happy tone as she replied, "Well I'm still married but that didn't stop us from hooking up. It didn't stop Calvin joining in either."

It was clear that tension was in the air now, "Like I don't understand that or something?"

She cut me off, "No, you don't understand. Pierre may have caught me with Calvin yeah but let's be clear here, it could've easily been all three of us or just us. None of us stopped but you tried to be mad that it was just me and Calvin sometimes. Like I said, he was my first too."

I rolled my eyes, "Okay chill out. Me and you vs me hooking you up with somebody is two totally different things. Besides, I didn't even know about you and Calvin so please shut up about it. Both of y'all were lying to me about even liking each other so yeah that's all on you that you got caught."

"It wasn't different when you hooked me up with Calvin though."

"Aleccia, we were teenagers and I'm sorry. I really am but let's be real clear I respected you when you didn't want to deal with Calvin anymore. I respected that and that was long before Pierre. I also respected you being done with me." I looked her up and down and shook my head wondering when she would see, it was ultimately her decision to not only give it up the first time but to continue even after being married! I didn't even know about her and Calvin having a thing until all of this. I won't pretend like I don't have some fault in this but it's not all on me. I just wish she'd accept her part in all of this as well. I'm being fussed at by Pierre or arguing with Aleccia. I'm so tired of arguing about the same thing every few days or getting beat because of it.

Aleccia uttered softly, "I'm sorry Harper. I shouldn't have said that. Tell me more about Omari. Sounds like a good friend if he's the only person to file a missing person's report."

I sighed. Disdain dripped on every word, "It's really nothing to tell about Omari. We're just friends."

"Did you know he would file a missing person's report?"

I hesitated. Omari and I wasn't even cool when I left, and I didn't tell anybody when I was leaving or where I was going. It's been plenty of times we've stopped talking and started back but after this last fight we had, I didn't think there was any coming back from that. At least I know the fight didn't mess up our friendship. This missing person's report has given me assurance that there was somebody in the world actually caring for me. I'm quite certain that my mom has thrown me away. Why would she care about the daughter that was sleeping with her husband? She doesn't have to forgive me but if I could ever get away, I'd tell her I'm sorry. No matter what issues we had, it wasn't right for me to continue with Calvin like that. If only I could've realized sooner just how wrong I was, maybe all of this could've been prevented. I

sighed from the reality of it all, "I'm just as shocked as you."

A few minutes later, the room door opened, and Pierre was back. Aleccia looked at me and smiled. I knew exactly why. Luckily for us he was still in a good mood. She preferred him happy over angry even though both were sadistic, torture obsessed, psychopaths. When he's happy, he's just horny all of the time. It's not romantic. It's not passionate. It's just a lot of it. One day, he's into BDSM to the fullest and the next it's just a moment that just passes by. I don't know what to call it really. That's something I can handle compared to the torture he could inflict when he's angry. He looks for new ways to inflict fear without being physical until that bores him and then it's nothing but slaps and punches for a while. Those angry days can last for weeks, and anything can set him off. There is no escaping the anger because he never stays happy. He finds things to get pissed about. He looked at Aleccia and then said, "Find another room." She quickly left out of the room. Shit.

I already knew the two options I had left when he fixed his gaze unto me. Should I be happy with not getting beat right now? If I just had a choice, I guess this is what I'd choose. He doesn't care to hear me moan or to pleasure me. This is strictly for him. If it makes him happy then he can do it as much as he wants to. Mentally, I'm never here anyway. There's always an island waiting for me to enjoy the view while sipping on some colorful daiquiris with umbrellas in them. I always picture myself out dancing on the beach under the stars while feeling the cool breeze of the beautiful island waters across my body. I always shed a tear when it's over. There are days when I believe this is where my life ends. I can't leave and nobody is going to find me. There are days when I believe I can escape and get myself back home. I could wait until we're walking around freely and give Aleccia the slip but that's the only way it would work. She says she wants to escape but she acts like she's just as messed up as him. It's as if I must have the courage for both of us and to be quite frank, I barely have enough for myself. If she wants to escape, she must be just as ready as me. My thoughts were interrupted when Aleccia said, "Pierre! Get off of her!" The beats of my heart sped up. She's never raised her voice at this man so what the hell is she thinking? Could I have been wrong? Maybe last night she really was ready and if I'd just listened, we could've escaped last night.

Appalled, he got up saying, "Excuse you?" She stood in the doorway and handed him his phone. For about 15 minutes, he stood there with nothing but his muscle shirt on and socks, texting somebody and as soon as he was done, his anger had returned, and he charged me with a closed fist. I blocked his punch. 'FUCK!' I thought to myself. I wasn't really thinking when I blocked it. I'm just tired of being beat on. I have no idea what's even happening right now. He stepped back for a moment and then he charged me again. I figured it was time to fight back. I didn't mean to block his punch but that's not going to stop him from beating me until I'm at the brink of death. I'm ready to do anything to leave this place no matter the cost but regardless I'm fighting back this time. Seeing Aleccia stand up to him, gave me a little bit of hope for her. I

know I'll lose by myself, but it seemed like Aleccia has finally found her courage. Together I do believe, we can take him and get away from here. That's not what happened though. I kicked him between the legs. As he was bent over in pain, I jumped up to finally run away. Aleccia was already to the basement door trying to get it unlocked. I was just a few steps away when he snatched me up by my hair and slung me into the floor. We fought around the basement, while Aleccia stood her distance. She could have ran but instead she stood a few steps back. She could've done something though. This is what we've been preparing for. While I tried my best to bite and claw him up, she could've gotten a vase or picture or something. It's plenty of stuff sitting around in this room. I did my part. I fought as hard as I could, but Pierre ultimately pinned me on the floor. He had me locked down with his entire body while he cuffed my hands.

Before he stood up, I could feel the fire from his hand once again on my cheek.

# Chapter Twenty

When you start to believe that you are officially living in your worse and last days, that is when you think, oh it could not possibly get any worse than this. Yeah, and that's when life accepts the challenge and takes it like fifty steps further. I suppose that is what Pierre thought he was doing by locking me in this little room alone. It is not necessarily dirty but more so dusty and forgotten about. A room in need of a little tender loving care to help it glow again. There is a sealed in space where a window used to be on the left wall. He took the cuffs and to my surprise I did not wake up with a collar on. I have been here since our fight in the basement. There's no sense of time here. No outside light to help me keep track of my days and nights. I was terrified to learn what my punishment would be for that fight. I guess I lucked up. This is the freest I've felt since walking back to my hotel room however many nights ago that was. A false sense of freedom is exactly what I need to bear each day with this deranged man. I've finally made a friend within the darkness. I'm only able to see the room when he turns the lights on and comes in. A lot of times he doesn't care to turn them on. He'll come in and handle all of his filthy dirty deeds in total darkness, then he'll walk back out. I wouldn't know it's him until I smell that sour cheap vodka on his breath. The silence has been quite alluring. I have found the most pleasure in being alone and out of the way.

I could hear footsteps at the door. My body tensing at what was about to happen next. He gently turned the lights on and slowly walked in. I pretended to be sleep because I got tired of seeing his face with that creepy ass smile whenever he'd turn the lights on. I felt his hand on my shoulder. The touch was light,

SECRETS OF MY HEART'S DESIRE

tender and different. It threw me off guard and that made me turn over to see Aleccia instead of Pierre. I inquired, "What's going on?"

She sat down beside me, "I just wanted to check on you. I don't want you out here forever."

I turned back over to avoid her seeing my annoyed facial reactions, "What do you mean?"

She laughed, "Don't be silly Harper. He has you in this make-shift bedroom that used to be our shed. I want you back in the house. I know you're lonely and so am I."

Not finding a thing amusing in this moment, I asked, "What's funny though?"

She started to walk us out of the shed and back to this big ass house as she spoke, "You baby. You're funny!" I was silent as she escorted me back to the basement. I watched her walking around rearranging stuff as she spoke, "Harper, I love you. I have loved you forever, you know that. Why do you think I was always there for you in middle school and high school? I know I hurt you by messing around with Calvin, but he was a piece of shit. We both know that now. I loved what we had. I did not want Pierre to do all of this. I mean I wanted him mad enough at Calvin to scare him away, but did I think he would kill him. Hell no! He certainly committed to the role of whacked out husband, am I right?" She paused with a smile on her face, but I had no reply, so she shrugged and kept on, "I knew it would take some time for you to see the truth about Calvin and what better way than to piss my husband off. Granted I didn't know about the whole sister bit, but you have to admit, it made it so much better. The anger was really natural."

I could not believe what I was hearing right now. Maybe I have been drugged or something. I chuckled in disbelief, "Aleccia, what are you actually trying to say? You set up being caught by Pierre to break me and Calvin up?"

She hesitated as she thought about her next words, "When you say it, it sounds kind of bad but yes I did do that. Girl, I was so caught up in you and Calvin. I could not let you go but that also meant I couldn't let Calvin go. Y'all were a packaged deal, right?

I sternly replied, "No."

She continued, "Right! You see, Pierre forgave me as soon as I explained everything to him. That was not stopping him from wanting to make us all pay. It's okay because I made a new package deal. There is no me without you. That meant you had to be here with us, and Calvin had to die. I knew you would lead him to Calvin and the only way I knew to get to you was to stalk you and scare you." The truth behind her words were too much to bear but she didn't stop, "I made him a promise that I'd train you. That way he doesn't have to make you suffer too much but Harper, you haven't made any of this easier on you. We could all be one big happy family if you would just allow him to love you and stop resisting. If you could love Calvin and me, you can only imagine how amazing loving me and Pierre will be."

After everything that's happened, I honestly cannot stand the thought of either of them. They both make me sick. I wish I never met their fucked in the head asses. Can I just go back to the shed?! I don't care where I am. I just want to be left alone. I could not understand why he wouldn't just kill me. For six months I've been waking up in a hell that Aleccia helped create. She hasn't been trapped. She's been helping and coaching and who knows what else. I couldn't contain my anger as I replied, "All of this time you've been helping him because you wanted me to be y'all trained girlfriend?!" I was screaming and throwing anything I could get my hands on.

Pierre heard the commotion and rushed downstairs. At first, he quietly stood there, arms folded with that creepy ass grin going from ear to ear. I guess this was the moment he had waited on for the longest. My breaking point. He shouted upstairs, "Come on down Darius." I stopped and watched Darius come down the stairs. He does not have a reason to be here. Darius comes in and goes, "Hey y'all might want to gone head and get rid of ol girl. She making a little too much noise and we don't need that kinda pressure on us." My mouth dropped. Did this man just say to kill me? Who gave him permission to give the orders?

Aleccia spoke nonchalantly, "What are you talking about?"

He sucked his teeth, "What I'm talking about is how I had to sit down with Detectives Bibbs and Stewart yesterday. Her picture is all over the news and somehow they done found out about me hacking her shit and sending those damn text messages. They even got search and rescue teams looking for her from Jackson to Memphis."

Pierre had an uneasy look on his face after Darius finished talking, he spoke firmly at Aleccia, "The police are sniffing around. I told you that missing person's report was going to be a problem."

She sighed, "I asked her about the guy. She said he's nobody important. I believe her. It'll all die down soon enough. As far as the media is concerned, she is irrelevant. She is nothing but another black person that they don't care about. They are probably down on ratings and need some kind of news story. Trust me Pierre, nothing is going to go wrong."

He wasn't trying to hear that, "That's what you want to believe but that's not what's happening. If Darius is getting questioned, then it's time to get rid of her. I'm not going to jail over this bitch."

She rolled her eyes as she replied, "Nobody is going to jail. Nothing connects to you or me or her." She paused and nodded towards Darius as she said, "Especially, if Darius didn't give away any vital information."

Darius was silent while Pierre and Aleccia awaited his reply. His agitated body language made it clear to me, he had thrown them under the bus. By the time he opened his mouth to answer, little beads of sweat had formed on his forehead, "I only said what you told me to say. They still think Aleccia is dead, but they had a lot of questions about Pierre and some dude named James." At once, Pierre pulled his gun out and shot Darius in the side of the head. I screamed out in horror, while I watched his body drop to the floor. I couldn't believe this was happening. Pierre went on to say, "He said some shit."

Furious, Aleccia replied, "Well obviously! But now we'll never know exactly what, now will we?!"

Pierre yelled, "It doesn't fucking matter what was said. His ass shouldn't have said shit in the first place. I told you we couldn't trust his ass. They probably know everything thanks to this bitch boy."

They continued to argue while I sat balled up in the corner of the basement next to the foosball table staring at Darius' lifeless body. My mind ran with a million or more thoughts, trying to understand the truth I was facing. My best friend has been the mastermind behind all of this. She set herself up to get caught by Pierre, so that I would find out and we'd break up. She then faked her death and made a deal with her crazed husband to train me as their personal sex slave, only for Pierre's teammate to sell them out to the police. If Darius was questioned about hacking me and sending text messages, then what else did the police have on them? What did Darius know? We could've talked this out like the best friends that we are. It didn't have to be all of this. Granted, I would've said no because Pierre isn't my cup of tea. I like him for her not for me but at one point I loved Aleccia as much if not more than Calvin, maybe I wouldn't have said no.

All I want is for this to be over. I don't think my heart can break anymore. She looked at me and noticed I was balled up in the corner. She walked over to me and sat down beside me. Aleccia gently stroked my hair and softly spoke, "I'm sorry baby. You know how he can be sometimes but that's no reason to be afraid. He loves you and he's not going to kill you. I promise. You just need to trust me." She stood up and reached her hands out to me, "Now come on. You need to freshen up." I knew I couldn't trust her or him, but I had to listen. I'm certainly not about to fight Aleccia just to deal with Pierre later. She was the mastermind, but he was the crazy brute force needed to enforce any plan. I took her hand and she led me to the bathroom where water had been waiting on me. Her touches were gentle. They could've been mistaken for love. She undressed me with ease while she hummed a sweet tune, I'd never heard her sing. She helped me into the tub and while I sat there, she began to wash my back. She pulled me into her, I leaned on her in response and stared at the tiles on the floor. Tears fell that I couldn't control. I was sobbing on the outside and on the inside, I was empty. Still, all I could do was sit there and silently let the tears fall. Aleccia was happy and humming. All of her dreams were coming true. They both finally broken me. I could have gone through this never knowing Aleccia's part and I would have never broken down like this. Pierre is crystal clear out of his mind and is a psychopath that needs to be locked away forever. I wanted to get through this with my mind intact somehow. When I thought Aleccia was in this with me, I wanted us both to escape. Of course, we would tell everybody it was Pierre and all that we had to endure but what exactly did we endure. I know what I can say has happened to me. I can't recall what has happened to Aleccia. Aside from her saying what happened, I haven't seen her experience anything. Yeah, I should be angry. I should blow us all up. I'm exhausted. Is it possible to get a time out?

# Chapter Twenty-One

As I peeled the potatoes, I watched Aleccia sashay around the marble countertop island in the kitchen. She was carefree and glowing as always in this grey sundress that hugged every inch of her body perfectly. One would say I'm happy too, but no, I'm not happy at all. I could try to deny the truth and say I hated being here, but I don't hate it. The only feelings I can muster up are numb, empty, and dead. I only speak when spoken to and I do as I'm told to do. Every day is easier to bear when I smile and go along with everything. One day, Aleccia bragged on how happy she was that I had signed the contract, saying that she'd have to be the one to kill me if I didn't and she didn't want to kill me. She laughed and told me not to fuck it up or else he'd have to sell me, or we'd all have to deal with The League. Remembering Calvin's bloody face and watching Darius' lifeless body fall to the floor, helped me to realize exactly how much I wanted to live. I don't know when but one day, things will not be like this. At least that's what I hoped and prayed for as I began to get up and sway to the smooth sounds of Mel Waiters blasting through the big speakers sitting outside.

Aleccia and I made our way around the kitchen island and joined hands. The last time we danced together like this was five years ago at a club in Dallas off of Northwest Highway. You couldn't tell us nothing that night. In our minds, we were the finest things walking in that club. Those bottles had us loose. While I was grinding, she was bumping and there was no getting tired that night. I smiled and she smiled back at me. I suddenly remembered how I cried and wished for another day like that with her. That day came sooner than expected and not at all in the way I had hoped for but here she was, dancing with me. As we started our bump and grind routine, Pierre walked in through the patio doors with a pan of ribs he had been grilling outside. The sweet aroma soared through the air and hit me with ease. I'm such a sucker for grilled food. My mouth watered while I watched him sit the pan on the stove. He did a little two step our way. That big creepy ass smile crept across his face. It affects me the same as it did before. Nothing has changed about that. I smiled back because he was happy and glowing like Aleccia. His happiness has lasted a lot longer this time than any other time before. We danced together until the song was over. That's when he kissed us both and went back outside to finish grilling, and I went back to helping Aleccia with the sides that we were going to eat.

The outside looking in would say we were perfect together. These last few months hasn't even been remotely considered bad. It's like everything has been turned inside out and sent into orbit. I mean we're laughing together and talking like we used to when they first met. Every day, we wake up and it's like Calvin, Darius, nor the abuse ever happened. Pierre is now this wonderful man that's a loving sweetheart. He's so caring, attentive, and eager to please. His lovable actions aren't only towards Aleccia. These are his actions towards me as well. After a couple of weeks or so of this new Pierre, I wondered how long it would last. Pierre isn't the only one who has changed. She's back to being the fearless and outspoken person I've always known her to be. She has Pierre wrapped around her pinky finger. Hell, she has me wrapped around the other pinky finger, but it doesn't matter because I'm just here to do as I'm told and to be honest, I'll do literally anything to keep them happy. Especially, if their happiness meant I didn't have to get whipped, cuffed, shocked, or killed. They trust me a little more now than they did before. On extra special days, I get to go with them to the store instead of being locked up in the basement. People walk by and see nothing wrong. They don't see me screaming with my eyes to save me. It's been moments where I've looked out at the street and hoped for the day where I could simply run away as far as

I could in the opposite direction. Aleccia has caught me in each and every moment daydreaming at escaping. She'll come over, hold my hand, and give it a slight squeeze. A reminder that I'm under contract and there is no running away. I guess I'm lucky because those moments always stayed between us. If Pierre had known, it would've cost me some days in the closet or the shed. The thought of it made me rub my wrists.

Aleccia took the mac and cheese out of the oven at the same time Pierre announced he was finished grilling. We sat down at the table and Pierre blessed the food. Aleccia complimented his cooking as she tapped my hand and smiled at me, "Isn't this awesome?" I smiled back as always and nodded. My silence has always been best because some questions were strictly rhetorical. She continued, "We should all watch a movie together." The back of her hand slowly slid down Pierre's face until she was stroking his beard. On days like this when they were both happy, ecstatic to cook and spend time with me meant it was time to be their human blow-up doll. Daily I was the maid and the chef. Some days I was nobody. After cleaning and cooking, I'd get escorted by one or the other, back to my room in the basement, where I'd be left and forgotten until the next day. There are times when Aleccia comes down and has girl talk with me but that's only when Pierre is away. She talks to me as if I'm not here against my will and forced into slavery. I haven't cared about anything she has been saying to me. Too busy trying to understand how the girl I once knew for eleven years could change so much. It's easy to assume it was Pierre brainwashing her but maybe she's been this way the entire time and Pierre only helped her to be her natural self. I've grown tired of trying to figure it out. Pierre started to clear the table and Aleccia set up the living room for a movie night. She motioned for me to join her, and I obeyed without hesitation. The nine o'clock news came on and Aleccia announced, "Kiara said their community outreach program was featured on today's 'What's Hot in the Community' news segment. It's because of the job fairs and ged classes she's been having lately."

Pierre yelled back, "It's about time she made the segment. She's been doing this for what four years now?" Aleccia nodded while turning the volume up on the seventy-two-inch flat screen that was mounted to the wall above the fireplace. I haven't met Kiara but I'm pretty sure the picture plastered across the television screen was mine. Within no time, I became nervous. I didn't need anything making Pierre mad and this was something I knew for a fact was about to piss him completely off. I didn't need to see his face to know he wasn't happy anymore. Even Aleccia could feel the change in the atmosphere because she pulled me up by the arm and escorted me back to my room. By the time we made it down into the basement, Pierre was only a few steps behind us. I stayed quiet. I didn't want to anger him. I was already terrified by what was taking place. This was one of those moments where I wanted so badly to be locked away and forgotten. Aleccia didn't have time to leave the room. Pierre had grabbed her by the hair so fast, she jerked, and I jerked with her as she held onto my arm. He pushed me away and I sat balled up on the floor next to my room door. I watched in horror as he threw her into wall after wall. He was ruthless and quiet. I closed my eyes and looked away. I couldn't watch him beat her like this. Hearing his fists connect with her face, arms, and chest, the whimpers she made like a scared puppy being handled wrong, all brought tears to my eyes. This went on for what felt like hours. From punches to slaps to glass vases shattering from her being thrown around the room, the only thought in my head was, *'I'm next'* The power in his steps grew louder as he made his way to me. I wanted to plead and beg but I knew that would only make it worse. He dragged me away from the wall by my feet. His animosity still seeping through his skin, he ripped my clothes off. With my head turned to the side staring at the baseboard, I laid there as still and quietly as I could possibly be, escaping to my fantasy world where my island and pretty drink awaited. After he finished, he got up and left. He didn't say anything except to stay our asses there. I helped Aleccia to the bathroom so that she could clean the blood off of her face. It wasn't hard to figure out what she was feeling. She didn't have to tell me since the past eight months made me an expert at the feelings of being immobilized. We showered together and laid down in the bed beside each other. Tears fell from us both while we laid there in silence, reminiscing the moments we experienced hours ago.

Five nights later, Aleccia was more than ready to leave the basement and work at making Pierre happy again. She didn't lock me in the room since it was just me and her. Although she had a ton of bruises on her body, she acted as though it never happened. Her face lit up when she heard the basement door open. Her smile abruptly disappeared when he walked through the door with another female on his arm and that creepy ass smile on his face. I figured it was another swing week paid for by one of the many wives of The League. They literally pay for a swing week where they can swap out their spouses with some-body else in The League for however many weeks they paid for, but no longer than a month at a time. The only problem is that Aleccia is unable to get swapped out thanks to the bruises he put on her the days before and I'm not allowed to be swapped out as I am only a slave and not a wife. As a wife you don't get a lot of privileges in The League, but it's a hell of a lot more than you would as a slave.

Pierre introduced his new arm candy, "Ladies, I want you to meet the new Mrs. Bennet. This is the beautiful Nicole."

Aleccia sighed, "You married her?"

Nicole held up her left hand where this huge sparkling wedding ring sat proudly on her ring finger, as she answered with a smirk, "He did."

Silence consumed me, while Aleccia asked Pierre, "Why would you do that?"

He laughed and shrugged, "I don't have to explain shit to you. Instead of questioning me, why not fix us some dinner." He kissed Nicole with a smile and asked, "Baby, what do you have a taste for?"

She looked at Aleccia and replied, "I'm thinking of steaks and baked potatoes with maybe some asparagus. Do you know how to cook that?"

He placed his arm around Nicole and answered, "Oh, she better know." They turned around and walked out. Aleccia was furious! She flipped completely out as soon as the door closed good enough. She took the cue stick and started swinging it at everything, not caring where it landed. The curio cabinet and all of the little glass trinkets inside were destroyed. After breaking the cue stick in half, she began carving the letter A into the black leather couch and matching chair. About three different hookahs flew from one side of the basement to the other. I stayed back until she flopped down in exhaustion, that's when I went up to her and tried to comfort her. I had led myself to believe that this was more Aleccia than Pierre and even if it was, it's clear to me that Aleccia is much more damaged than I could have ever imagined. My heart was aching for her.

It only took seconds for her to connect whatever dots she needed and then her frustrations turned my way. The disgust in her voice as she said, "You stupid bitch!" She flung herself unto me at the same time as she grabbed my neck and began punching, clawing, and slapping me. Her actions had me taken aback, she had the best of me as she managed to grab my hair and place me in a choke hold. Aleccia picked up another cue stick during the walk across the basement to my room. I already knew she was going to lock me up in the room and forget about me or at least that was my hope. She proved me wrong when she let me go and pushed me into the room. Within seconds she was beating me with the cue stick. If I had known that comforting her would've led to this, I would've easily stayed my ass in my corner of the basement and left her alone. When she finally stopped, she started tying my hands up and dragging me to the closet door. I was in entirely too much pain to run or fight. I didn't say a word as she hung me in the closet like a wet rag doll and closed the door. Tears flowed from the sounds of her leaving and locking the room door.

# Chapter Twenty-Two

The light from the room peeked through the opening of the door as Aleccia slowly opened the closet door. Despite the bright light that blinded me behind her, I forced myself to see her as I didn't want to give her a reason to leave me in this closet any longer. She walked up to me with a smile while untying my hands. My legs were weak and tingling. It started to feel like ants crawling up my calves and thighs. She helped me to the bed where a food tray sat. Seeing and smelling that food made my stomach jump for joy but I kept my composure. After I sat on the bed, Aleccia helped put my legs in the bed. She fluffed my pillow and then placed the food tray in front of me on the rolling table beside the bed.

After she pulled up a chair and started to feed me, she sighed, "I think it's time that we cleared the air between us, and I don't mind starting. First of all, you meeting up with Darius put a huge dent in the progress I was making for us. I didn't want you here until after Calvin was already dead. I just needed a few more months and then I would've snatched you up to be our forever girlfriend. Instead, you've only made things worse. I could have never imagined that you would be all over the news like this. What the fuck do you think he's going to do with you now that he's gotten married?"

The words that would convince her that I cared never surfaced. I shrugged, "I'm sorry."

She laughed, "Sorry! You're not sorry! Oh Harper, you're not sorry. No, what's sorry is Nicole but not you. No, sweetie you're worse than sorry. You're too pathetic for words to be quite frank. I cannot believe I used to be so jealous of you. Oh my god! Every guy that laid eyes on you, wanted you and you refused to even talk to them but me? I was invisible compared to you. How would anybody see me when you've always had the perfect black girl body that every man wants?"

She couldn't possibly be referring to me. I hear her speaking but I'm not processing what she's saying. She continued, "If I wasn't getting compared at home to my sister then I was getting compared to you, my best friend. I wanted somebody to see me! I was young, skinny and naïve when I met you and even more naïve when I met Calvin." Aleccia stood up and checked to see if anybody was near, but she asked, "Do you remember that guy I told you about when we first met? He was my sister's boyfriend's cousin. He was the first guy to ever notice me, and I told you about how I had the biggest crush on him."

I vaguely remembered the conversation. A lot of times I'd zone her out if it had anything to do with her sister because she was always whining about how she could do stuff that Aleccia couldn't. Being an only child, I couldn't relate. I somewhat remember her liking somebody, but the conversation never came up again. I nodded and that angered her. She snapped, "But that didn't stop you from jumping up in his face every time you seen him! We used to talk on the phone constantly and no, he wasn't just sweet talking me as you love to say. We talked about some of everything. He even helped me to find my inner voice. If it wasn't for him, I would've never even done that fashion show. The week before he convinced me to do it was also the week, I learned that I was pregnant with our first baby."

It wasn't until now that I realized this girl was talking about Calvin. As if hating myself for sleeping with my mom's husband wasn't enough, I now learn he was my best friend's first love before I even introduced them. I never felt the need to confide in her about how Calvin and I met before I met her, but I also never paid attention to how she felt about him? Was I really that caught in him that all I seen was him and no wrong or right? I carefully listened to her words, "He was so happy. We were going to run off together until I lost the baby. He didn't stop loving me though. He made sure to be there for me every single day.

That's when I knew he really loved me and not you."

Somehow that last sentence really gutted my heart out. Being over a man is one thing but to learn he never loved you is another. He could have. He should have but who cares about that? What about the years I've wasted being a fool for a man that married my mother and was sleeping with my best friend all behind my back? To hear her say, "He was right to think you'd go crazy if you knew about us." Almost made me risk it all again listening to the secrets of my heart's desire. She spared me no pain as she went on to say, "I knew it would be impossible to ever be friends with you if you knew about me and Calvin. I loved you like a sister, and I didn't want to lose our friendship, but I loved Calvin too."

I watched as she cleared off the table. It wasn't hard to see she still loved him. She can love him, but I wish he never existed. I whispered, "Aleccia, you didn't have anything to be jealous of and you could've told me how you felt about Calvin."

She scoffed, "Is that right? Yeah, tell that to everybody that compared us. Even Calvin compared us to each other from time to time."

Her anger was misplaced in ways she just could not begin to fathom. She acted as though I created myself. I've had issues with my appearance for years and the entire time it's been a problem with my best friend too. I'm just not comprehending how it is my fault that she looks different from me. Her exhaustion turning more into frustration as she ranted on, "Every guy I thought actually wanted to talk to me, only wanted me to hook them up with you. As far as they were concerned, I was just the bridge to you and nothing more. I started charging them for my phone number. It was funny how they thought they were talking to you when really it was me. You always wondered why certain guys were cussing you out. It's because they thought y'all were in relationships until you'd ignore them in public. That was always the highlight of my day. Those dusty mop ass niggas still never seen me beside you though. It wasn't until I got the modeling deal that I started being noticed. Sad shit, right? So, tell me

Harper, what changed from then to before I died?"

I spoke softly, "What do you mean?"

As she shook her head she replied, "Of course you don't know that Pierre noticed you well before the afterparty. If you remember correctly, it was like the third NBA draft afterparty we had been to. He had approached me at the first one just to get at you and naturally I gave him my number. He didn't know the truth until much later that he was talking to me. He wasn't upset about it and that's when we agreed to meet up at the next afterparty. Why do you think we flowed so well at that party? You didn't notice how he already knew our names. Sad shit. You're always blind to what's right in front of you. Him noticing you first is what made me think that you could be our unicorn."

I grabbed her hand, "Why not just ask me then? Why fake your death? Why stalk me? Why the abduction?"

She turned her head to face me, "I suppose you do deserve the truth." She sighed and sat on the bed beside me, "When Pierre caught me with Calvin, it was maybe a few weeks before I faked my death. Somebody told him I had been cheating on him. He wanted proof. Just as I told you before, he flipped out. He wanted to kill me and Calvin, but I worked out a deal. I'd help him kill Calvin and that was our plan until he went and got us a girlfriend. I wasn't involved in the selection process or even the thought process. Yeah, we'd had threesomes but a girlfriend? I went along with the shit just to be treated like the red headed stepchild in my own marriage. I

set up an argument over the phone between me and her after I had already cut the brake lines in my car as she was driving to supposedly meet me in Jackson at your apartment. She actually thought I was about to introduce her to you. The accident killed her instantly while I was here waiting on the news report. I called Pierre and told him what I had done and because he loves me, he agreed to vouch and say that she was me."

Her soft silk like fingers lightly brushed my cheek as she spoke, "He may have noticed you first, but conversation is everything. He loves me like crazy. Calvin did too." Aleccia smiled at me, "I thought blackmailing Pierre would've been a great plan. Let him collect the insurance money and then pop out and get him arrested for insurance fraud as well as murder. The League was already 10 steps ahead of me with him a new wife lined up, ready to submit. That's when I suggested you as his new wife so that The League would leave it alone. He agreed and I said I'd get you here. So, when you had to meet up with Darius randomly, I had to take my chance then. I snatched you up but somehow this bitch outsmarted me Harper!" She stood up and started pacing back and forth, "I had Darius to drug you and bring you here. It was perfect until he came home and wanted to celebrate this huge win. He poured us some wine like nothing was wrong and I woke up the next day tied to the bed beside you and Calvin. Oh trust, I was just as surprised as you."

Stunned by the words she was saying. I didn't want to hear anything else and yet I needed to know more. I urged, "Is this even the truth? You've changed your story so many times."

She nodded, "You're right. I have. I needed my plan to work. I needed you to get over Calvin so that you could give Pierre a chance that wouldn't kill us both. I made a deal I didn't lie about that. There's no me without you. Darius stalked you for us so of course I knew you and Calvin were still seeing each other but I didn't ask for information about anybody else. I only wanted to know about you and Calvin. Darius gave me that and I fucked up by not giving that information to Pierre first. I withheld it. I didn't want him to kill Calvin. I was going to send him away but The League ain't shit to play with. Pierre joined them in response to catching me with Calvin. Now he has an abundant amount of resources from anonymous billionaires to help him with whatever needs or wants he has when it comes to the women in his life. It doesn't matter if you've signed a contract or not. I signed a marriage license and I'm not seeing much of a different. Are you?"

I shook my head no in response trying to process everything that she was saying as true. At this point I could've lived a thousand lifetimes and still didn't need to know this truth. What can

I do with it? I have no words for the whole love story of Calvin and Aleccia. I mean no words and watching her finally sit down in the chair just to rock her leg told me that she had more to say. Calmly I answered, "Let's say I believe you. What happens now that he's married Nicole?"

She looked me in the eyes and said, "I suppose he's going to kill us both Harper. He has no use for me anymore and that would obviously mean that the deal is dead. I figured it was time you knew the truth. One less lie I don't have to be buried with."

Her words were as cold as frozen icicles in the dead of winter. The realization that any day now would be our last sent chills down my spine. I started wondering how the end would be but soon I would know.

# Chapter Twenty-Three

Last night I silently watched Aleccia drink an entire bottle of Remy in celebration of her latest attack on Pierre. These random moments of Aleccia talking to me has been the only interaction I have had with anybody now that Pierre has remarried. Aleccia is celebrating the idea of her putting an anonymous tip of Pierre committing insurance fraud and murder to police. I've urged her not to do it because of what's going to happen when he finds out and he hasn't been arrested yet that she did this. I thought she knew better but this sudden need to get revenge has consumed her. Pierre marrying Nicole has been the only thing Aleccia can think about. Anytime she comes down here it's to talk about Nicole and how she's been sent from The League. A few of the things she's shared with me has given me a little hope. One little tidbit is that Pierre has been gone a lot lately, parading around his new little wife. Aleccia feels invisible and my name is never mentioned in any of these talks. Thanks to Aleccia, I'm allowed to leave the room in the basement. With her focus centered on all things Pierre and Pierre focused on all things Nicole, I figured I could at least try to escape. I know exactly where the door is and on the few times we would leave, I believe I can make it to the nearest store to get help. The only thing I'm afraid of is The League. They could be anybody. Aleccia has confirmed that those random guys in the beginning were all familiar faces to her. That's the only reason she went along with it. None of it was new for her. I didn't want to believe it at first, but it was making a lot of sense. These people know that Aleccia is still alive, and when she killed their girlfriend, it was enough to convince The League that she needed to be eliminated since the girlfriend was part of The League as well.

SECRETS OF MY HEART'S DESIRE

The courage to run made the plan so simple, however the fear of getting caught hovered above my head pouring out every ounce of bad luck the universe had to offer. I should've made sure that Pierre was gone before I tried anything because if he catches me then I know my time is up. He used to have these designated date nights with him and Aleccia before he caught her with Calvin. Well now he's given them to Nicole and I'm hoping tonight is date night. This would be great for me since I know that it takes Aleccia a couple of days after her drunken cries for attention before she can function correctly. She was well past wasted because she was crawling up the stairs. Even her farewell words were distorted and lagging at the same pace as her feet. I was surprised when she made it out the door without falling down the stairs. A few minutes went by, and I hadn't heard the keys locking the door. Just as I had hoped, she was too drunk to lock the door as always. A smile made its way across my face. Maybe it was the anticipation or anxiety? It was uncontrollable. It felt like now or never. My heart was pounding about three hundred beats per minute while I was crept up the stairs. I was on the verge of a heart attack at the time I placed my hand on the doorknob. I thought I was ready. I thought I'd be in the hallway inching to the front door within no time but instead I stood there as if I was a statue frozen forever holding this doorknob. I could've made it out of the door, but I didn't even turn the knob. Every fiber in my body was frozen stiff. I wanted to leave it all behind and yet I was fighting fear at the door. Another battle I would evidently lose. It's amazing how quickly I
could retreat to my room. Only seconds had went by and, I heard the keys locking the door. The one chance I thought I had was destroyed by fear.

For over a week, I've listened at that door for their voices. If I heard none then I'd pick at the lock on the door. It seemed to take forever but after only a few days I was able to unlock the door. I had to practice getting it opened faster while Aleccia was still making random visits which didn't feel all that random once I started to keep up with my days. If Pierre had guests over, then

Aleccia would come down here to drink and be loud. I can only assume his guests were members of The League. This happened every Friday from what I've been able to gather. I sneak a few looks at her phone when she's sloppy drunk and every single time she staggers out the door, she leaves it unlocked. It's helped me to know that today should be the first of December, making it almost a year since I got here. There's no telling all of the things I've missed out on. The date was shocking to see at first, but it was also the motivation I needed to get away from here as soon as possible. If tonight I'm successful in escaping, then it's only so many options I have. I know I won't be able get help from anybody nearby because Pierre trusted going to only a few places when I was allowed outside, and they were always close by. Those will be the places I avoid without a doubt.

As I sat at the door listening to Pierre and Nicole giggle, I knew I couldn't allow fear to win again tonight. This entire time I haven't heard anything from Aleccia or about her, I'm pretty sure that she's sleeping that liquor off. So far, everything is lining up perfectly. It's been fairly easy to know when somebody leaves and comes back, I can see now why I'm not supposed to leave the room. I could hear the garage door opening and the chirps of a vehicle along with the sounds of scuffling feet making their way down the hall, getting closer to me but veering off in the opposite direction instead. I wait patiently for confirmation that they have left so I can make my escape. My heartrate slowly increased when the sounds of the garage door closing was the signal I was waiting for. I took a deep breath and started to pick the lock. My hands were sweating causing me to constantly stop and wipe them on my gown. What used to take days only took four hours tonight. The first step was completed. Gently I twisted the knob and softly pushed the door open. It was dark as all of the lights downstairs were turned off. I stayed against the wall hoping that with each step I didn't bump into anything. If something were to fall, it would certainly wake Aleccia up because it was too quiet. I even had to get a handle on my breathing after first walking out of the basement door.

Getting from the basement to the front door is a huge accomplishment for me that I'm going to have to wait to celebrate after getting away from here. I started to unarm the alarm when I seen the headlights of a car rolling across the wall. I ducked down and peeked from behind the wall into the foyer and hoped it was just a car making the wrong turn and turning around. The lights around me turned on as I quickly struggled to hide. Pierre had come back earlier than I had expected, slamming doors, and screaming at the top of his lungs for Aleccia to wake up. As he stormed up the stairs, I swiftly made it out of the front door. The night was still, dark, and cold. There were only a small number of houses in our vicinity, so I hid on the porch wondering if Nicole was in the car or not. The only sounds I could hear was Pierre and Aleccia screaming. I thought with them arguing, it would draw attention away from me and the dogs wouldn't notice me running but that was a big fat lie! They started barking as soon as I sprinted off towards the road. As luck would have it, they were still chained up and I didn't have anything to worry about them. Once I got past these houses, I wasn't sure which way I should've taken but I knew I

couldn't stop running. Being in the middle of nowhere wasn't a good enough excuse to stop!

Real freedom was within my grasp. I couldn't wait to get to the police and turn them both in. My hope is that the police will find The League as well. I don't want to look over my shoulders for the rest of my life in fear of them. I've ran from one street to walk past 3 streets because I wasn't sure who was a part of their organization. Knocking on one of the member's houses late at night in an attempt to run away from my master would be my death and not at my master's hands. I needed to get further away to the next town at least, and I can't waste time doing it. I darted across the street into an old KMART parking lot. There's a gas station in the far distance that I've psyched myself to believe is just a few more steps ahead when in reality it's a mile up a hill and I'm already about to freeze to death. The only logic as to how I got this far is adrenaline. I cared nothing about the cold weather when I jolted from that porch wearing nothing but a gown and socks. It's catching up to me now though. I continued to walk to towards the highway. There was no turning back.

I was abruptly stopped in my tracks by Pierre's car slamming into the side of me. I laid on the ground in agony hoping he'd finish the job by putting me out of my misery right then and there. Instead, he jerked me up and slung me into the backseat. What I thought took me at least 2 hours, seemed to take Pierre about ten minutes. He pulled me out of the car and back into the house to push me down the stairs. I hit the floor lighter than I did the pavement when he hit me with the car, but the pain remained the same. I was once again moaning in agony clutching my stomach. I heard Aleccia laughing during my return. I glanced at her and she had a black eye with a nice, busted lip to match. I also noticed the shock collar was back around her neck. It wasn't hard to understand the type of shit we'd both stepped in. Pierre shut the door with a loud bang announcing that he had entered the basement. He violently escorted us both to the couch where we awaited our final judgement.

He snapped, "You two evil bitches!" His focus towards Aleccia, "You think you did something huh?"

Aleccia hissed, "The same way you thought marrying that hoe was doing something?"

Pierre shook his head as he groaned, "Aleccia." He started to clap his hands, with an overwhelming sigh, "Congratulations, you done fucked up now! Do you know what happens when the League doesn't want you in their little club anymore? Well, my dear wife, they make it seem like you've never existed."

Aleccia's laughs interrupted his rant, "Well I'm dead so I already don't exist."

He scoffed, "Oh, this shit is funny to you huh? You know for a dead bitch, you laughing real loud." Aleccia laughed harder and he punched her in the mouth. She was spitting out blood when he asked, "Ain't shit funny no more?" He grabbed her face and whispered, "I ain't going down for this shit by myself." Aleccia spit in his face and he returned the favor with the butt of his gun to her face. That's when he walked up to me and stroked my face with the gun. He began to slide the barrel from one side of my face to the other. He stopped at my lips after the third slide, forcing the gun into my mouth while threatening, "Suck it before I blow your brains out."

# Chapter Twenty-Four

During the moment of me tending to Aleccia's busted lip, she asked, "What made you think you could get away?"

I shrugged, "I never thought I could."

She nodded, "A suicide mission in other words?"

I agreed, "Whatever gets the job done."

She placed her hand on mine, "I wish I could be you."

My silence was my reply. I didn't have the energy to entertain her many sad excuses as to why I had to be here for a year enduring any of this. I continued to nurse to her wounds. Pierre has been out of control for the last two days since he was arrested. He's been a complete monster without any remorse for his actions. Even in the midst of his rampage, Aleccia says she understands him and that she shouldn't have sent that anonymous tip to the police. It's caused Nicole to leave him and the League to mark his file as dismissed. Now, he's on his own without any help to battle the murder charges and insurance fraud that's piling up against him. He wants to keep Aleccia alive so that she can admit to her part in all of this. She's already said she's going to do everything she can to help him because for whatever reason she loves him and doesn't want to lose him. She sounds like a fool if you ask me, but my opinion doesn't hold any value in what they do.

Pierre came back waving this gun around with his feelings of authority still in question from the stunts we've done. He pulls me away from Aleccia with one swift move. He motions for me to go sit down on the couch while grabbing Aleccia next. He sat in a chair across from us and looked us up and down as he scratched his head in silence. I felt powerless and fragile from watching him decide what he wanted to do next. He had no need for either one of us. He now knows that Aleccia tipped the police off which apparently has been the ultimate betrayal for them. Here I am attempting to run away which makes me a flight risk. What Aleccia and I did, gave him the perfect reasons to beat our ass black and blue and if that wasn't enough Nicole straight sold the man out to the police. She blew the whistle all about him holding us hostage in the basement even though he wasn't holding Aleccia hostage. She simply refused to leave him, but the police now have a different story.

He fumed, "I want to tell y'all a little story. When the police showed up at the restaurant to arrest me, I wasn't worried because I knew they had nothing on me. Then they fucked me and made my wife turn on me and this is before they told me my first wife sent in the anonymous tip." He paused for a moment as if he was recalling what happened, he chuckled, "By the time they got to questioning me about you Miss Harper, I was already screaming it was Darius from the rooftops!" Frustrated, he sighed, "These summabitches had the nerve to tell me they found his body in a burned abandoned house." That creepy ass smile seemed to appear out of nowhere as he continued, "Shit, I was honest! I told them I didn't know anything about a burned abandoned house. Called my lawyer and got my ass out of there."

The lines of coke he's been snorting for the past couple of days is starting to get to him as his face glistened with sweat. The gun laid on his lap as he tried to wipe the sweat from his face with his black muscle shirt. The sounds of a can dropping outside of the basement door made Pierre alert and ready. He looked back and forth with the gun in his right hand and placed his left index finger on those big soup coolers, instructing us to be quiet. Aleccia agreed with a nod, and I did the same but deep down everything in me wanted to scream out for help. I knew Pierre would shoot me dead if I made a sound. He inches up the stairs and opens the door slow and with ease. When he didn't see anything, he was convinced it was in his head but on his way back in somebody kicked him down the stairs. His gun slid across the floor while this other person came charging down the stairs in full STF uniform. I wondered where the rest of the swat team were, but it wasn't anybody else and Pierre didn't stay down for long. In mid step, Pierre swung and knocked off the helmet. Aleccia and I moved near the foosball table in order not to get hit as the fight ensured. Pierre was weak and off balance in the beginning, but he didn't allow that to stop him. He still tried to fight but this other guy overpowered him. The guy had Pierre in a headlock from behind until Pierre flipped him and he hit the floor. It didn't affect him has he popped back up like Muhummad Ali ready to box. When he turned around, I realized the other guy was Omari. He was handling his own just fine until Aleccia slid Pierre's gun closer to him without me seeing her. As I thought for a second to run to Omari, I seen Pierre reaching for the gun. This caused me to scream out, "Gun!" Luckily, it was enough to get Omari to kick the gun away. Pierre grabbed his ankle and Omari hit the floor sounding off like thunder in a storm.

My hands trembled at the sight of Omari wrestling to get Pierre off of him. The last thing I wanted to see was Omari get killed. I wouldn't be able to live with myself being the cause of his death. Pierre had the advantage and reached for the gun again, but Omari jabbed him in his side causing him to ball up giving Omari the upper hand as he struggled to get the gun from Pierre. It was too much to watch. Every second lasting longer than an hour and yet if I blinked my eyes, I'd miss it all because it was happening too fast. Pierre tried his best to punch Omari in the face without letting the gun go, but every punch Omari blocked it and then the gun sent off a shot. Instantly, I turned away and buried my sweat drenched face into my gown. I allowed the tears to freely fall wherever they wanted to. A minute passed by, maybe more and I could hear crying and the words that came through, "Baby wake up! Wake up baby please! I'm sorry. Okay I'm sorry!" A hand rubbed my back. I turned to face Omari in his attempt to help me up while pointing the gun at Pierre. I stood up with my eyes glued on Pierre. Aleccia laid in his arms as he pleaded with her to breath and come back to him. She gasped her last breath as the blood poured out of her chest.

She was gone, and we all knew it. He continued to hold her as he started to rock back and forth crying.

Omari thought we could slip out the door while Pierre grieved Aleccia. Pierre stopped us in our tracks when he sobbed, "Harper, wait." I stopped but Omari lightly tugged my hand, urging me to leave while I had the chance and yet I stood there waiting for something I knew I didn't want. Pierre sat on the floor soaking wet from sweating and covered in Aleccia's blood. He looked at me with his red tear-filled eyes and shouted, "It should've been you! You should be dead! Aleccia didn't deserve this! This was the love of my life, but you and that pedophile ruined her." He paused, looked down at Aleccia and gently stroked her hair. He placed a kiss on her forehead and started back speaking, "I only got married to make you mad baby." His eyes shifted from Aleccia to me as if he were looking for confirmation that him marrying Nicole was forgiven. Even though Omari continued to urge me to leave, I stood still. Pierre spoke with a broken heart, "I know I could never be James but baby nobody could ever be you." I had hoped she would move, a cough or something. The only reason I've been standing here this long is to see if she'd come back. I related to Pierre's disbelief, but his intentions were never pure.

This was somebody I loved from the very day I met her. Granted we indulged in things we should've never done but my love for her was real and seeing her dead was the one thing I never wanted to see. Maybe Pierre was right. Maybe it should've been me after all I am still the one that encouraged Aleccia and Calvin to have sex never knowing they were already talking. I am still the one encouraging the threesomes. It was me that enabled all of the behavior, but I never forced her to do anything. I loved her and only respected her when she declined. Aleccia was broken long before she ever met me, and Calvin was a pedophile on the day he approached me. I hate to even think it but maybe I'm not the culprit. Maybe just maybe, I'm the victim. In a spilt second, he had drawn a gun from behind him and pulled the trigger with the gun aimed at me. There were two shots that sounded off before Omari shoved me up the stairs and out the door. We ran out of the house at the same time the STF and police ran in to arrest Pierre. Everything was in a blur as the paramedics tried to assess my wounds. Pierre didn't put up a fight and walked out cuffed with ease and that creepy ass smile on his face. The coroners rolled Aleccia's body out behind him. When he seen the black body bag, he became hysterical which made the STF taser him. The squad car pulled off with Pierre still going berserk in the back seat. The coke and the pain of Aleccia's death was stopping him from even feeling physical pain.

The feeling of being free from Pierre didn't set in until I was at the hospital. Omari rejected any notion of him leaving my side after detectives entered the room to get my side of the story. I replied with what I knew and when I wasn't answering their questions, I wondered how I would go on to live a normal life. It wasn't a lot of information to give to them because I didn't know names of any members in the League. To top it all off, I didn't even know where I was being held. The detectives decided they would talk to me at a later time so that I could rest and heal. When they walked out of the door, Omari stood up to hug a female waiting in the hall beside the door. I thought she could've been Tia, but she was too tall. I didn't think anything else about who she could've been until she made her way in the room, and it was Nicole. Omari introduced her as his cousin. I stayed silent. It was clear to them both that I was uncomfortable. My body had tensed up and I was gripping the rails with the last bit of strength I had. Nicole held both hands up as she stepped forward speaking as softly as she could, "Harper, I am so sorry for what has happened to you. I'm an agent in the Special Task Force with the Mississippi State Protection Agency. I was assigned to go undercover with my brother, Richard, to infiltrate the League. We've been trying to take them down for at least six years now because of them operating a sex trafficking ring, drug smuggling, money laundering and a bunch of other charges. Thanks to Omari we were able to take down everybody in connection to Pierre." My eyes drifted to Omari as she continued, "If he hadn't asked us to look into who was terrorizing and stalking you, we would've never discovered it was Darius. He was the thread we needed to pull to dismantle the entire organization."

With my hand in his, he stated, "I wanted to tell you everything about what Nicole and Richard were doing, but I couldn't or else it would hurt their sting operation. I'm sorry for pushing you away. I only did it to protect you."

He didn't need to apologize for saving my life. If anybody needed to apologize, it was me for accusing Tia of being a jealous stalker and treating him like a suspect. I wouldn't be alive right now in this hospital bed, if it wasn't for him. I smiled, "It's okay. I'm sorry for being crazy and please tell Tia I'm sorry as well." I turned to Nicole, "I'm really happy to know you're an agent and not a part of the League."

She smiled as Omari replied, "What are you apologizing for? You had every reason to be crazy."

Nicole chimed in before leaving, "You are an amazing woman. A true survivor and that's nothing to apologize for." She hugged Omari and went on her way.

I was thankful to have a friend like Omari. He stayed the night with me at the hospital despite me telling him he should go home and get rest. He refused to leave me alone, since he felt I wasn't ready to be left alone yet. I stopped trying to get him to leave because he was right, I wasn't ready to be left alone.

# Chapter Twenty-Five

The door opened after the third knock. I had hoped Shirley wouldn't answer and I could have left knowing I tried without the extra work that's required. She stood there in nothing but her bra and panties looking like she had just woken up. The early morning sunlight made her squint her eyes and cover her face and yet it didn't stop her from recognizing me. She grunted, "Well, aren't you a sight for sore eyes?"

Waiting patiently for her to move, I smiled, "Hey mom."

You'd think she'd be more excited to see her only child with the recent events that's happened. I was abducted and tortured for a year by my best friend and her husband and of course my mother didn't care. She stood to the side as if I was a salesperson and she needed the entertainment. I walked in remembering that the last time I was here was Christmas and that damn party she insisted I come to. I looked around and the decorations were still up. Nothing was different from that night that I was here. It wasn't hard to figure out that Calvin must've been snatched up after leaving my apartment that night. We sat down in the living room across from each other and before I could start talking, she asks, "So what do you want because I don't have any money?"

"I didn't come here for money. Am I bothering you by being here?"

She cleared her throat as she replied, "Of course, I'm bothered that my one and only daughter has been back for months and haven't come to see her only mother."

Baffled by her words, I took a second before replying. Normally I'd be pissed at the utter display of bullshit she was giving me but in these days I'm unable to hold true anger in my heart for even a second. Her goal with every word that comes out of her mouth is to belittle you, manipulate you, and completely make you think that you're crazy. It was the reason I kept my distance for so long but even distance didn't stop me from feeling worthless because of her words and actions. My deep breathes gave her the pleasure she needed in knowing her words had affected me negatively and yet I was more surprised at the care she didn't give versus the attitude she always had. I didn't want to say the wrong thing and cause an argument, but I wanted to be honest with her. I replied, "Ma, I haven't done anything in the months I've been back but try to heal and recover. I would have come to see you sooner, but this transition hasn't been easy. I'm here now though. Better late than, never, right?" I smiled.

My words didn't transfer as funny as she spoke with her natural condescending tone, "Had you been here, it would've been easier. Always in the fucking streets running up behind some damn body that don't want you." I sighed.

Silence filled the space between us. I didn't think something such as trying to get back on my feet would be a big deal. I didn't come here to argue with her. I just wanted to talk to her and expose my truths and feelings but it's like she knows why I'm here. I wouldn't put it past her to deflect this conversation as it's happened several times before. Whenever I tried to come clean as a teen, she did everything in her power to not only dismiss my feelings but to validate her actions. I had nobody to talk to but Aleccia and in the end Aleccia used everything I ever said to her against me. I could relate to the story Pierre told about his sister with Calvin because a lot of times I wondered how my mom didn't know what was happening in her own house. I remember a friend tried to tell her she needed to watch Calvin around me because he seemed like the type that would touch on a little girl. In response my mom stopped talking to the lady. I never seen her come around again. Was she that blinded by love, or had she given me to the very man she called her husband? There is never a moment when she's not playing the victim and I knew before we really got to the bottom of this that she would start faking and shaking with tears running down her face. I contemplated leaving before things got worse. It was already starting on a sour note, and I have only been here maybe thirty minutes. She reached for a white torn open envelope on the table beside her chair while my heart sank. I could feel the moisture in my mouth began to disappear. Staring at the letter in her hand, I could picture her on the news while Pierre read the same letter to me. It was like it happened yesterday.

Shirley sneered, "I'm not BooBoo the fool. I know this is what you came for."

Tears filled my eyes while I dropped my head in guilt, listening to her read the letter aloud. I have said a thousand times and more that I was done with this woman and still I try to find ways to get her to see me and love me because being her daughter isn't enough to receive that love. Granted, she's won the Toxic Mother Award a few times, but I've messed up too. I think it's possible for us to forgive each other and move forward from this. I was too caught up in how I should explain myself when I heard her say, "That bitch got some nerve lying on James like this. She'll say anything to protect that brother of hers. I hope his ass gets the death penalty for what he did to James. My man didn't deserve that!"

I think she was mixed-up in what she was saying so I asked, "I'm sorry ma I don't know who you're talking about."

She rolled her eyes, "That nigga that killed my James. You know him, right? You were with him for a year!"

Annoyingly I sighed, "Yeah ma I was."

"His bitch of a sister done wrote me a letter accusing James of molesting her and that being the reason her brother killed him. Claiming she sorry for all the pain that nigga done caused me. I almost wrote her ass back and told her some thangs." In disbelief from what she was saying, I stood and went closer to my mom to look at the letter. It read....

*Dear Mrs. Kersh,*

*I am writing this letter to apologize on behalf of my brother*

*Pierre Bennet. My name is Trinity and when I was younger, our mother married James. He was a bad guy. He molested me for years and whenever I tried to tell my mother, she never believed me. I told my aunts who ran him out of town. They also adopted me and my brother Pierre. My mother later killed herself because she was heartbroken. She ran her car off the bridge one night when Pierre was just a baby but when he was old enough, he wanted to know the truth about our mother, so I told him. I do not know how he found James, but I am so sorry that he felt it was best to take his life causing you and your loved ones' pain. Although James was a bad guy to me, it has been my hope and prayer that he turned his life around so that he was not harming other little girls the way he harmed me. I pray that you find it in your heart to forgive my brother as I pray, he forgives himself. Again, I am sorry for your loss, and I pray healing and strength over you and your household in Jesus' name.*

*Sincerely,*
*Trinity Bennet*

By the time I finished reading it, my mom said, "Do you believe this bitch?"

As I sat back down in my seat on the couch, I pondered at the question she had asked me. It wasn't hard to see that Pierre was just as much of a compulsive liar as Aleccia. He never sent the letter to my mom and his sister was alive. He didn't even kill their mother. She committed suicide! There was no trial because there was too much evidence along with my testimony, so Pierre had no other choice but to plead guilty. I was happy to not have to sit through that, retelling my story to complete strangers. I would not have been able to move forward with cameras in my face constantly. I turned down interviews for the same reason. I just wanted to be left alone. I'm still considering legally changing my name so that I'm no longer associated with him from an introduction of my name. The mean mug that sat on my mother's face was one that would make you drop dead. The look of Medusa is what Aleccia called it. The feelings that would arise when she gets this look reminds me of every day when she blew up at me over nothing. One day, I was getting cussed out and beat on because I was fat and eating up all of her food. I only wanted a second piece of chicken from a 20-piece box of chicken that had to be split between 3 people. Another day, I was a lying lazy bitch because I wanted to do nothing on my first off day in three weeks. After the look, she'd incite an argument and by the end of it all she would threaten to beat me or call the cops on me if I didn't leave her house.

Angrily she spoke with her hands balled into fists, ready to swing, "If you've got something to say, then Harper I suggest you say it."

Softly with a timid tremble, I uttered, "I'm sorry ma."

"What exactly are you sorry for? Don't tell me you were sleeping with James too?"

My silence and body language was all she needed to understand precisely what I was sorry for. She nodded as she sucked her teeth, "So what you're saying is I gave birth to nothing ass ho. I fed you, clothe you, and made sure you had a roof over your trifling ass head and in return you go and fuck my husband? That nigga should've killed your nasty ass too!"

Her anger was expected. Her words were not in the least surprising to hear. I gave an attempt at explaining my side and how it started, "There were times I wanted to come clean in the beginning when y'all first got married. I'd try to tell you about him, but you constantly dismissed me. You kept pushing me further onto him by making me ride everywhere with him. He took advantage of every car ride. Every overnight shift you worked, it was my room he slept in and creep out of by six in the morning so that you wouldn't catch him."

The waterworks started going and the blame rained down on me, "I did not make you have sex with him. All you do is lie. You ain't never tried to tell me nothing. Your nasty ass was fucking him because you wanted to fuck him and you're not going to blame me for that shit."

"You know what ma. You're right. At the end of the day, I

was doing it because I wanted to. I never said you made me do anything. I'm saying it wasn't hard to do it when you treat me like a piece of trash on the side of the road and he'd come along behind you treating me with love and affection. Oh yeah, I definitely did it because I wanted to. I do not deny that, but I tried to tell you. It was you that wouldn't listen."

In the middle of her screaming at me, I stood up to leave when she said, "Bitch I wish you would try me!"

I shook my head while she got in a fighting stance ready to defend her reputation as a wonderful wife and mother. I walked right past her and out of the front door. For all of the times I tried to reconcile with her after a fight, I promised myself that this time I would never look back. Only I am responsible for my actions, and I have admitted that I was wrong. When I needed a mother, she was not there. I had to learn to be my own mother and patch up my wounds the best way I could. When I needed love, it was Calvin who gave me his messed-up version of it. When I needed protecting, it was Aleccia that came through no matter how jealous she was deep down. She is too self-absorbed to ever truly care for me but that's okay. I love her and wish her nothing but the best in life.

After leaving Shirley's house, I received a phone call from Blue Pointe Apartments informing me that I was approved for the 2 bed 1 bath apartment I had applied for. They told me I could move in today! This was the pick me up I needed after that argument. I rushed to get to Omari's house so that I could pack up the little stuff I had accumulated since staying there. Omari has gone over and beyond for me, and I couldn't have been more grateful. I have lost everything from being held captive by Pierre and Aleccia. I came out alive, but I came back to nothing. No job. No place to stay. No car. No money. No clothes. I mean NOTHING! I've been staying with Omari until I can get back on my feet but that hasn't been easy. It took me a couple weeks to adjust after leaving the hospital. When I wasn't able to sleep through the night, Omari would be there with laughs and snacks. We'd binge watched different Netflix series before he'd eventually fall asleep from exhaustion while I stayed awake. He was able to work from home during that time so that he could help me if I had an episode. Once I was able to sleep through the night and the nightmares decreased, I knew it was time to try and get back to working. Of course, I had the option of getting a job with my previous employer but the job I had was no longer available. Omari suggested I apply at JDL where he works, but he never once mentioned how he put my name out there with the big heads in the company. He's the reason I got the job two months ago as their Creative Director in the marketing department. The interview was more of a formality than it was actually seeing if I was a good fit for the position. It's great being able to have somewhere safe to stay with a great paying job. Things are starting to look up but I'm almost back to the independent woman I once was.

I pulled up just as he was walking back inside the house. I quickly hopped out of the 2010 Ford Fusion that Omari helped me get and excitedly screamed, "Guess what?!"

He nonchalantly replied, "You're really an alien."

"What? No, shut up. I get to move into my apartment today!"

Without a care, he said, "Oh, the ones around the corner?"

Blinded by the excitement of having my own place again, I darted for the door as I replied, "Yes sir!"

He came into the guest bedroom he had loaned out to me. I noticed he wasn't actually helping me pack as he would get an article of clothing from my suitcase and place it back inside of the dresser draw while casually talking about eating some hibachi for dinner. I stopped him by saying, "Hey my guy what are you doing?"

He shrugged, "Trying to see what you want to eat tonight. What are you doing?"

I motioned to the suitcase as I said, "Uh trying to pack. What you're not tired of me yet?"

"I just don't understand what I did to make you want to

leave. I mean are you sure you're ready for this? You do know you can stay here for as long as you like Harper."

"Omari you haven't done a thing wrong. You've been more than a friend to me. You're like the big brother I never knew I had. I wouldn't be ready if not for you. Thank you but every grown woman needs her own place."

He sighed, "You don't have to thank me. What are friends for?" He finally started to help me pack and even trailed behind me to the apartment so that he could inspect it. Some would say he was going overboard but I appreciated everything he did no matter how overboard it might seem. When I was getting stalked, I took this overboard nature for granted. That's something I will never do again. It feels damn good to know somebody is protective of me and cares for me without wanting anything from me but my friendship. After shopping for a few household supplies, we ate Chopsticks on the floor of my new but empty apartment.

# Chapter Twenty-Six

"You've made a lot of progress since our first session. Are you still having nightmares?"

"Some nights I do. Everything replays over and over again. I still can't get Aleccia's face out of my head. I've tried just about everything I could think of and still I jump out of my sleep. I can say it's slowed down a bit. The nightmares are here and there now. I suppose it could be adjusting to my new apartment."

"Harper, this is all very normal. It's only been seven months since you've escaped. There's no guarantee that the nightmares will ever stop." I took those words in with a grain of salt. It wasn't what I wanted to hear her say but everything she said was right. Overall, I was still healing, and there was no sure-fire way to get rid of these nightmares. She continued, "Have you finally spoken with your mother yet? In our last session you mentioned your desire to mend the relationship."

I sighed, "Yeah that's not something I really want to do anymore. I think it's best if I stayed out of her life for good."

Dr. Juelz nodded, "You'd be surprised at the outcome. Communication is a start."

I started to fidget with my fingers as I glanced out of the window. I shrugged, "I understand that but regardless I know she hates me plus I tried the communication thing last month. Nothing changed."

Dr. Juelz leaned in and held both of my hands in hers as she sweetly explained, "The only thing that should be of importance to you is that you don't hate you. We as humans cannot control the emotions or actions of another person and we are not required to. If hating you is what she chooses to do, then acceptance is what you have to do for you."

I smirked, "I accept it and then what? Endure her toxic evil ways until she just randomly decides to love me?"

Calmly she spoke, "Accept not endure. You should never stay where you are not respected. Accept your life for what it is with her and not what you want it to be. We all want wonderful loving mothers; however, we do not get to pick our parents. Harper, you are grown, you do not have to endure anybody's toxicity or evilness. You must love yourself enough to leave a person that treats you like this no matter who that person is."

I nodded, "That's something I realized after talking to her. I love her and ultimately, I forgive her, but I have washed my hands with her with love in my heart. I still only want the best for her, but I am no longer worried about her the way I used to be. I am only concerned with getting my life back on track and seeing what the future holds for me."

Meeting Dr. Juelz has been one of the best decisions of my life. Based on my track record it is probably the only good decision I have ever made. Our session ended on a positive note even though I was expecting Dr. Juelz to say I needed to look over my mom's toxicity and continue to endure her ways since that is my one and only mother. I am happy at how refreshing it's been to talk about my darkest secrets without being judged or ridiculed in the process. This is the main reason I am not going to stop therapy simply because I feel good for a moment. I was happy to hear something different for once in my life. The memories of my childhood flooded in as I thought to myself how the conversation should have gone. I cannot deny that I love my mother because she is my mother. I used to crave those mother-daughter relationships I had seen in the movies and tv shows. If only Clair Huxtable could've have been my mother or the dark-skinned Vivian Banks. Nothing against the lighter one but man the dark skinned had a certain razzle dazzle about herself, especially in that episode where she showed out in ballet.

I have kept my mother at a distance since I left her house at seventeen, but I loved her still and wanted to be around her. When I tried to be a good daughter that she could love, she reminded me of how I could never be that person in her life. It was not until the thought of having a baby with Calvin that I realized how wrong sleeping with him was, so I did what I thought was best for us both at the time. After everything that's happened, I'm even more convinced that I did the right thing in sparing that child the ridicule and torment it would face having been born to me and Calvin. I knew the conversation was long over-due between me and my mom, but I did not think it would go so far left making that the end of our relationship. I

pushed those thoughts to the back burner as I left Dr. Juelz's office with a smile on my face. I no longer felt the guilt for not wanting to deal with the toxic traits of others even if that meant not dealing with my own mother. It may be a while before I see Dr. Juelz again, but I am thankful that I have someone I can see when I need to.

A candy blue 2007 Toyota Avalon sat parked in Omari's driveway when I stopped by. The windows were tinted but I could still see the Tinkerbell seat covers. It was enough to put me right back in my car. Respecting Omari and his relationship with Tia is all I want to do but I do not have the energy to put up with her today. There will be a day when we all sit down and get on the same page with me apologizing for my wild and crazy antics as well as the accusations I placed on Tia, however, that didn't stop Tia from being a cheating ass hoe. Omari has been an amazing friend to me, and I cannot see him give his life away to her knowing she's cheating on him. Aside from being a cheater she was still a very jealous individual and I was in a good mood that I did not need it ruined by jealousy or betrayal, so I went to see Charmaine. I have yet to see her and her handsome little baby boy. I could not think of a better way to give them some space even if that meant driving all over Jackson.

She welcomed me in with open arms and the biggest smile on her face. I sat down at her dining room table while she picked up her son's toys in the living room. Watching Charmaine in complete mommy mode was an eye opener. Her apartment was completely different from the club going girl I once knew living across from Westland Plaza. She had committed to being a mother and it was a wonderful thing to see. Jokingly I stated, "From bottles of Cîroc to bottles of breastmilk huh?"

"Girl, yes! I still can't believe it and he's here." She looked and said, "Amir, baby no!

Don't put that in your mouth. That's nasty."

Charmaine seemed to be an amazing mother and her son was too adorable! She laid Amir down in his playpen so that he could watch cartoons without destroying her place again. Watching them interact with each other made me wonder if I would have been a good mother. Hell, it made me wonder if I would ever be a mother or even a wife for that matter. I did feel like I was damaged goods. Who would truly want me after everything I've been through and done? I barely wanted me but that's why I'm learning to love myself again. One day I would love to be a mother and a wife. My feelings on being damaged was all thanks to what Pierre and Aleccia had done to me. What did I have to offer to anybody looking for love? It took over a year before I tried to just love me, and after a setback like that, I'm learning how to do that correctly. I do not know what love is, and I do not know how to love somebody. What I thought was love was just figments of my imagination. The love that has been presented to me over the course of my life has been dipped and stained with abuse. I learned the hard way that this was not love.

Charmaine placed a glass of some mixed concoction she had made and said, "Taste this."

I took a sip and replied, "You made this? Girl, you need to sell this. It's too good!"

"Already ahead of you boo! I started me a little daiquiri business."

Surprisedly, I replied, "Stop it! I know business is booming too!"

She stood up and started to dance, "And is! I'm not letting my son want for nothing! Not with a mama like me."

I nodded, "That's how it should be. Is his father in his life?"

She grunted, "Girl yeah. He loves Amir. I guess he's a good father when he wants to be."

"Every kid needs their dad though. Especially a boy and it's good Amir has both of you even if y'all ain't together or whatever."

Her phone buzzed on the table and the name 'BabyDaddy' appeared on her phone. Annoyed she said, "Speak of the devil and he shall appear." She turned her phone on silent mode and placed it face down on the table while she explained, "He's a great father but being a parent isn't something he should be able to pick up and put down whenever he wants to. He is only around because I stay on his ass and make sure he is around. If I do not, he'll forget about my kid and act like he doesn't know anything about him or me."

It was not shocking to know that a baby daddy did not want to be a baby daddy. I shook my head and began to reply when a random knock disrupted our flow. Charmaine looked confused and did not move at first. More knocks came and she eventually got up and answered the door,
"Hey, right now isn't a good time."

He sounded annoyed in his response, "Well when is a good time Charms?"

She pleaded, "Just come back later or tomorrow. I have company right now. It was unexpected okay!"

I felt as if I was going to be the reason these two argued and I was already trying to avoid drama at one house just to cause it in another. I probably should've just taken my butt home after the therapy session. He continued to stand his ground, "You always do this. Every time I try to come and pick my son up, it's an excuse why I can't. What nigga you got around my son?"

She tried her best to keep her unwanted male guest from getting in, but she failed miserably. I didn't have to assume that this was Amir's dad since it was pretty obvious from the phone call she ignored and the tension at the door. He came in fussing about how Charmaine does not answer the phone when he is trying to see his son. She was firing back all kind of insults as he walked over to the playpen picking up the baby bag and then Amir. Charmaine tried rushing him out of the door before he could notice me. She had nothing to worry about. I do not want her baby daddy, her neighbor's baby daddy or anybody's baby daddy. I am way too busy trying to stand on my own two feet again to get sucked into a world wind romance with anybody.

Charmaine failed at making sure he did not notice me because when I raised my head up, we locked eyes. I was not expecting him to look at me with the same face as my ex-Mike. Charmaine stood to the side looking at the floor biting her thumb nail as the realization crept upon my face. Immediately I knew, it was time for me to leave. I did not need an explanation as to how or why this even happened. What was done was done and I needed to dismiss myself quickly before anybody felt the need to make this more awkward than what it already was. Mike stood frozen in his steps when he seen my face.

I gathered my things and headed for the door when Mike broke the awkward silence in the room, "Harper, you look great. It's good to see you again."

I stared at him with a raised eyebrow trying to make sense of the current picture I was looking at. What was good about seeing my ex that broke up with me on my birthday holding a child he shares with my now ex best friend. I chuckled to myself while shaking my head at the reality of it all and walked on out of the door. Charmaine followed me to my car as she said,
"Harper wait! Listen just come back inside so that we can talk."

I stood at the car with the door open as I replied, "There's nothing to explain. The picture is crystal clear. I wish you both nothing but the best and congratulations on being parents together." She started to reply but I did not let her words stop me from getting into the car and driving off. I would have cried but the situation was not as dire as what I've been through with Aleccia, Pierre, and Calvin. The first time I learned that my best friend was sleeping with the man I loved, I was truly heartbroken. To learn a second time that a guy I liked is messing with my friend, is like been there done that. I remembered the feelings of inadequacy when he broke up with me on my birthday and how she dismissed me on that same exact day. The way they stared at each other when I introduced them should have told me something and yet I pretended not to see a thing. I was not hurt nor angry, simply disappointed in myself. I have known since high school that Charmaine was this kind of person. The kind that has no regard for friendship and sleeps with whoever, whenever. It was the reason she never met Calvin. Let us just charge this to the game. She won that and she can certainly have that! I am happy to lose out on a man like Mike and a friend like Charmaine.

# Chapter Twenty-Seven

Awe filled silence was in the air as the DJ started to play a song while the lovely couple begin to dance their first dance for the second time with the pictures from their first wedding flashing across the wall behind them. A lot had changed in their appearance, but time was still on their side. Five kids and thirty years later and she still looked amazing in her peach-colored wedding gown. Her locs were longer now with beautiful salt and pepper streaks that were pinned up under her crown. His hightower fade had faded away as he was now bald. They swayed together in harmony until the music stopped. An uproar of applause came as they walked hand in hand from the dance floor with smiles wider than ever. The epitome of black love at its finest. I yearned for the day I could look in the eyes of my forever love with a burning desire that lasts for decades. They walked around thanking family and friends for attending their vow renewal. When I seen that they were coming my way, I wanted to run because I didn't know these people from Adam, and I didn't want to explain how I was a last-minute invitation and not crashing their beautiful ceremony. They approached me at the table and the happy bride wasted no time, "I'm so happy you could make it! I have been wanting to meet you. You are just so beautiful!"

Her husband chimed in, "Where is that knucklehead boy of mine? I can't believe he'd leave you over here by yourself. You're too beautiful to be left alone. It's some vultures in this family and he knows that."

Understanding the confusion, I replied, "Oh no I'm not who you think I am. I'm Omari's friend. I'm not his girlfriend, Tia." She smiled, "It's Harper, right?" I nodded with a smile.

Her husband said to her, "Baby don't butt in."

Her side eye was hilarious. I giggled to myself as she said, "Frank will you hush. Now Harper I know who Tia is but I'm happy that you're not her and I'm hoping to see much more of you."

Just as I was about to reply, Omari walked up and said, "Mama, you're badgering her. Let her breath a little."

She glared at him as Frank replied for her, "Boy where you been? You're supposed to be with your date. You know how your cousins are when they see a new pretty face."

Omari stepped to the side to speak with his dad while his mother continued to get to know me, "I have heard so much about you. Omari talks about you all the time. I am thrilled to finally meet you. We have this annual church trip coming up soon. We'll be heading to Florida, and I hope you'll be able to attend."

"Oh wow, I didn't know he was doing all that but umm, I hope so. This has been a wonderful ceremony. You two are just beautiful together. I mean the love just flows."

She nodded with a smile and spoke as she stared at Frank, "It still amazes me how we've made it work for so long. Not every day has been filled with roses and lingerie and despite having five kids we've managed to keep our eternal love flame burning for another ten years. Oh yeah there were days that I could've really bopped him upside that bald head of his in the name of Jesus but the days like this where you say the love just flows, those days happened with ease way more than any bad day we've had. I've prayed that all of my children find a love like ours if not better."

As nervous as I was to watch them walk over to me, sitting beside her at this table looking at Frank and Omari was not so bad after all. She loved her family, and it was something I had not ever seen before in my life. A mother's love. Is it possible to possess this kind of love for a child when you never experienced it yourself? I want to one day look at my husband and my children with the same prayers in my heart. After today I'm probably going to hound Omari about any and all family or church events now. Being around a family filled with love and morals is something I didn't know I was craving for until now. I might meet a cousin that's right up my alley! I agreed, "I'm sure they will. They all have these great role models as parents. I don't think you have anything to worry about."

She looked at me, "I like you Harper. I hope my son sees what he has before it's too late."

I shook my head, "Oh no we're just friends."

Frank and Omari stepped back to the table as she stood up and said, "Yeah I remember saying those words about 30 years ago. As a matter of fact, I didn't even like him the day I met him, but his charm grew on me. Now, he's my best friend."

Frank smiled, "Janice get your nose out of that and come on and cut this cake with me."

They walked off while me and Omari shook our heads in laughter. The older generation stay with the hooks up especially during a wedding. They see two people in a crowd smile at each other and immediately they think those people should get married and have babies. That is not how relationships and love work. At least I don't think it is. I'm still learning but I'm confident my future husband is not Omari, although I wouldn't mind my in laws being people like Frank and Janice. It seems like they got it right. The marriage, the kids, and the careers. I could learn a lot from people like them.

Omari waved his hand in front of my face while saying, "Earth to Harper."

"Sorry. Your parents are beautiful together. It's hard not to watch them."

"Yeah, I hear ya. They got their own vibe going on. I hope my mom didn't get on your nerves too bad though. She can sometimes be too much with her spidey senses that she thinks she has."

I laughed, "Really spidey senses? Sounds like my mom but in a good way. That's cruel of you to say but no she didn't get on my nerves at all. I enjoyed talking to her. I would like to know what all has been said about me though. She said she's heard a lot about me." I nudged his side, "So spill. What have you been saying sir?"

With a straight face he replied, "Huh? What you mean?"

I raised an eyebrow, "Dude, what have you been saying about me to your mom?"

He smirked, "Nothing. Just told her who you were since you were coming to the ceremony."

I mocked our favorite movie, "You ain't gots to lie Craig!" while rolling my neck and snapping my finger in his face.

He gently grabbed my hand while looking me in the eyes. It was something about this moment that made me feel a tingling sensation over my entire body. Omari has never made me feel faint before and I couldn't understand why I felt the way I did as he asked, "Would you like to dance Miss Ward?"

I uttered, "Sure." And we hit the dance floor. The dj had the building bumping with best sounds from the 70s, 80s, and 90s. This caused us to form a soul train line because why not. We both had beads of sweat forming on our noses with shiny foreheads to match. Most of the men had pretty much gotten undressed from the formal attire they were wearing. If their shirts weren't completely off, then they were wide open or had a few buttons undone. If I didn't know any better, I'd think somebody came along and poured gallons of water on all of them. The ladies that wore heels were now barefoot with the heels pushed to the side as they tried their best to drop it low in their gowns. My favorite slow song blasted through the speakers. Those without dance partners left the floor as well as the ones too tired from twerking and jigging. I couldn't dare sit my favorite song out and Omari knew this. He placed his arms around my waist with my arms around his neck. This style of dancing wasn't something that was popular in Jackson. Maybe it was too sensual for their taste. Some prudes refer to it as sex on the dance floor but to me it is the black Tango and I love to do it every chance I get. A cameraman walked circles around us causing the crowd to form a circle and watch as we grinded to the Haitian beat that played in the background. Omari had never heard of the Kompa until I showed him years ago during a spring break trip in Miami. Aside from the grinding of our hips in close proximity, there's the in and out swaying of our bodies as we dance together in harmony to the beat of the music. It's as if we are a stream of water flowing with the music. At the end of the song, Omari dipped me and as I slowly came back up, he held me closer as if he wanted to kiss me. When an uproar of applause and praise for our dancing broke our trance, we quickly left the dance floor and headed outside to cool off and get some fresh air.

The sun had went down showing the dark star filled sky while the wind blew slightly here and there. A storm was coming in the coming up days but tonight the weather was as perfect as it could be. Standing amongst parked cars and chatting it up, there was a vibe that I hadn't felt before. An undeniable chemistry between us that I was trying my best to deny. I guess weddings and vow renewals do bring out something in you that you never knew existed before. I'm sure it's just the scene or maybe it was the energy from the dance, but I was seeing Omari in a different light. He has always been fine to me and there was a time I wanted him, but we settled into this friendship because of his playboy ways and me being caught up in all the wrong things. That has been so long ago though. We have graduated, gotten jobs, and have grown mentally. He's no longer the playboy he once was. He's actually become a real faithful dude. It just sucks that it's with Tia. She doesn't deserve him but what do I know really. This is not only my best friend but hell my only friend and I'm not about to mess up this friendship because of lustful hormones. At the same time, if Tia is doing him wrong, I feel I should say something, but my only goal is to stay drama free and I know if I say anything about his relationship, then drama will follow. I am happy with the friendship but how do you turn this energy down? I don't want him to think because of these random misplaced feelings that I'm jealous and trying to break them up.

He must have felt what I was feeling though. It certainly

wasn't hard to do. After that dance anybody is bound to think we're in a whole relationship. He stood in front of me saying, "I don't know if I said this, but I love this dress on you." I looked down caressing the black strapless velvet felt gown that hugged all my curves and draped around my ankles. The spilt came up to my thigh in which I thought it was too much showing at first, but I didn't have time to find anything different. I purchased this online and by the time it came in the mail, I had no other choice but to wear so here I am. He continued, "You feeling all over yourself is only making my view better."

His comment had me blushing. Oh yeah, he was feeling something. He hasn't really flirted with me in years, so I asked, "Are you high?"

He chuckled, "Not at all. Just trying to shoot my shot and missing is all."

I wondered as I nodded with a smile if his shot was meant for a one-night stand or something more. I was too scared to ask, instead I replied, "It's not the first time you've missed."

He stepped closer to me until we were inches away. Our energies becoming more intense as he said, "Why don't you stop blocking my shot then?" He paused and stared at me. The man had me scared. This was too much because a part of me felt like he was serious knowing he has a girlfriend. I should have pushed him back and laughed it off. I've learned my lesson with being with involved men, but I was more intrigued than ever as to what would happen next. I wondered how far he would go if I allowed his advances. As he leaned in closer, my eyes closed in anticipation of his next move. I heard the words, "Where the fuck is Omari?! I want to see him right fucking now!"

He jerked away from me and turned around to see Tia wobbling through the parked cars trying to get to the building. I watched him meet up to her and try to get her to leave only to realize she was completely hammered and should not have been driving in the first place. Tia fought him while trying to lick his face. It looked like she was trying to take him down in front of everybody. Whatever she was drinking I wanted no parts of it. She was going to feel horrible in the morning. His younger brother came out and seen the commotion and offered to help figure something out with her. She was not listening and constantly yelling not realizing where she was at. This had a few more people come out and watch them try to tame her drunkenness. I slipped away and left. I was lucky enough to park on the side of the road away from everybody else. It probably would've been better to let Omari know I was leaving or to even say goodbye to his parents and siblings, but I was too ashamed to face him or them after that moment we had before Tia came. For a split second, I wanted to do some of the nastiest things to my best friend at his parents' vow renewal. What was I thinking? His dad is a freaking pastor! I can't get caught up in the sauce like that. Luckily, Tia did come and set us back on the right track. I had to leave though.

If I had stayed, I feel like it is highly possible that he would have wanted to pick up where we left off, but it was obvious that we were both just caught up in the moment of things. We do not actually want each other. It's obvious that he's in love with Tia because he hasn't let her go as of yet! I do not want to lose the friendship I have with him over lust, so I took some time to cool off. I went home and for the first time I took a cold shower. I hate cold showers, but my body was like a volcano ready to erupt, and I needed something to cool me down and get my mind back focused on the right things. Moments like this is the reason I bought the multi speed detachable showerhead. Seeing Tia was a sign for me that I needed to keep respecting his relationship and remain his friend. I didn't think he deserved her, but I didn't want to ruin this friendship either. I needed some space from him and I'm not sure how I'm going to get it when I now live around the corner from him, and we work at JDL together, but I was certainly going to try my best to keep a distance between us.

# Chapter Twenty-Eight

Jamal has been arguing with me over this design for the last hour. He's determined to present his idea and dismiss mine although I have met the requirements that the client has made. His design looks like something that should be on the bottom of a shitty holey moley nasty ass shoe which is not at all what the client wants. He says that my design is too girly and looks like it smells of bubblegum and baby powder. I would've walked away from this project and just let him have it, but the boss gave it to me and Jamal. He's refusing to be a team player and take his L. He didn't do any research on the client and that was his biggest mistake. He can either get on board with this bubblegum and baby powder smelling design or he can kick rocks. He ain't thought that we were going to present his dead as a doorknob idea. I would not present that idea to a funeral director. It should be tossed and burned. This entire ordeal has me trying to figure how did he even get hired. I was just about to walk out and request his name be removed from the project when Omari startled us both, "Why not let him present his idea first and then you present yours?" He stood next to both of the big bosses as he made his suggestion.

Jamal eagerly replied before I could, "Yeah let's do that then you can see for yourself that mine is better."

I forced a smile as I sighed, "Sounds great." I gathered my paperwork and headed back to my office. Omari followed and closed the door behind us. I looked up from behind my desk and asked, "What was that?"

He sat down in the chair in front of my desk and shrugged, "I was trying to help you Harper. You've been arguing over designs all morning. Both of you were on the verge of making a scene."

I scoffed, "I can't help it if I'm right. His idea is garbage. It's like he didn't do any research on the client nor their expectations."

He nodded, "Jamal never does research. He's only here because his uncle is part owner of the company, and he wants to make his resume look good."

Irritated, "So if you knew this then why suggest he present his idea? Why not just tell his ass to trash the idea. How could you not back me up in there? And in front of our bosses at that?!"

I flopped down in my chair full of despair as he replied with a smile, "I told you why. You both needed to let it go. Besides your design is great and the client will love it. Plus, I needed you alone so that we could talk about how you've been avoiding somebody for a month that you work with and stay down the street from, and claim is your best friend."

I looked away, "I haven't been avoiding you. You've just been missing me somehow. I mean we're both busy. It's just life really."

He chuckled, "You're right I've been missing you. Well, it's Friday and somebody has a birthday tomorrow. You got plans?" I shook my head no while continuing to avoid eye contact.
He continued, "Good because I'm picking you up tomorrow."

I looked up at him, "Oh no tomorrow isn't good. I have so much to do."

He stood up and tapped my desk, "I better be able to find you and you better be ready tomorrow. Bright and early!" He walked away and all I could think was damn. I haven't been avoiding him but the conversation surrounding his parents vow renewal that I know we are going to have tomorrow I certainly have been avoiding. He's going to want to know why I left like I did. I'm trying not to mess up this friendship and yet I see now that I'm still doing just that. As if that wasn't bad enough, I was still feeling like jumping his bones as he sat in my office. It's safe to say, I've developed feelings and now I needed to figure out how to place them inside of Pandora's Box for good.

The next day Omari was banging on my door like the police at five in the morning. He didn't get a key this time. We managed not to open that door this time around but the way his banging was going, I might end up giving him a key just so he does not bang on my door like this ever again. I opened the door and let him in, and he was in full workout attire. I looked at him crazy as I said, "You're taking me to the gym for my birthday? I'm going to be honest; I

don't want to do this. We can literally order a pizza and hang out here or at your place. Better yet you could cook to save some money."

His smile was even mesmerizing at this point. Damn girl! Get yourself together! He replied, "I'm not telling you where we're going but you are going to need to wear this." He handed me some black gym clothes and reluctantly I went to my room and got dressed. I was surprised at how well they fit me. When did I tell him my size? It must've been the man whore deep down that just instantly knew a woman's size and here I thought boys went to Jupiter to get more stupider. Guess I was wrong. When we left, the sun was barely starting to peek out. We hit the highway heading to Natchez which left me confused but I stayed silent and enjoyed the ride. As long as we weren't going to the gym then I was cool with it.

After a two-hour drive, we made it to the Tomahawk Trails. I glared at Omari and was met with a smirk. Buddy was taking me on a nature walk for my birthday. I suppose this was punishment for ignoring him for a month, but it was not so bad since I didn't have plans for my birthday anyway. Omari went to the trunk of his car, opened it, pulled out two huge bags. He put one on his back and helped me put the other one on my back. I only obliged because of the guilt I was feeling. We started to walk, and I realized it was really a hike up a mountain. We stopped here and there because I could not walk more than a couple of steps before a spider web, or a bug was attacking my face. It was a great idea, but I was on the verge of full snobby girl complaining before we eventually made it to the top. We kept walking until he stopped at a clearing in the woods. It was around noon and if it had not been October, I would have died from a heat stroke. Noon is not the time to take a hike or be in the woods. He took his bag off his back, and I did the same. He looked at me with a smile and asked, "So what do you think?"

I looked around at the trees with a disgusted look on my face until I seen the lake. The sun was shining down on it in the most beautiful way. I walked closer to admire the view. It was one of the most beautiful scenes I had ever witnessed. I was not too happy to see a bunch of trees at first, but this was like a painting out of an art gallery. It left me speechless. He walked up behind me and held me saying, "Happy Birthday."

His touch was the warmest and yet it sent chills down my spine causing goosebumps to raise on my arms. I uttered, "Wow. I gotta admit this is really cool. Thank you."

We unpacked the bags which contained a tent. One tent. I had hoped there would be two has this was starting to feel more like a set up than a birthday surprise. A camping trip in the fall by a lake, my best friend had done it again. He's given me another amazing gift for my birthday. I am really not a nature girl because of bugs but after a spraying on some bug repellant, I can get with this anytime. Omari cooked us dinner on a cast iron skillet over an open fire. I just knew animals were going to attack us for the food since it was smelling so good but thankfully not one furry little woodland creature attacked us. When we were finished, we sat down watching the sun set behind the trees. The way the lake sparkled with the sunset was a view I wanted to remember forever.

It was perfect until he said, "You want to tell me why you left my parent's vow renewal way you did?"

Damn. I sighed, "I just wanted to clear my head but to be honest Omari, we're lucky that Tia was drunk when she showed. I want to respect y'all and that means you need to respect y'all too. I appreciate everything you've done for me, and I couldn't ask for a better friend but let's be honest, we almost messed up. If she had seen us, then what?"

Nonchalantly he replied, "Then nothing. I'm single."

Assuming this was because of us, I chuckled with my eyes squinted, "Yeah right. And when did this happen?"

"Two years ago, on Christmas."

Taken aback I exclaimed, "Two years ago? Does she know this?"

He laughed, "Yes, she knows. She thinks I will forgive her cheating on me with Mike."

Bewildered, "Wait she was cheating with Mike?!"

He nodded his head, "Yeah, she went through my phone and seen a long Merry Christmas message from you which started the biggest argument. She accused us of sleeping together and admitted to stepping out as a way to get back at us. She's been trying to get me to forgive her since Mike went and got some girl pregnant, but I don't want Tia."

Shame fell upon my face as I replied, "Wow I didn't know my message caused all of that drama. I just wanted to apologize for being paranoid."

He nodded, "I understood you being paranoid. The accusation hurt but I understood it. I tried to apologize for how I reacted and when I didn't get a reply, I figured you wanted space. It wasn't until I tried to pop up at your place like I always do and seen it was empty that I knew something was wrong. I went by your job, and they hadn't seen or heard from you in weeks." He paused and looked at me, "I'm sorry it took me so long to find you."

I smiled, "It wasn't your job to find me but I'm happy that it was you did. I didn't know life could be so crazy until I was in that mess. It made me turn to the only person I had to turn to and that was God. I really don't know how I made it a year in that."

"I had all the prayer warriors in the church praying for you too. You asked what I had told my mom about you. Well, she always knew about you because she'd call sometimes when we hung out but when you were missing, I confided in her and told her how I felt about you."

I teased, "Oh did you express your undying love for me?"

In a serious tone, he replied, "If I did?"

Butterflies filled my stomach while my best friend was becoming the man of my dreams before my very eyes. We continued to talk until we both were too tired to keep our eyes open. When I stood up to retire to the tent, I took a moment to embrace the scenery since tomorrow we'd head back to Jackson. The sunset was gone, and the night air came in a little cooler than before we arrived. Suddenly, a cool breeze blew past me and gave me goosebumps. Omari noticed my shiver and wrapped big warm arms around me. It was the most comfort I had ever felt. His breathing was slow and steady on the back of my neck while the beats of his heart were like the drums of an African love song. The vibe had returned stronger than before. This is my best friend, and he will always be my best friend but here I am wondering how bad one kiss could be. When he whispered, "Are you ready to lay down?" I quickly replied, "Yes!" not processing his words nor caring about the consequences of my reply. He chuckled as he walked over to the fire and started putting it out. I walked up behind him and said, "Hey, thank you so much. You are an amazing friend." He smiled and we hugged as if we were about to start our dance. His embrace once again tantalizing. I pondered at letting him go or not, but I knew I would have to. Tia or not, he was still somebody I didn't want to mess over and aside from the constant flirting that he does with every female he sees, I cannot allow pheromones or vibes to mess up a good friendship. With his arms still around me and his beautiful brown eyes staring into my soul, made it hard to let him go. He started to make his move while I stood there lost, confused, and looking foolish. He leaned in and as I closed my eyes, I felt his soft lips plant the sweetest kiss on mine. I could have melted into his arms.

How could I deny him when all I really wanted was him? He lifted me up and cupped my butt in the most perfect and gentle way ever. The kissing never stopped. If anything, they became more intense. He walked us inside the tent where he kneeled with ease and laid my body down onto our sleeping bags. When his lips touched my neck, I bit my bottom lip as I moaned out in pleasure. I could not believe this was happening. I could feel his hand on my thighs slowly moving up my shirt and back down to my thigh when abruptly he stopped and looked at me. We stared at each other breathing heavily until he broke the silence, "You are so beautiful. I have wanted you forever, but Harper I don't want to hurt you." I shook my head in response and he smiled, "Harper, I love you. I want to be with you. I want to be your man and show you how a man should love a woman. I have been in love with you since the first day I saw you in the plaza. We can keep going if you want to and I understand if you don't feel the same way. I just wanted you to know before we went any further."

His honesty was everything I needed as I pictured his parents and how their love seemed to transcend through space and time. I realized he was my forever love. I placed my hands on his face as I smiled, "I love you Omari."

# Epilogue

Standing in my full-length mirror that stood in the corner of my master bedroom examining another online purchase I had finally received in the mail last week. I needed to stop ordering so late because I always get stuck with the purchase whether I actually like it or not. It was a white romper that has hints of green, yellow, and blue. I thought this was too cute when I came across it on Fashion Nova's website. I think I love how the back has this see-through tail that is open in the front. My original choice was a cute flowy dress, but it is the end of March, and it is already too hot to wear anything other than shorts. My goal was to be cute and cool, and this outfit had met my needs. I knew I was wasting time in the mirror when I heard the music start up from the backyard. I went downstairs to check on how the setup was coming, and it was beyond everything I had hoped it would be. There were pretty light green, white, and clear balloons as well as matching streamers that led from the kitchen to the backyard. The food table was looking the bomb.com especially with the beautiful array of fruits on one table and grilled kabobs on another. Brinae startled me when she said, "Girl where is your ribbon?"

I had contemplated pinning the handmade ribbon on my romper but was too busy caressing the basketball size stomach I had developed over the last eight months thinking back to the day I took the pregnancy test. Brinae and everybody at the office had already begin to tease me about the weight I was putting on and I had snappily confirmed it was just happy weight. The annoyance in my tone only made them tease me more. I had no reason to believe I was pregnant until of course Aunt Flo didn't come like she was supposed to. It was no denying the pregnancy but even when the test turned positive, I was still in doubt that it was even real. After everything I been through how could I be pregnant? Granted I had been getting it in nonstop after I started going to church more and getting in the bible more, I started praying as well, but I mean come on let's be real. With what I've done in the past, I wondered did I deserve to truly be a mother. I

was terrified, excited, shocked, and perplexed on what my next move should be. They tell you how forgiving God is in church and how real he is if you just believe and repent. I did all of that only because of Omari. He told me to just try to have a little faith that everything they were saying was the truth. I did but when it all boiled down, I still wasn't in full belief until the pregnancy test turned positive. I cried for days realizing that I was going to be a mother. I cried because God saw fit to bless me despite what I had done or even been through. Being pregnant was a miracle to me and I walked in that miracle every day with my head held high until I was four months pregnant. After all I had been through, I didn't think I would get another chance at motherhood. Imagine my surprise when the doctor discovered a second baby snuggled behind the first baby four months into the pregnancy. I knew God was real when the ultrasound tech said, "Oh you're having twins." Twins? I cried even harder at the fact that this was happening to me. What did I do to deserve this? I wasn't worthy!

They couldn't keep me from church after that. I started shouting and praising every Sunday as if I was the original church mother from back in the day. The praying mothers covered me and my babies in prayers with blessed oil. It's nothing anybody can tell me now about God being real and being a forgiving God. I smiled as I replied, "I got sidetracked when the kicks started up."

She laughed and went upstairs to get the ribbon she had made for me. I've known Brinae for the past year now. I was so happy when Jamal got replaced with Brinae. She actually knows what she's doing in the office. We've brought in a ton of clients and knocked out some highprofile accounts together. This is my work bestie turned real life bestie. She's been planning this baby shower since the day I told her I was pregnant. The girl is a craft goddess! She makes homemade ribbons, cups, shirts, trays, and I don't even know what else, but I bet she can do that too. She walked up to me and pinned the ribbon on my romper while saying, "Listen your ass better not go into labor during this shower. You need to sit down somewhere!"

I smiled, "I can't promise you a thing. Girl with the way my back and feet feel, I'm just about ready to do anything to get these babies out. Besides, does it look like I could stretch any further?!"

She laughed, "See that's why I stopped rubbing your belly. I was afraid you'd pop from being touched."

I took her advice and wobbled to the nearest chair. I hadn't even been walking around long and already my feet had started to swell up. Brinae pulled up an ottoman and said, "You know damn well you need your feet up! You gone make me whoop you soon." She walked away shaking her head. The girl was acting like she was my mother, doctor, and baby daddy. It wasn't annoying to me though. I knew she had genuine love for me and of course I enjoyed the catering for the most part. From the second the test turned positive I knew I wanted to cherish every little second of this pregnancy, but I was terrified to learn that I was having twins, a boy, and a girl. We have been going overboard with buying newborn clothes and items. I literally cannot walk in a store without going to the newborn section and getting something for both of my babies! Brinae started calling them 'The Doublemint Twins' hence the green and white décor for the baby shower. Now the entire JDL building is awaiting to meet 'The Doublemint Twins'

The guests started to arrive and that's when Brinae put on her hosting hat. They were required to put safety pins on from the door and at any time if they said the word baby or twin, they had to give their pin to the person that heard them said the word. I was seeing pins getting jacked left and right. People were taking this so seriously and it was amusing how they were all slipping on the words and trying to act like they said something else. I saw a few people slip and look around hoping nobody heard them. My face was starting to ache from the permanent smile I had on, and the babies kicked in joy with every hearty laugh I made. The funniest moment was when the biggest pin jacker slipped. The entire party reacted in laugher as Brinae jacked her pin. I think my favorite and funniest game to see play out was watching the men race to change the baby diaper on the baby dolls. Brinae figured the women would do better in a baby bottle drinking race and boy was she right. These ladies played no games with those baby bottles, had the men cheesing and whispering over in the corner. Just nasty is what they are! Whoever invented this guess the size of the belly game is just wrong! I felt so huge when some of the guests had to estimate my size with toilet paper, but I loved it and certainly loved Brinae for doing such an amazing job on this baby shower. She's been a true angel from the moment I met her. I pray for the day she meets her forever love and have some little ones running around playing with mine. How perfect would that be? When the party was over, a few stayed to help clean up which I thought was so sweet because I certainly wasn't helping. Others had dipped out as soon as Brinae started to thank everybody for coming. My only concern was going to lay down and Brinae agreed. Only problem was I wanted everybody gone before I went to bed so I sat downstairs eating grapes until they finished cleaning. Brinae walked up to me, "You are always eating grapes. Did you eat anything else?" I nodded and she sat down near me, "Do you know that guy in the backyard with the red polo shirt?"

I said with a smile, "No, I only know the fine dude that's beside him."

She looked at me from the corner of her eyes with her lips tooted up to the side and chuckled, "Well, duh he's ya husband! Why not come out there with me since you're clearly not going to go lay down?"

I did the pregnant rock to get up which made her burst out

laughing. I rolled my eyes and headed towards the patio door. She helped me down the stairs of the deck and to the guys. It took no time for my babies' daddy to say, "What are you trying to do go into labor?"

"Boy hush! Now who is this guy with you?"

Omari shook his head, "Every day you sound more and more like my mother." He looked at his friend and said, "Vincent this is my wife Harper and her friend Brinae."

He was very handsome, and I could see why Brinae noticed him. When he smiled, he showed off his pearly whites with the cutest dimples. I shook my head at how Brinae almost drooled all over him. If I didn't know any better, I'd say they had fallen in love at first sight from the way they were eyeing each other being all extra cute and lovey dovey. It was nice to see. Omari continued to tell us about how they've been friends since childhood. Vincent grew up in South Jackson off Siwell. Omari would sometimes visit his cousins and one day he met Vincent. They used to be some bad ass kids jumping off houses, shooting squirrels with BB guns, and playing WWE on the trampoline. The stories they shared had me and Brinae dying laughing. Vincent suggested we play a game of spades and that's when I seen for myself just how perfect we all were together.

After maybe two hours I had Brinae meet me in the kitchen, "Listen I see you really like him so my suggestion to you is to be his friend. I promise you can't go wrong by being his friend. Yeah, he's fine and all but you'll end up with something so amazing by just being his friend."

She looked at me with a raised eyebrow, "Now girl you know it's been a minute since I done had some and like you said the man is fine. We can be friends but I ain't stopping nothing!"

I laughed so hard that I peed myself, "Damn. Now I done peed on myself."

She looked down and looked back up as if she had seen a ghost, "Harper I don't think that was pee girl! I think your water just broke!"

I chuckled because her words had my nerves rattled. I didn't know what that felt like but maybe she was right. I looked down and I still had what I thought was pee trickling down my leg to the big puddle on the floor. I looked back up at her shrugging, "I guess it did break."

Her facial expression was priceless as she replied, "You guess!"

Omari and Vincent walked in smiling at us as Omari said, "Baby, when are you going to go lay down. It doesn't matter if the house is clean or not. Let me help you upstairs to the room."

Brinae calmly interrupted him, "It's a little too late for that. Her water just broke."

Omari stood frozen and shocked while Vincent begins to panic, "Well, why the fuck are y'all so calm. We need to get you to a hospital." He shook Omari out of his trance, and they all helped me wobble to the truck. Brinae grabbed the hospital bag that I had packed and was sitting beside the front entrance of our house. We all hopped into the truck and traveled to River Oaks. After what seemed like forever, I was holding my son and daughter for the first time. I looked into their eyes and sobbed tears of joy. The hospital had a visitation limit, but Omari's family cared nothing about that. His parents and siblings were there to awe over the two new additions to the Richards family. We asked if Vincent and Brinae would be the godparents and they happily accepted.

Within the six weeks I needed to heal, Brinae and my mother-in-law Janice were by my side through it all. Janice refused to let me even lift a finger. They helped me with everything from cleaning to cooking and allowing me moments to myself. I didn't endure the suffering of somebody coming over only to hold the babies while I tried to do everything else. They were everything I never knew I needed. As soon as my six weeks were up, we took Noah and Grace to church for their christening. After a double blessing like this, I had to give these babies back to the Lord because I knew I wouldn't have them if it wasn't for his loving grace and mercy in my life. Grateful was an understatement.

It was on that day that Brinae said to me, "So I have something to tell you." I wasn't sure what the problem was. We had just left church, and everything was going great. Sunday dinner was laid out like picture from the movie Soul Food.  I prayed it was nothing bad as she continued, "I'm pregnant." I was shocked!  This girl had been at my house every single day for six weeks helping me with the twins.  When and how could she get pregnant?  Then again it doesn't take much to get pregnant.

I shrugged, "So who's the lucky guy?"

She smiled as she looked up at Vincent.  I squealed and she hushed me, "Shhhh he doesn't want anybody to know just yet." I motioned me zipping my lips and throwing away the key.  I was more than happy to hear the wonderful news.

When the day ended and I was snuggled in the bed with my boo after feeding the twins and putting them to sleep, he confided in me, "So Vincent is going to propose to Brinae tonight and he asked me to be his best man.  I'm sure she's going to call you tomorrow with the news." My excitement couldn't stay contained at how beautiful life turned out to be.

# Acknowledgements

*I am eternally grateful for the support and love
that I have received on this writing journey.
I thank God and my Lord and Savior for providing me with
the experience, wisdom, and creativity to fill this book with
a story worth reading. A special thank you to my sweet
Jellybean, sassy SnuggleBug, and funny valentine Boobie
for being the apples of my eye. Thank you to my amazing
readers for taking the time to journey through this novel.*

***Peace, Love, & Blessings
KC***

# About The Author

Katrina Chanice is an entrepreneur as well as an author of adult romance. A native from Quitman, Mississippi, she's known for being an avid reader and having a passion for writing poems, short stories, essays and so much more.

KC has a way with words and the ability to captures a plethora of emotions through pen and paper. These writings serve as a safe space for KC's daily thoughts, pain, and escape from reality. Everyone needs an outlet and when you don't feel like talking writing is a creative way to go.

Katrina Chanice hopes to motivate and encourage those that may be struggling with the same issues in these stories. Creating an avenue for conversation among family, friends, and co-workers. A safe space for personal issues that are too complex for society or the media.

Made in the USA
Columbia, SC
11 September 2022

66865766R00129